Sarah Tucker is an award-winning travel journalist, broadcaster and author. A presenter for the BBC *Holiday* programme and travel writer for the *Guardian* and *The Times*, she is also the author of *Have Toddler, Will Travel* and *Have Baby, Will Travel*. She has also presented award-winning documentaries for the Discovery channel.

Sarah lives in Richmond, Surrey and France with her son. Find out more about Sarah at www.mirabooks.co.uk/sarahtucker

Sarah Tucker

the last year of being single

MIRA

MIRA Books, Eton House, 18-24 Paradise Road,
Richmond, Surrey, TW9 1SR

ISBN 978 0 7783 0196 7

60-0108

Printed in Great Britain
by Clays Ltd, St Ives plc

ACKNOWLEDGEMENTS

How I came to write this book is a story in itself. At a
Christmas party, talking to a fellow guest about life, I made a
casual remark that I had a novel inside me.

She gave me her card and said she worked for a publisher…
This book is the result.

A huge "thank you" to: Karin (the woman with the card),
who gave me the break; Sam, the editor who made it happen
and who is the kindest, most astute and enthusiastic person
you could ever meet – thank you so much for believing in me;
and to Paul, who struck the deal without pain and helped me
to my first Mini Cooper (S) (yellow with white roof).

To my son, Thomas, who is, and will always be, my sunshine,
my true love and inspiration.

To my coterie of friends – especially Jo Moore, Amanda Hall,
Claire Beale, Helen Davies, Steve and Paul – who over the
past year have proved to be the best friends anyone could ever
hope for.

To Simon and Caroline, who both think I should put on my
gravestone "Sarah – someone who was so very frustrating but
gave incredible pleasure." I aim to do both. To Kim and Linda
and Karin, for listening. Lots. To Hazel and Doreen. I love you
both loads. Thank you for being there.

the last year of being single

AUTUMN

SEPTEMBER

ACTION LIST

Have fun.

Join gym and work out three times a week. Kick-box and yoga.

Buy goldfish and put in wealth area (have attended Feng Shui class and am told fish in wealth area brings in money). Unhappy as wealth area has toilet in it, which means most goes down the drain. Instructor recommends I put toilet in dining room. Or move.

Buy lots of goldfish and make sure they don't die.

Buy lots of orange candles and light them, ensuring they don't burn anything.

Be wonderful to Paul.

THE DARK PRINCE

1st September

I've met the man of my wet dreams.

Well, almost. I imagined some six foot two, dark, olive-skinned, firm-torsoed prince of a man, on a dark, steamy-breathed steed, thundering mercilessly towards me through a forest full of bluebells (aka sex scene from *Ryan's Daughter*) and whisking me off my feet and then ravishing me almost senseless amongst aforementioned bluebells. In my dream I have huge, voluptuous breasts and long dark eyelashes—two wish-list firsts. Alas, I have neither in real life. There are no mosquitoes, worms or spiders to distract from the pleasure—and it's a warm eighty degrees and the breeze is light. He takes me in his arms and then he takes me. Ripping clothes (aka sex scene up against wall and over luxuriant sofa in *Basic Instinct* with Michael Douglas and tall brown-haired actress wearing brown underwear can't remember name of but she looked like she enjoyed it). I try to resist his advances. Fail, obviously. He always respects me afterwards.

The dark prince in reality is dark and brooding and has deep black-brown eyes which are set too close together. His eyebrows meet in the middle, which means, according to all *Cosmopolitan* articles, he is not to be trusted, undoubtedly a wolf and ruthlessly dominant in bed. He has the look of Rufus Sewell. Shiny jet-black hair, curly almost tight ringlets which look good enough to pull. He has a strong, defined masculine body. Harvey Keitel in *The Piano* masculine body. I visualise him gently toying, stroking, softly kissing my ankles as I play on a piano at least to Grade 7 level. He is completely overcome by the beauty of my calves. I revert back to reality. He looks how men should look rather than how men think men should look. I scan further. He has large hands. No wedding ring. He stares unsmilingly, never lifting his gaze from my eyes.

His first impression of me is my backside. I am leaning over my desk. Trying to get my briefing notes out of a drawer so crammed with briefing notes that it refuses to open. He 'h-hum's. I turn round.

'You Sarah Giles?' he snarls.

'Me Sarah Giles,' I joke.

He doesn't smile. I flush. Sort of Tarzan meets Jane intro. I am meeting this dark, brooding Keitel look-a-like for lunch. He hasn't arrived on a black steed. He's arrived on the 11.25 from East Croydon to Victoria. He is briefing me on how newly privatised Rogerson Railways is supposed to communicate with its customers. He is a specialist, I am advised, in management consultancy gobbledy-gook. The current buzz-words are 'customer focus.' Not passenger focus. Must learn jargon. Passengers are out. Customers are in. This makes loads of difference to the service provided, according to the management consultants. The trains still fail to arrive on time. But the angry passengers are now called angry customers. So there's a difference. I'm told.

The man of my wet dream is a regional director of a regional headquarters of a region of Rogerson Railways. He thinks he is important. I don't care if he isn't. I wanna be his customer, for lunch at least.

'You're taking me to lunch,' he snarls again, still staring, unblinking at me.

'Er, yes. Pizza Express.'

'Whatever. I prefer pubs myself. A beer man. English beer only. None of that foreign muck.'

I don't like beer—English or foreign muck—so I make no comment. He asks me to lead the way. I wish I'd worn something short and tight and sexy and, as the Brazilians do, 'dressed to undress'. Instead I'm wearing eight-year-old Laura Ashley blue and pink flowery culottes and a white T-shirt which leaves everything to the imagination. I do as he asks, realising that everyone in the office is now looking at me. At us. Leaving the office together. I turn round, realising I've forgotten my bag. He's a few paces behind me. Staring at my bum. He looks up, unabashed, unblushing. I flush again.

'Forgot bag,' I explain.

He says nothing. He just stares.

We say nothing in the lift. We say nothing as we cross the road to one of the few decent places to eat in Euston Square. I've pre-booked, but every other table is taken by people I know in the office. They all look up and smile at me and stare at him. This dark prince has a reputation. I am warned he is a womaniser. That he is amoral. That men hate him. That I am to stay away from him and keep him at arm's length. That he is dangerous. Of course this makes him utterly irresistible to me and any other girl who has been told to keep clear. Half the people sitting on the other tables have told me as much. All eyes watch as we sit down. I feel as though the wolf will pounce any moment and start nibbling at my calves. Actually, I fantasise about it. Then I revert back to reality.

The only downside of my dark, brooding anti-hero is his name. John Wayne. How can an anti-hero be called John Wayne? There is something almost Easter Bunny about that name. The name denotes someone stoic and noble and macho, but ever so slightly cuddly and loveable. How can anyone live up to that? The Hollywood actor was always the good guy. The faithful husband. The leader. The man's man. The saviour of every Western, who married Maureen O'Hara in *The Quiet Man* and never even got to see her naked. He never ravished anyone in his life. How could I take this cowboy seriously?

'You don't look like John Wayne,' I say

He looks bored. Disappointed. 'Everyone says that. That is the first thing everyone says to me. No, I don't look like the actor John Wayne. My mother, however, thought it was a good name. He was a good actor and a nice man and played good roles. So she gave me this name. And I like it. Sarah Giles, on the other hand, is ordinary and bland. And you, Sarah Giles, are unoriginal.'

He is obviously from the treat-them-mean-keep-them-keen school of how to talk to women. Either that or he utterly detests my company already.

Enough of the small talk. I tell him that I've been told to speak to him because he knows about customer focus and that I've got to write this report on customer focus and why the regional part of the regional part of Rogerson Railways is failing to communicate with its customers when disruption occurs. He tells me it's because management is bad and no one communicates. He then asks me if I have a boyfriend and what he does.

I have a boyfriend. His name is Paul. I tell him he works for a bank.

I ask him if he has a girlfriend.

He says this is very personal.

I say he's asked me a personal question so I've got a right to ask him one too.

He says he has. That her name is Amanda and that she is curvy, has fat calves, short squat legs, likes pink, has big tits and large eyes and eyelashes and long blonde hair. I visualise Miss Piggy. Then I revert back to reality.

'What have you been told about me?' he says, unblinking and staring straight into me rather than at me. I swear he has not blinked for a good hour.

I tell him that I've heard he is a womaniser. That I am not to trust him. That he is amoral and that he will probably make a pass at me and try to seduce me. But that he is also well thought of professionally and has a good mind.

He smiles. It scares me. It looks very unnatural. Like when Wednesday smiled for the first time in *Addams Family Values*. I ask him to stop smiling and look mean and brooding again. He laughs, which looks more natural than the smile, but the laugh still looks out of place on his face.

We order.

John has a pizza. No fuss. With everything on it.

I order salade niçoise. With dressing on the side. No potatoes. No anchovies. No dough balls. Extra tuna.

John says he will have my dough balls.

I say I will have the dough balls after all, but can we have them on a separate plate?

I order Diet Coke.

No, they don't do English beer. Only the foreign muck. He orders Diet Coke too.

I ask him why he has a fetish for English beer. He says he always has. He says he lives in Surrey in a yellow cottage by a railway line and is surrounded by five pubs within walking distance which all do good English beer. It makes him salivate just thinking about it. At which point he starts to salivate just thinking about it. Methinks this is unsexy, so I ask him what else makes him salivate.

'Cats and women's legs. I can't see your legs, so I don't know if you would make me salivate,' he says straight-faced, 'but I have two cats. Hannah and Jessica.'

I try to flirt. I tell him I have nice legs because I used to be a dancer and that I would like to have a cat. He says that he can't tell me if my legs are good because I'm wearing a disgusting pair of culottes. He also says he will report me to the animal cruelty society if I get a cat, because as I am working full time I won't be able to look after it properly. He is not joking. Or at least I think he is not joking. He doesn't smile while he is saying this, which is some relief.

I interview him about customer focus. I fantasise about him drinking beer in a pub in Surrey. It's the summer. There's him and me. I'm wearing a short white dress. Hannah and Jessica are there, rubbing their bodies round my ankles and his ankles. And I start to run my fingers through his hair. Very slowly. Then I revert back to reality. Get real,

Giles. I'm talking to a guy who works for a regional part of a regional part of the railways called John Wayne.

2nd September

7 a.m. Flatmate Karen is still not up yet. Completely scatty, she makes me feel and look organised. I love her for it. It's some feat to do that. She is nanny to a four-year-old who is being hot-housed by his financial advisor parents. He can speak two other languages fluently. French and pocket money. She gets a taxi to pick her up every morning at six forty-five a.m. The taxi driver knocks on the door. He usually bangs it a few times. She is always asleep. She gets changed, washed, brushed in five minutes. Between the change and wash I tell her I've met a man called John Wayne. She laughs very loudly.

'Does he ride well?'

'Er, no. He has a girlfriend. And, Karen, I have a boyfriend.'

Door slams. Boyfriend Paul is two years younger than me. Very sensible. Good with money. Attractive. Charming. *Everyone* likes him. *Everyone* thinks he is sensible, good with money. Including me. Been going out with him for five years. Not all good, but *know* I love him, been through a lot with him, and he is a 'good catch'. *Everyone* likes him. Except Karen, who thinks he is too straight for me and has something missing and has a dark side. Her most affectionate nickname for him is Flatliner.

'You need someone with some va-va-voom, Sarah. He's a non-starter. He's insecure and controlling. And a potential bully. And you don't want that.'

My friends also don't like him much. They thought he was OK in the early years but as he did better at work gradually became an arrogant, boorish, self-serving prat. But I don't see much of them these days.

My insecure, sensible control-freak Flatliner lives in a two-up, two-down in Chelmsford. I have a two-bedroom flat in an old Victorian house in Brentwood. Largest commuter town in the country. Full of back-office suits wanting to be front-office Ferrari-drivers. I have a flatmate who pays her rent on time and is fun as well as funny and sensitive and has a boyfriend who doesn't understand her and lives up the road and is in awe of her and threatened by her and treats her badly. And I have a job at the railways as Situation Manager (I recover situations, or cover over situations—whatever is more pertinent to the issue). During the six months I've been there, the company has sponsored me to go on three positive thinking, power and assertiveness training courses in wonderful country hotels in the Lake District and New Forest. And I still can't say no.

So life is sweet. Ish. Boring but sweet. Until I meet John Wayne.

3rd September

I disagree with Karen. My boyfriend is not boring. I met him at his twenty-first birthday party. He was going out with someone called Gillian. I was going out with someone called David. I thought he was cute, had a smooth dark brown voice and had the most amazing long eyelashes. He told me later he also thought I was cute but that I wouldn't stop talking about David.

I then met him two years later. At Liverpool Street Station. He liked my legs. He saw me from the back. He told his friend he knew me. His friend bet him fifty pounds he didn't. He came up to me. Introduced himself and won the bet. He also got a date with me.

The date went well. In a local pub, called the Dead Duck, beamed, mid-eighteenth-century, lighting so low you couldn't see what you were eating or drinking. And it had an unfortunate sewer problem. Despite the stench of sulphur in the pretty beer garden outside, we managed to make each other feel good. He had lovely eyes. The sort you get lost in. An open, honest face. And a wonderful smile. No pretension or artifice other than he worked in the City in a bank and was aware he was surrounded by people who were full of both.

He invited me back to his two-up, two-down in Chelmsford, which he'd just bought with a heavily subsidised mortgage. He asked if I wanted to see his etchings. The charm of it is that he genuinely *did* want me to see his etchings. Fabulous and imaginative drawings of dragons and horses and knives and outstretched hands, and swords and leopards and weird and wired shapes and images. Some quite disturbing, others quite delicate and poignant. He had a wide and diverse interest in music. A passion for everything from heavy metal to gentle classics. He played the electric guitar very badly. His rendition of Status Quo's 'Whatever You Want' was diabolical but I said he played OK. He spoke eloquently and with sincerity. He made me laugh. He intrigued me. He loved to cook (although not to wash and dry). He was sensitive and interesting and was interested in me as a person. He asked insightful questions. He gave open answers. He didn't try to impress and smiled knowingly when I did. He didn't try to kiss me, and I said I would call him some time next week.

He called the next day. I said I was going to Monte Carlo and would he like to come down for the weekend? Other men had asked if they could join me, but I'd said no. But I asked Paul. Instinctively I knew he was the one. The one you know you are going to love. I suggested we have lunch before I left. On the day I was due to fly out. I took the train to London and met him for a lunch. Neither of us touched the food. We just looked at each other. I told him I had to rush home to get my suitcase so I could then come back into London and get on a flight from Heathrow. The madness somehow seemed logical then, and in keeping with the surreal nature of our relationship.

I went. I didn't hear from him for a week and thought he'd changed his mind. I then received a call.

'Hi, it's Paul.'

I had forgotten who Paul was.

'Er, Paul who?'

'Have you forgotten me already? Paul O'Brian. Etchings. Brilliant guitar player.'

'Er, ah, yes. Etchings.'

I remembered. But lots can happen in seven days. Monte Carlo had turned my head in a week. I'd forgotten this unpretentious doe-eyed boy for the bright lights and fast cars of the principality. When I heard his voice I felt he was coming to save me from myself. Almost heaven-sent.

'I'm driving down tomorrow and should arrive tomorrow evening. Where are you staying?'

I was staying with a 'friend'. Andreas Banyan. Fifty-five. Wrinkled, rich and worldly. Half-Egyptian. Half-American. Sounds so sleazy, and perhaps it was. I'd met him when I was in Monaco before and he had introduced me to some of the stars who waft in and out of Monte Carlo like feathers at the Pro Am Celebrity Tennis and Golf Tournaments held there annually. He was old enough to be my grandfather and I kept him at arm's distance because I knew he wanted more than just a smiling companion.

'Women should be treated like fabulous works of art. They should be put on display and appreciated, and if you can't appreciate them any more they should be passed on to a collector who knows how to appreciate them.'

He considered himself a collector and his logic made me sick. I wondered how many ingenues had been seduced by the money people. Andreas was surrounded by many other 'collectors' who made me aware they would be happy to appreciate me should Andreas ever fail to do so.

Into this den of iniquity arrived Paul in his blue Golf GTI and his Quicksilver shorts. I wasn't there to greet him, but arrived the next morning and told him I was so pleased to see him. He didn't know how pleased.

We ate at the same restaurants I'd visited with Andreas, but with Paul they were somehow so much more romantic. Most of the couples who were eating there weren't looking at each other. They were looking at other couples. What they were wearing—their jewellery, the labels—but never who they were with. We only had eyes for each other. We only talked to each other. We held hands. We kissed in public. We made love in private. We slept very little. Ate very little. Drank very little. Danced a lot.

On Day Two, we both made the decision to leave early. I introduced Andreas to Paul.

Andreas pulled me aside and whispered in my ear, 'Sarah, he's only a boy.'

I whispered back, 'He may look like one, but he's a man and I love him.'

I didn't say what I thought, which was, Anyone would look a boy to you. I thought this too cruel. And honest.

We drove back slowly through France. We'd planned to stay in Monaco for a week, so hadn't booked anything en route, but somehow every hotel we stopped at and asked had a room—only one—left. Admittedly usually at the top of the hotel. And there was never a lift. I spoke the French. Paul carried the suitcases. That was the deal. I got the better end of it, methinks.

In Avignon we stayed for two nights. I danced along the river and we ate breakfast overlooking the medieval city. Mealtimes were spent gazing into each other's eyes and talking and talking and talking. Complimenting and in turn being complimented. Needing to touch one another—even if it was only by the fingertips. The electricity was there. In Vienne, our hotel was near to the Cathedral. Perhaps too close for some, as the bells rang out on the hour every hour. But it didn't matter. We didn't sleep much anyway. In Versailles I danced down the steps of the palace and practised my best *Singing in the Rain* skit when it poured on us when we took a picnic in the gardens. It didn't matter. Paul told me he used to row at school and rowed on the lakes in the Versailles grounds. He almost fell in while pushing the boat away from the side. Somehow he didn't, but it was funny and we both smiled and I was so very happy and in love and he was so very happy and felt loved.

By the time we arrived home we were totally smitten. In love as in not needing food or drink or sleep. Just needing each other. Nauseating bucket stuff. We ate at his favourite restaurant. Well, we didn't eat. We just stared at each other for five hours. We emptied the restaurant, despite having been the first customers to arrive that day. The waiters got concerned that we didn't like the food but we said it was fine. So he ate half the steak and I ate two potatoes. New. After our non-lunch, we meandered to the nearby cricket green, sat on the grass, and watched the local teams play abysmally on the sort of day that only exists in Miss Marple films. Sunny, balmy, no dog turds on the grass. Bees that don't sting but just buzz happily. No mosquitoes to distract from the pleasure of furtive fumblings. No background noise of car radios or road-rage drivers wishing each other dead. Just hours of kissing and being held and holding and being wanted and wanting and being smug and happy, somehow both knowing we'd met the right person, and weren't we very lucky, and *Room with a View* was right and I knew how Helena Bonham Carter felt in the last scene.

Most weekends we would spend all Sunday in bed. Antisocial and not good for the back. Occasionally we would venture to our favourite restaurant by the cricket green. Remembering and creating new memories to tell our children. Making love and sleeping and making love. He was a wonderful, caring, considerate, sexy lover. He taught me ways to please and how to please myself and I became consumed in ways of how to please and tease him. Each Sunday we would get up at five p.m. and I would accompany him to his local Catholic church. We would sing hymns and pray for forgiveness for an hour, then return and make love again. Until we fell asleep in each other's arms.

I didn't want to see anyone just in case they took me aside and slapped me awake. I didn't want to break the spell and perhaps discover it was a dream. A high I couldn't maintain. I wanted to marry him and have his children and live happily ever after. And this had never been my dream before. I had never met anyone I would want to share an evening with, let alone a lifetime. But this man was good and kind and sexy and honest and made me feel special and told me I made him feel special. Neither of us was stupid. I had split from boyfriend, David, who'd kept disappearing off to Saudi Arabia to 'find himself' in an endless desert and strangely always returned a few months later more lost than ever. He had eventually moved out of our flat to Notting Hill, where everyone, it appeared, was as lost and nutty as he was.

Paul had just split from his girlfriend, Gillian, who was still 'hanging around'. He told me it wasn't until he met me that he realised how unhappy he was with her. He said he'd continued to see her, but only for sex. Occasionally Paul would say something that would make me stop and think, That's cruel or mean, but there were so many pluses, what of the negatives? Of the little snide comments about past girlfriends? How they had hurt him and weren't quite up to his standards—which were high. I felt sorry for her. This pre-Sarah girlfriend called Gillian. She would stalk the house occasionally and ask to see him. He once returned to the house two hours later than he'd said. I'd cooked something simple. Steak. So it was about two hours over-done. And he explained that he had seen Gillian and that she had been very upset and wanted him back but that he had told her it was all over. That he had been very calm about it. That she had looked dreadful. Her nails were bitten and she had started to smoke, but he had moved on. This wasn't for him. He then kissed me, told me he loved me, and allowed me to go down on him. Bless. And he wasn't hungry—for food—so not to worry about the steak.

Sometimes Paul came out with lines—as in well-rehearsed verging on the corny 'I need space/must move on' variety. I felt somehow he had probably told Gillian the same story when he had dumped his previous girlfriend for her. I occasionally got the feeling he used the same lines, because they came out as sing-song. I knew this because most men I knew did it and most women I knew did it. But, hey, I was guilty of that too. And I felt he was genuine when he looked into my eyes and said he loved me and called me his angel and little pixie and that I was wonderful. And I thought he was wonderful and special because he loved me. And deep down I didn't want to believe him. And I did.

We got on to the subject of past boy and girlfriends, as you do. And shouldn't.

Paul—'What were yours like?'

Sarah—'I had one, really. David. Who kept buggering off to Saudi Arabia to find himself in the desert and always managed to find his way back home after a few months. But that was it. How about you?'

Paul—'Well, before Gillian there was Eve, and before that there was Isabel and a girl called Tracy, but she didn't count, really. I was embarrassed to be seen with her. I used her a bit. I liked Eve. She was short and plump. Sort of like a moped. Fun to ride but not for best. Gillian, who you know of—well, I just got tired of her coz she moaned a lot in the end and wanted to get married and I didn't want that. And she did. Very mature for her age she was. So was Eve. Isabel was sort of a school romance. You're breaking my criteria, really. You don't have a chest, you're not shorter than me— or really short, which is what I usually go for, for some reason, and you're not the mature type.'

Sarah—'Sounds as though you want someone to look up to you and want to fuck your mother.'

Think he was a bit shocked by me being so up-front, but, hey, I'd met the type before. In fact, methinks that most of the men I had met were hunting for their mums. They said they wanted independent-minded feisty women but bottom line is they didn't. Not really. Problem with independent feisty women is that usually they also like their own space, want to move on and are capable of doing so—and don't want to do anyone's cooking, cleaning, ironing, washing. At a push, only their own.

Paul—'No, I'm not looking to marry my mother. But you have broken the criteria. Most men have a wish-list. Just depends when they decide to break it. Sometimes it's tried and tested. Sometimes it evolves. Mark, my brother, always goes for townies. Girls who work in London, good job, must be beautiful and have a brain and humour and conversation. Do you have a wish-list of things to look for in a man?'

Sarah—'Kind, loving, intelligent, funny, nice hands, nice eyes, nice hair, over six foot. Handsome, if possible. Good dancer.'

Paul—'Well, I'm most of those things. Just six foot, though. And I think you can ask any of my friends and they'll tell you I'm not a cruel person. As for the rest. You decide. I like a woman with her own mind.'

Sarah—'Really? Most men I know say that, but what they really mean is that as long as their opinions are the same as theirs, they're welcome to have an opinion. If they're not, well, they might as well not have one.'

Paul—'I'm not like that.'

We'll see, I thought. But as the weeks rolled on he proved himself to be kind and considerate and generous and loving, and occasionally boorish but a very good dancer and very sexy—in and out of bed. I remember him looking at me one evening and calling me his angel with tears in his eyes and me thinking, Hey, I would love to be your angel. Just yours. Just the two of us. As he would say to me, 'Two of us against the world.' I never really got that bit. I never thought the world was against me. I always felt I had to make it work for me. Somehow I had to work with this gritty, nasty world rather than against it. I had to be kind to it, and it would be kind to me. But Paul had other qualities which more than made up for some of his reasoning.

For a start, he was romantic without trying. He never sent Valentine cards. Which miffed me as friends received bouquets and dinners at the Ivy or Samling in Windermere. Instead, on one February fourteenth, he wrote a card…

Dear Sarah

As you know, I don't believe in celebrating Valentine's Day. It always seems a pity that people need something as commercialised as VD to show each other they need each other. However, it would appear that you feel you need reminding.

Well, let me take this opportunity to make sure you realise that you are the most important thing in my life. You cause such extremes of emotion. I love you so much sometimes I need to come up to the surface to breathe before I can dive again to be surrounded by your love.

My feelings for you go beyond just affection. I think about

*everything that affects you. Sometimes you catch me just star-
ing at you—it's as though I don't even have to touch you.
Just looking at you I feel our love. You are the only person I
have ever met who in the same minute can drag me to the
edge of despair and desperation and as I'm about to fall grab
me and hold me close. You should always know that even
when I'm not with you you are in my thoughts and that I
can't experience love unless I'm in your presence, because only
then do you release my heart from the prison you've built for
it, to let me really feel what love is.*

*You must never doubt me—because through all that has
happened to us in the last two and a half years I've never
really doubted you.*

*Together, Sarah, we will be something very special. Like
everything that's good in life it has to be worth waiting for.
Trust in me as I've trusted you. Let me into your world as
I've let you into my heart. Words can only say so much. Just
believe.*

Love, your Paul. xxxxx

I desperately wanted to believe. At the beginning we
would write notes to each other—at least three a week. My
feelings would inspire poetry. Sounds naff, but I sent love
poems and letters. Do people do that any more? The old-
fashioned way. Handwritten in cards. I was always getting the
length wrong and having to use the back cover to complete
my work. E-mail and text messaging are so deletable and lazy
and quick. Not as clever. Writing takes longer. Means more.
Mistakes, smudged by tears, crossings-out and all.

To Paul...

*Your name means strength and valour
You come from noble stock*

You'll travel like your father
To find what others mock

You're a leader and a driver
Leaving passengers behind
You act when others wonder
How quickly works your mind

You understand the Game of Life
As though you've played it all before
Aching as each new morning breaks
To improve upon your score

You have few faults in my eyes
But my eyes are blind to see
All the faults and contradictions
That you often find in me.

I've never felt this hurt before
I've never known this joy
Echoing through my heart and mind
Becoming as fragile as a toy.

Love Sarah xxx

First Christmas I wanted to spend with him. But his father didn't think it right.

'You haven't known this girl long.'

'I've known her for four months.'

'Not long enough. Just our family should be here, Paul. Can't she go with her own family?'

'She doesn't want to.'

I didn't want to. Mum was driving me nuts.

So I didn't spend Christmas Day with my love. I spent it with my ex. With David.

David had returned from one of his Saudi I-will-find-my-focus trips, to discover his long-suffering girlfriend had found a focus of her own and he wasn't in it. After taking all his furniture from the flat we'd shared (i.e. three-quarters of it) when I was away and leaving me with minimalist decor—which had up sides (less to clean and I didn't like his stuff anyway)—he calmed down. Realised he was a prat. And asked to see me. To have dinner. I declined. But he called after Paul told me we wouldn't be spending Christmas together. I said I was fine. David said I couldn't spend it by myself. He said he'd take me out to dinner.

He took me to Paris. By Eurostar. First Class. Montmartre and Sacre Coeur on Christmas Eve and top of Eiffel Tower on Christmas Day. At the top he proposed.

David—'Sarah, I have something to ask you.'

Sarah—'What?'

David—taking little black box from his pocket—'Will you…?'

Sarah—realising what little black box contained and thinking on feet—'Stop. No. Don't. I'm not right for you. You know I'm not.'

David—looking shocked and dejected—'I understand.' (He didn't)

Long hug. Saying nothing. Him in tears. Me trying to be.

I said no. I said I was saving him from himself and myself and that in years to come he would thank me. He looked crestfallen, but I was adamant. Plus I didn't love him. Not that way. We ate at the restaurant in Gare de Lyon. Ornate and grand and value for money—a rare combination. We then returned home, still friends. He dropped me at the bottom of Paul's parents' road. I walked up to be greeted by Paul and family as though I was one of them. Although obviously not on Christmas Day.

Looking back, my relationship with Paul in those first years was innocent and special and wonderful and naïve and I wish it could have lasted for ever. But, like the ink on the cards and letters, over time it faded leaving only the impression of happiness rather than the reality of it.

I keep a box of the letters and cards. They stopped about the fourth year. The last note I wrote was a contract of love. I'd applied to so many jobs over the years, I thought I could work the format. A request for a full-time position in his life.

Dear Mr O'Brian

RE: POSITION AS LIVE-IN SPOUSE

I'm writing to express my interest in the position of best friend, lover, occasional domestic, gardener, sexual arouser, hostess, intelligent wit and sleeping partner to Mr Paul O'Brian. My relevant experience and learning points to date include:

- *How to balance precariously on knees without using hands, and bending over at an angle. The only thing stopping me from toppling over is will-power.*
- *How to prove Paul wrong about women drivers.*
- *How to prove Paul wrong.*
- *How to sexually arouse myself.*
- *How to sexually arouse myself keeping Paul guessing as to whether I know he's watching me.*
- *How to ring the same person over three times a day, having just seen them in the morning and about to see them that night, and still feel you miss the sound of their voice.*
- *How lucky I am to be as supple as I am.*
- *How lucky Paul is to have someone who is as supple as I am.*
- *How cuddles take on a new dimension when you're with someone you love.*

- *How everything takes on a new dimension when you're with someone you love.*
- *How I hate electric guitars and never knew it.*
- *How I must never speak after ten o'clock when I'm in bed with a very tired man who has been working hard all day and needs his rest, unless he's feeling randy, in which case I'll have my mouth full anyway.*
- *How I have a cute arse.*
- *How Paul thinks I have a cute arse.*
- *How other people probably think I have a cute arse but Paul won't tell me.*
- *How although Paul likes my chest he would like it to be bigger.*
- *How although I like my chest—I would like it to be bigger.*
- *How I can watch TV, play records and have a meaningful conversation at the same time.*
- *How I have a meaningful relationship with little black dresses.*
- *How having fun and being loyal are not incompatible.*
- *How I love you…*

I would be grateful if you would consider my application in your loyal and gentle care, and hope this temporary position will one day evolve into a permanent one.

Yours sincerely…

See. Sounds naff. But at the time, writing it, it was funny and wonderful and just right. I would keep the letters and cards in a little red box and occasionally look through it on quiet Sunday afternoons if Paul was out with friends. Reading it back, somehow it made me feel just sad and very lonely.

The letters and poems and cards grew less frequent as the months progressed, until the only cards sent were for birthday and Christmas. And, on the fifth year, he sent a Valentine.

Five years in, the romance had faded. We'd forgotten to respect each other and do what agony aunts enthusiastically call 'working at it'. There was almost a laziness in his attitude towards me. We both, perhaps arrogantly, thought that relationships if they were meant to be didn't need to be worked at. The agony pages were for other couples who had problems. We didn't. We were intelligent and sensitive and in tune with our emotions and other people's.

Well, we did have some problems. I had been through an abortion after going out for nine months, to which he had agreed and paid for. We had planned a long weekend in Suffolk at the Angel Hotel. I had forgotten to take the Pill. Well, I had taken it, but I'd been ill and it hadn't worked. Obviously, because two months later I'd discovered I was pregnant. I didn't know if I should tell him. Hindsight is such a wonderful thing, don't you think? In hindsight I wouldn't have told him. In hindsight I wouldn't have told him a lot of things. But I didn't have the benefit of that, so I told him.

'Paul. I'm pregnant.'

'Is it mine?'

'Of course it's yours.'

I didn't expect that question.

He came over to me and hugged me. I think he wanted to be hugged more than hug. I think he was dazed.

Then, 'What do you want to do?'

'I don't think we should have the child. We love each other but we've only been going out for nine months. It's too soon. We want to do so much. Achieve so much. I think if I had the child you would resent me and it and I would resent you and it. That's not fair on either of us or the child. Will you tell your parents?'

Paul—'No, of course not. They're Catholics. They don't even know you're living with me, or we're having sex. This would break their hearts. They wouldn't understand. They wouldn't get it. Couldn't comprehend it. So it's not worth going there, Sarah. Will you tell your parents?'

I was bemused by the fact he thought his parents were naïve enough not to realise we were sleeping with each other, but, hey, like so many things Paul increasingly said, let it pass for now.

Sarah—'No. Likewise. They're not interested. They have their life to lead. They are busy and my mother doesn't want to know what will or could hurt her. So I tell her nothing. My dad's not well. He thinks of me as his little girl. I don't want to spoil the illusion. My mum wouldn't forgive me if I did.'

Paul—'So we tell no one?'

Sarah—'We tell no one.'

One week later. Local clinic. Paul drove. Seven a.m. No traffic on the M25. Leafy lanes. Pre-warned there might be demonstrators outside. Anti-abortion. There weren't. It would take a morning. I could work the next day. They were very kind. Efficient. At twenty-five I was the oldest in a ward of ten women. It was quick. Physically and emotionally numbing. Offered Rich Tea biscuits and sweet tea when I woke from the deepest sleep. Feeling relieved and relief. The other women in the ward were still sleeping. One was awake. She was crying. She'd had a local anaesthetic and she told me she'd seen the baby.

'I saw the baby. It looked like a proper little baby. I didn't think it would look like a baby, but you could tell. You could tell it was a baby when it came out. I didn't expect that. I didn't expect something like that. I expected a little cell and I don't think I would have had a local if I'd known. I don't think I would. I don't think I could go through that again.

That will haunt me, that will. That will haunt me. Wish I
hadn't seen it. Wish I hadn't.'

I hadn't seen the baby. I hadn't seen what had come out
of me at twelve weeks. I had been asleep. And I closed my
mind to it and just thought it was a joint decision and something that both of us, Paul and I, had decided together and
agreed upon. And that it was a dreadful decision to make,
but it was the most practical decision, and it would have been
unfair on Paul who was just starting out on his career and
me who was trying to start one. And there would be plenty
of time to have children and we loved each other so it wasn't
a case of that. And we loved each other. And we loved each
other. I kept saying that over and over in my head because
it made me feel better. Not good. Just better. Reassured.

And I cried, just a little bit.

We drove home in silence. Two hours of it. He cried and
went to Confession. Alone, I stayed in the two-up and
two-down in Chelmsford and made tea. My mother
phoned on the mobile to ask how I was, but really to tell
me what she had been doing with Dad that weekend. She
asked me if I was OK. I said fine and that I was… She
didn't wait for me to finish and said she had so much to
do and had to look after my dad and there was a dinner
party they had to go to and she had to get ready and get
my dad ready. And she did. I didn't tell my mother. She
was not the sort to listen or offer calming advice. She was
the sort to scream and consider every bad thing that happened to me an affront to her ability as a mother, and every
good thing something she could either credit to her own
influence or, in some cases, feel jealous that she hadn't done
herself. In her youth. Even the good things that happened
in my life I think potentially hurt her. I would often think,
what she doesn't know won't hurt her and she can't hurt
me by reacting to things the way she does. Pity. I would

have liked a mum. I spent my life in search of surro-gate mums.

Paul returned from Confession an hour later, having confessed nothing.

Paul—'I couldn't tell the priest anything. I felt ashamed.'

Sarah—'Isn't that what the confessional is for? To relieve the guilt? To relieve the sin?'

Paul—'You're not Catholic. You don't understand. Don't even try to understand what I'm going through. Don't talk about it any more. Don't mention it. Ever.'

Paul didn't tell anyone. I told my friend Helen and my friend Steve. Helen, an old schoolfriend, had had an abor-tion herself and was wise beyond her years. Steve was matter-of-fact, straight and honest, and I wanted and needed a man's perspective. Paul didn't want to talk about his perspective. So we didn't talk about it again. The abor-tion was never mentioned. The baby was never mentioned. The weekend in Suffolk was never mentioned. It was a black hole of time we lost. And into it went our innocence.

I locked it away. We weren't as intimate. We got up at ten a.m. on Sunday mornings and always met friends and had lunch out. Paul stopped going to church.

As an Irish Catholic, he had felt an impact on him greater than he or I could have imagined. The relationship strained under the weight of guilt and reprehension.

Paul—'You should have told me you weren't on the Pill.'

Sarah—'I was on the Pill. I was just unwell and it obvi-ously didn't work.'

Paul—'The Pill always works. Now I've got to live with it as well.'

Sarah—'Are you honestly telling me you wouldn't have had sex with me that weekend if I'd told you there was a chance the Pill might not work? It was a lovely weekend and I didn't want to spoil it.'

Paul—'Well, you did, didn't you?'

Sarah—'It was a shared responsibility.'

Paul—'You didn't give me the option to share it.'

Sarah—'I didn't think there was danger.'

Paul—'You knew there might be.'

Sarah—'You've slept with girls who weren't on the Pill before.'

Paul—'That was different.'

Sarah—'How different?'

Paul—'I knew about the risk and I took it. I was given no option here.'

Sarah—'That's not fair, Paul. Give me a break.'

Paul—'Why should I? You didn't give me one.'

Tears. Both of us.

Within the next six months the sex died. I quietly mourned. In silent desperation I would get up and go to work and come back home and go for a workout and organise birthday parties and Christmas drinks and dinner parties and be the devoted girlfriend and feel very lonely. And I knew he felt lonely too but I couldn't reach him any more and somehow he didn't want to be told I loved him any more. I loved this man in a spiritual as well as emotional sense. Paul had only a single bed, and we would snuggle up, spoon-like, so close all night. Somehow we managed to sleep and it was fine. We would ring and text each other every day. E-mails were long awaited.

Paul—message received
Thanks for a lovely evening. I love spending time with you. I wish we could have spent more time together but there will be other times I know. xx

Sarah—sent
You are a wonderful human being. Think of me in lacy

black knickers. Nothing else. That's how I'll be when you meet me at the door 6pm tonight. Maybe... xx

After dinners out or the cinema the last message would always read something like:

Paul—message received
Night beautiful. You are very special to me. Thanx for putting the sun into my summer. And I wish you were here with me in my bed. Lots of love. xx

After work lunches or meetings he would always remember and send:

Paul—message received
Hi gorgeous one. Hope lunch went well. Wish I'd been there. You are fabulous. Thinking of u. xxx

We'd go to weddings and listen to the vows. I never caught the bouquet, but friends would always ask in their subtle-as-a-brick sort of way 'So, when are you two getting married?' It was a naff cliché and we both ignored it, but as years progressed it started to bug. Breeding insecurity and resentment and cutting communication of how I felt, because I knew it might open the wounds of the abortion again. Which he never talked about. Even when others opened a conversation at one of the many dinner parties we went to and were talked at.

He had been my white knight in his Golf GTI. He had helped me to gain confidence about my body and sexuality. And then he had taken it away. He didn't feel it was right any more and so we didn't have sex any more. We hugged naked. We occasionally, in drunken stupors, made love or had sex, but he was always slightly irritable in the morning—as though I had made him to do it against his will. I had tempted him against his better self.

We started to organise dinner parties. To meet his friends and acquaintances. Some of whom initially talked about Gillian a lot, but who eventually realised that Sarah existed too and she was a person in her own right. Paul told me he loved me every day. He e-mailed and texted and called and wrote and every day I felt loved. But not physically loved. Not touched. Which doesn't matter. Sex isn't everything. But when you don't have it at all, it gradually becomes everything. And he hugged me a lot. But it wasn't like the first nine months. I'd got the chastity belt without even realising it was on.

So by September I was feeling a bit tired of a no sex, no going anywhere relationship—despite the fact I still deeply loved him. I was happy in my little world.

Meeting Paul for lunch today. Our favourite. The Punch Bowl. Posh country restaurant with fine wines. I remember Paul took me here first when we started going out. Arrived at twelve midday. Stayed until six p.m. in the evening. Romantic. Then we walked to the cricket ground and watched them play. Perfect. Fell in love with him.

Five years going out with each other. Perhaps he will propose. Perhaps he will go down on bended knee at the restaurant where we went on our return from that French trip. Perhaps it will be a birthday—his or mine—or perhaps a Christmas or perhaps a holiday overlooking a golden sunset or perhaps at dusk when music is playing in the background. Or perhaps at a concert while the music is live and throbbing. I've gradually forgotten to wonder any more. Forgotten to think that maybe this month he will ask me. I didn't want to ask him. Not even in a Leap Year. Still thought that naff.

Anyway, I knew I would be with him for a very long

time. Perhaps not a lifetime. But still for a long time. But not quite like this.

We arrived at twelve midday. We left at two p.m. Food was good. Fine wines still fine. Conversation still OK. Ish. But less room for gaps somehow.

Sarah—'How are you, Handsome?'

Paul—'Very well, Pixie.'

He still called me Pixie. It was an endearing nickname. I liked it. Felt perhaps when it was in my forties it might not be so appropriate.

'I will always think of you as my little pixie, Sarah,' he would say. 'Even when you're not little or pixie-like any more.' Ahhh. Warm gooey feeling inside. Perhaps this was the real thing. Perhaps. Had got fingers burnt before with David, so did I want to do this again?

Paul—'What would you like to eat? The usual? Melon with Dover sole and new potatoes—right?'

Sarah—'OK, OK, I know I always have the same thing, but I like it.'

Paul—'Why don't you try something new?'

Sarah—'I have and I don't like anything else on the menu. We could always go to a different restaurant. And you would think in five years they would have changed the menu a little more than they have. But they tell me it works, so why change it?'

Paul—'OK.'

Sarah—'How is work?'

Paul—'Fine—busy. Love working with Richard. He's fun and he's thinking of getting married to Caroline. But she's a fickle girl; she likes someone else and keeps going back to him.'

Sarah—'Perhaps it's not meant to be.'

Paul—'He'll win her over, I know.'

Sarah—'Do you still love me?'

Paul—'Of course I do. We've been through a lot together and I still love you very much. I sometimes sit and think that we could so easily have split at the time of…well, you know…and we didn't. I love you so much I ache sometimes. I hope you realise that.'

Tears in his eyes.

Sarah—'I do.'

I didn't. Tears in my eyes now.

Sarah—'I love you so much, Paul, but we must try to be kinder to one another. I know that other couples take each other for granted over time and I never want to do that with you. You're wonderful and I love you and I want to spend the rest of my life with you.'

Paul—'I will always be here for you, Sarah. I will never leave you. I will always love you. You lift my heart to the highest point and yet let me down to the deepest despair sometimes. But I know you are always there for me. Loving me. This is the real thing, Sarah.'

Sarah—'I know it is.'

He leant across the table and with his forefinger wrote on the palm of my hand I LOVE YOU. I reciprocated. It was something of a little tradition. Even when there had been rows we would always touch hands and somehow everything would be all right. Admittedly we did it less, but it was a sort of innocence that we had managed to salvage through the abortion.

We both wanted to fill silence with something these days. Before it was enough to look at each other in stunned silence, in awe of how lucky we were to have met each other. Today we were more in awe of the fact we were still together.

4th September

A Sunday. Am excited as tomorrow will be seeing or speaking to John again. Have to ask question of him about customer focus. This has put me in a good mood about everything. Am very sweet to Paul. Paul reciprocates and is sweet to me. A master of Latin phrases, Mr O'Brian. Oral pleasure a house speciality.

5th September

I've phoned. His PA stops me from getting through. Her name is Medina. I keep wanting to call her Medusa. I visualise snarling snakes emerging from her dandruff-ridden crusty head. Turning people to stone who dare to ask her the time of day. She sounds as though she is in dire need of oral pleasure.

'Who is this, please?'

'Sarah Giles.'

'Does Mr Wayne know what it's about?'

'Yes.'

'Could you tell me what it's about?'

'No. It's a bit complicated.'

'I'm afraid Mr Wayne is very busy and can't speak to anyone.'

'It won't take long.'

'Then you can tell me, can't you, dear.'

(Don't you 'dear' me, you sexually frustrated and probably bearded and moustached Medina–Medusa person.)

'OK. I want to know what his views are on the customer focus issue raised in the management document issued by Central Office last year and if he could provide me with a quote as I am now writing a report and it needs to be in by two p.m. this afternoon. OK?'

'I will see if he is free.'

Big sigh.

Muzak. Barry Manilow singing 'Could it be Magic'.

'He will speak to you.'

Click.

Silence.

'Er, hello?'

'Yes.'

'Is that John Wayne?'

'Yes. My time is precious. You need a quote. Do you have pen and paper ready?'

'Yes. Do you know what I'm going to ask?'

'Medina has told me.'

'Then fire away.'

'I have no views on it. Quote, unquote. Is that OK?'

'Yes. I mean no. I want a quote from you. You must have an opinion on this. You have an opinion on everything else. Cats, English beer, women's legs. Why not customer focus, which is your speciality?'

'On that particular paper I have no comment and no opinion. Is that all Ms Giles?'

'Well, if you can't give me a comment on this, then who can?'

'No one.'

'Great. Well thanks for, er, nothing.'

'My pleasure, Ms Giles. And thank you for an interesting lunch last week. Are you still wearing those culottes?'

I was. I lied.

'No.'

'Good. They looked disgusting on you. You should burn them.'

Click.

'Rude arrogant bastard.'

'Ms Giles?'

'What—er—?'

'Mr Wayne has handed you back to me. He has suggested I arrange another lunch with you as you don't seem to understand the issues revolving around customer focus.' Medina sounded less sexually frustrated.

More amused this time. She had obviously heard what I thought of her boss.

'Er. Right.'

'He can do a week on Wednesday. I will book Santini's. Is that OK with you?'

'Where is Santini's?'

'By Victoria Station. One o'clock. It's smart.'

'Fine.'

'Fine.'

Click.

I'm wearing those culottes again. Screw him.

14th September

I am meeting John Wayne today for lunch in Santini's. And, no, not wearing the culottes. And I've binned them. They were old anyway. Instead I'm wearing a dress. Sort of white, empire line and just above the knee and feminine. Not see-through. Just nice. Virginal. I feel virginal these days. Neat pumps. I look like a potential for the *Sound of Music*.

I arrive late. Ten minutes past one.

'You are late, Ms Giles.'

Dark, brooding, rude bastard scowls at me.

I make no excuse. It seems a bit churlish to blame the trains when I actually work for the railway at the moment.

We are shown to our table. Middle of the room. Harsh, unforgiving light. We order sole. And eat in silence. I start conversation.

'So, do you think Rogerson Railways will improve its customer service?' I ask.

Stares into my eyes.

'Who gives a fuck?'

Silence then smile (God, it makes me nervous when he does that).

'No, really. I think it will get better but it will take time and money, which the government are not prepared to give at the moment. Why are you wearing a bra?'

Somehow the sentences seemed a little incongruous together, and I wasn't quite sure whether to comment on the first bit or answer the second. So I did both.

'Do you think the funding structure will change with the new government and do you think privatisation will work? And this dress is slightly see-through and I didn't want you to see my nipples.'

'I don't think the funding structure will change within this government or the next. The petrol and car industry subsidise government coffers so heavily, and the catch-22 is unless the service improves customers will not use public transport over private transport. It's a pity I can't see your nipples. I think that would make you look quite sexy.'

I stare straight back into his eyes, which are now boring into me.

'How do you know all this about the government subsidy and the link with the car industry? Is it common knowledge? Surely there must be some sort of policing committee to stop this from happening or continuing to happen? Travelling by air is still the quickest and easiest way to get around the world. And, yes, it would look sexy, but I don't want to look sexy today. I want to look professional and have a conversation about airlines rather than my nipples. OK?'

'I know about the subsidy because we work closely with local government and we get told, like many journalists do—' (pointed look here) '—off the record about back-handers. What we need to do in the railway is change the culture so that we can better manage the limited funding we have and then we can progress from there. And I like talking about your nipples. Interesting. Are they very responsive to touch? And you have nice legs, Ms Giles. The dress allows me to see that you have very long legs. Long calves. Long thighs.'

John Wayne starts to salivate, which puts me off my sole. I get up, taking my legs and nipples with me to the Ladies'. I can feel his eyes following me, but he doesn't.

In the Ladies' I sit on the loo, pontificating whether I should allow him to kiss me. Or pat my bottom. Or hug me goodbye. Of course, he may not want or offer to do any of these things. And, hey, Sarah, *you have a boyfriend, right*! Yes, yes. Out of mind. Get John Wayne out of your head. Ten minutes later and no pee. I leave the Ladies' and go back to the table. John is coming towards me.

'I was going to send out a search party. Thought you'd flushed yourself down the loo. You OK?'

'Me OK.'

'Good.'

He escorted me back to the table, now soleless. And asked if I wanted dessert.

'No, thank you.'

'Coffee?'

'That would be nice.'

Two hours, two liqueurs, two coffees and wafer-thin mints later, I was beginning to relax in his company. As we sat at the table, he started very slowly to stroke my wrists. The inside of my wrists. Very gently with his fingertips and then with the back of his hand. It made me feel quite dizzy.

'Why are you doing that?' I asked him, knowing full well why he was doing that.

'Why not?'

Why not, indeed?

'When you were in the loo, it took me back to when I was a child. Do you know that if you prevent yourself from going for a pee for long enough you might orgasm?'

'I thought I would just wet myself, or worse get severe stomach cramps.' (God, this guy is weird.)

'No, it's true.'

'Did you read that anywhere?'

'No, one of my girlfriends told me this is what happens. It was always very exciting having sex with her when she was dying to go to the loo. She would have the most amazing orgasms.'

'I presume you weren't giving her oral sex at the time? Would be a bit messy, what?'

John smiled. (Ughh). 'Yes, I suppose so. But keep that in mind next time you go to the loo. Hold on and you never know—you may relieve yourself in more ways than you think.'

This guy was certainly different, and entertaining in a very unexpected way.

'Tell me about your boyfriend, Sarah.'

'I told you. He works in a bank. He is a trader. His name is Paul. I love him to bits.'

'Why aren't you married?'

'He hasn't asked me.'

'Why don't you ask him?'

'I don't believe in the woman asking the man.'

'Not even in a Leap Year?'

'No. Are you still with Amanda?' (Miss Piggy cropped up in my mind.)

'Yes. But she may be moving out. She was married before she met me. For a month. She realised on her wedding day she'd done the wrong thing. She was brave to do what she did. I met her on a management training course in the New Forest. She thought I was interesting and asked if I could take a walk with her round the grounds after dinner one evening. I did. She seduced me.' (Yeah, right.) 'She told me about her trick with chocolate cake. She said she could smear it all over her chest and I could lick it off her. I'm rather partial to chocolate cake so I tried that evening. Very good it was, too.'

All the while John talked about his chocolate-coated Miss Piggy he continued to stroke my wrists. Occasionally reaching up my forearm to the inside of my elbow. It was as though he was pretending my arm was my leg. That he was playing with the ankle and gently making his way up the calf. Then stopping, and gently pushing to go even further. I was so pleased I was wearing a bra. My nipples have a life of their own.

He continued…

'You see, Sarah, I went into the railway because after leaving university I trained as a research chemist, but there weren't many women in that job. Or not that I found attractive. I joined the rail industry, because I considered myself on the fast track in life—' (he smirks; I don't) '—because I liked the challenge it presented and also because I thought you'd find more women working in the industry.'

I must admit, I found this argument totally unbelievable and told him so.

'I thought you would have found other industries with more women in them. Advertising or marketing, for example. Far more women, and attractive ones. Or PR. That industry is full of women who give good head as well as PR…I'm told.'

He smiled.

'I know. They do. I've met quite a few.'

He pays the bill. Scowls at the cost. But he chose the restaurant—not me. I thank him.

'Thank you for a lovely lunch.'

'My pleasure.'

He walks and talks me to the station.

'I came here with a management consultant last week. Her name was Stephanie. She was very beautiful, soon to be engaged and she told me she was quite fixated by me. She pushed me into that alcove over there—' (he points at alcove in wall of station) '—and ripped my shirt. I had to go back home to Amanda and explain.'

I didn't quite know if he meant to tell me this because a) he wanted me to do it to him—and wanted to put the idea in my head; b) he didn't want me to do it, just in case I'd considered doing it, as Amanda might understand once but not twice in a fortnight; or c) he liked Stephanie and she was going to be Amanda's replacement after the chocolate cake fetish had turned mushy.

I said… 'Oh.'

Unimpressed by my lack of response and clever riposte, he said he would see me to Liverpool Street Station, to make sure I was safe. I said I would be fine.

'No, I'll make sure you're OK.'

And that's what he did. Made sure I was OK till Liverpool Street Station. Ten stops Circle Line. Standing up all the way. No conversation. Just lots of staring. Mostly at my legs and then into my eyes. No smile, laugh or sign of light. No wrist or calf or ankle-stroking. Nothing. Very peculiar end to a very peculiar lunch with a very peculiar, sexy, ravishable dark prince.

20th September

I'm bored. I have done nothing to report about. Nothing to recover from. John Wayne has not been in my life. Touched my heart or my wrists. Every time I go to the toilet I think about him. And he was right about the pee thing. I contact his office and get Medina, who says he's gone away for a fortnight with his girlfriend Amanda. I tell her to tell him he was right about the 'pee thing'. I tell her John will understand. She huffs that she's sure he will. I try to find out where they've gone. Some hotel in the middle of nowhere with a four-poster bed and an *en suite* bathroom with a bath for two and a shower for two. Probably. I wonder if he's tickling her wrists as I'm writing my appraisal on why Roger-son Railways fails to communicate with its customers while disruption occurs. I wonder if he's eating chocolate cake off her voluptuous breasts. I wonder if it's chocolate with or without milk, if it's home-made or from Marks & Spencer. I wonder if he's drinking English beer or the crap foreign muck and if he's eating sole in the evening and thinking ever so briefly about me, or about Stephanie, who tore his shirt.

30th September

'Hello. This is John Wayne.'

Unexpected voice. Unexpected pleasure first thing on a Friday morning. Indian Summer of a morning and John Wayne calling *me*. Not Medina saying John is on the phone. He is actually calling me direct.

'I wanted to know how you were.'

'I'm fine. Did you have a good holiday with Amanda? Not too much chocolate cake, I hope? Or ripped shirts? Or foreign muck to drink?'

'It was fine. Amanda is definitely moving out. I've suggested she moves out. She needs her own place. She moved into my cottage just as an interim measure. She needs to find her own space. I've told her as much. I got your message from Medina.'

'What message?'

I'd forgotten.

'About the pee. Good to hear it worked. Hope you've been practising. I find it quite exciting, the thought of you in the bathroom now, Ms Giles.'

'Whatever turns you on, Mr Wayne.'

Silence.

'Well, I'm at the Crime Prevention conference in November, which I believe you're organising. So look forward to seeing you there.'

'You too.'
'Goodbye, then.'
'Goodbye.'
Click.

What a weird conversation. Started so well. So promising. Sort of sexual innuendo. Literal toilet humour and then nothing. Just a goodbye, and a tease about his girlfriend moving out. The Miss Piggy I've yet to meet. Perhaps Stephanie will be the replacement. Anyway, girl, focus on your man. Your Paul. Your Rock. Leave the chocolate cake to someone else…

OCTOBER

ACTION LIST

Enjoy work.

Go to gym four times a week. Be able to do the box splits.

Try out new kick-boxing class.

Beat crap out of bitchy girls in office.

Try to seduce Paul into having sex with me.

Drink eight glasses of water a day. GMTV suggested this helps eyes shine.

Eat less low-calorie chocolate drink.

Take vitamin pills. Despite making pee very yellow.

TEXT SEX

1st October

My mobile phone is an extension of my right hand. It is almost a spiritual thing. It is another intrinsic sense. To smell, to touch, to see, to hear and to text message. I have discovered the power of text messaging. It was designed for me. Short and sharp and to the point. Ability to spell totally irrelevant. In fact, lousy spelling adds a certain charm. You can be as smutty as you like. It doesn't matter. You can say you meant to send it to someone else. That is, of course, if it doesn't continue to happen after repeated warnings.

Paul works in an office of men. Their bodies are full of testosterone. Their egos are huge and wallets are full. These testosterone-filled money bags are surrounded by women who work there with one goal in mind. To bag these money bags. Ideally by getting them in the sack and getting them to realise that they can't live without them. These girls are pros. They should work on the streets (albeit SW1 streets), and some of them (I am told) have done so. Anyway, out of every ten who enter the trading room, one usually gets her man. Or someone else's. Wedding rings are totally irrelevant.

Paul is different. He wears no ring (we're not engaged), but he's faithful and loves me. He goes to lap-dance joints because his brokers pay for it, but he doesn't enjoy it. He tells me so himself. Like a dog, really.

He texts me every morning:

I've arrived safely.
I love you.
Hi gorgeous, big confident kiss.
I wish I was still in bed with you.

At Christmas:

I've had my first mince pie. I wish you were in my bed. Miss you loads. Looking forward to seeing you this weekend.

That sort of thing.
Then I started to get:

I wish my cock was in your mouth. It's so hard at the moment. I loved you in those jeans last night.

Linked:
1/3
What a shame I am not there to ease your horny state. I could take off your knickers lift off your top. Kiss your lips then your nipples. Touch you with…
2/3
my finger then my tongue. Keep licking until you nearly come then turn you over and put my dick in your wetness pulling you onto me with my hands on your…
3/3
hips so I am as deep as possible.

Linked:
1/2
Every inch of my body is gagging for you. I loved you in those jeans last night. I wanted to rip them off you and come all over your…..
2/2
…face.

Sort of slightly different in tone.

I contacted him to find out that, no, these messages had not come from him but a salesman called Pierce, who was a close friend of his and was into bondage in a big way, was thirty-eight, on his third wife, and had at least four sex kittens on the go—all of whom worked (loose term) in the Square Mile as secretaries and salespeople, and all of whom liked to be 'fucked up the arse' and tied up. Nice.

The aforementioned Pierce was also a Harvard Graduate, played piano, guitar and saxophone and had a wonderful singing voice, lovely home in the country (used to be a pub, now converted with taste and money—the two are not synonymous). Background and appearances can be deceptive.

I contacted Pierce. First of all by text reply, after one particularly explicit 'cock-sucking butt-wrenching, I know you'd enjoy being fucked up the backside really' message. And then by phone.

'Hi, Pierce. I'm Paul's girlfriend. I think you keep sending me messages meant for someone else. Could you please delete my number from your phone as I don't want to get them any more? Have a nice day.'

'I'm so sorry, Sarah. Big apologies. Just that one of the kittens is also called Sarah. I'll change her name.'

'Thanks, Pierce.'

2nd October

Seven a.m. Beep on the phone. Message waiting.

I've got a real hard-on. It's really hard and I'm imagining you putting your lips around it and sucking it really hard and I'm aching to get my hands on your big tits.

Definitely not Paul.
I rang the number.
'Pierce?'
'Yes?'
'It's Sarah, Paul's girlfriend. You sent me another one of your "fucking" messages. Don't do it again or I will tell Paul and he'll be furious. OK?'

'OK. Very sorry, deeply embarrassed and mortified.'

3rd October

Seven a.m. Beep on the phone. Message waiting.

I can't stop thinking about you. You're driving me crazy. I imagine your wetness in my mouth. The thought of your nipples is driving me crazy.

Right. That's it.
'Pierce!'
'Yes?'
'It's Sarah, Paul's girlfriend. You sent me one of those messages again.'
'I didn't. I've sent nothing this morning. You must have got it from someone else. Perhaps Paul.'
'Doesn't sound like Paul.'
'Ring the number back.'
'Er. Well, sorry, Pierce for bothering you.'
'That's OK. Bye.'
Click.
I looked at the text message. Didn't sound like Paul. And now I looked at it again it had a little (though not much) more finesse than Pierce's drool.
I called.
'Hello.'
'Hello? Who is this?'
'John Wayne. Who is this?'
Heart stopped. Then beat very loudly.
'Sarah Giles.'
Silence.
'Have you just sent me a message on my phone…by accident?'
'What did it say?'
'Nothing much. It's just that it was slightly personal—well, very personal, actually, and you sent it to me. Was it meant for Amanda? I think it was. Or Stephanie, perhaps.'
'What did it say?'
I repeated it.

'Mmm. Sounds pretty strong, doesn't it? No, I didn't send it.'

'Well, it came from your phone.'

'Perhaps someone stole my phone and typed it in for a joke.'

'Who would do that?'

'I don't know. Anyway, how are your lovely nipples today?'

'You did send it, didn't you? Why?'

Silence.

'John? You have a girlfriend and a potential bodice-ripper in Stephanie. I have a boyfriend, who I love. Why are you contacting me with messages like this?'

Silence.

'Hi, you still there?'

'Yes, Sarah.' (God, I loved it when he said my name. He made it sound like *Sarah, I want to undress you now and make love to you* in one word. Amazingly no one else heard that, which is perhaps a good thing.)

'Did you send me the message?'

'Yes, Sarah.'

'Did you mean to send me the message?'

'Yes, Sarah.'

'Oh, er, right, then. Well. Don't send any again. As I said, we're going out with different people.'

'Fancy lunch some time soon?'

'Lunch should be OK. Next week?'

'Thinking more tomorrow, or the day after.'

'Er, haven't got my diary here. Wait a minute.'

I gave myself space to think. What was I doing? Lunch with John Wayne. Had done it before but then I hadn't had the message before. The signal. The idea of him thinking about me that way was firmly in my mind. Couldn't get it out of my mind. He wouldn't be able to do the chocolate cake trick on me. My breasts wouldn't fill a teacup, let alone a cake tin. I returned to the phone, having not found the diary but found some breath and balls.

'I can do day after tomorrow.' Anything or anyone that day would have to be cancelled.

5th October

Day after tomorrow. Don't know where tomorrow went. Lunch at one p.m. at the restaurant up the road from Pizza Express. None of the staff go there. Food is limited, service slow, you need more than two hours to meander over the courses and wines and coffee.

I was early. Chose the table. He was late. Ten minutes. I smiled. So did he. I went up to kiss him. Both cheeks. He smiled again. His smile was scaring me less each time. Always a good sign. Perhaps because he looked less like a wolf, or perhaps because I didn't see the wolf-like qualities any more. Only the deep brown eyes, the dark hair and his smell.

John Wayne smelt fabulous. I know women can smell great—but this man smelt of pheromones. I personally believe when he was a research chemist he concocted some artificial ones and impregnated himself with them. Whatever, they worked. I found him more and more irresistible every time I met him. Despite the fact he was just six foot and had a bit of a belly on him, I found the way his mind thought fascinating. Occasionally disgusting but always interesting.

I asked him about his cottage. He told me he'd got all the interior design done for free.

'What, did you sleep with the decorators?'

'Actually, yes.'

His story was that there were two girls who were designers that he had known from university, and that he'd kept in touch with them. That they had always liked him and he'd invited them round for the weekend. He'd propositioned them by saying that if they would paint his house inside and out he would sleep with them both all weekend. My mind was whirring round like crazy. Imagining them covered in paint, taking it in turns to sleep with this supposed sex god. I told him this was all bullshit. He said I could phone them and ask. I said it was bullshit and didn't have to. Anyway, the arrogance of the man was sometimes phenomenal.

He told me that Stephanie's brain was like a lighthouse to his torch. And that my mind was like a match to her lighthouse. I held in there for the pheromones.

He told me about his sexual prowess at college. How with one girlfriend he only had to touch her breast lightly and she would come.

'Really? That must have been inconvenient if you were in a pub with friends and you brushed past it by mistake.'

'It used to be my party trick.'

Why did I like this man? Arrogant, misogynistic, rude, undoubtedly bright and sexy, and pheromonal and animalistic and, and… Keep focused, Sarah. The guy is an arsehole!

He did more of the wrist-tickling and then asked if I would like to see his little cottage. And meet his cats. And have a drink in one of the pubs which do really good English beer (salivating here).

At three-thirty p.m. we get up and go back to the office. Kiss on both cheeks and he smiles again. I positively squeak with pleasure, floating off back to the office and fourth floor.

Text message:
Thank you for a lovely lunch. You are quite lovely Sarah.

Methinks was that quite lovely as in quite amazingly lovely, or quite as in quite almost OK lovely?

I return message:
1/2

Thank you for a lovely lunch. Wonderful company. Don't believe your story about the decoration, but am sure the cottage is fab. Can't wait to stroke your...
2/2
.....cats.

10th October

Text message:
Hello Sarah. We've never met but John suggested I get in contact with you as you specialise in recovery. I am working on a project for the Change Management Team and wondered if you could help me. My name is Amanda.

Amanda? Miss Piggy Amanda?

Respond:
Amanda—John's girlfriend Amanda?

Text message:
Yes. Can we meet?

Respond:
Yes, when?

Text message:
This afternoon.

Er. Right. Didn't expect this.

Three p.m. Amanda Cruise walked into the office. Beautiful, but then I looked at her legs. John was right about everything, but she looked nothing like Miss Piggy.

'Hello, I'm Amanda.'

'Hello, I'm Sarah.'

'I know. John described you very well.'

'He described you well too.' (I was wondering which Muppet I was supposed to look like.)

Amanda sat down and we talked recovery for thirty minutes, twenty minutes more than it deserved, and she said thank you, and I said it was a pleasure, and she asked if I would like to go out for a drink and I said fine (really thinking not a good idea) and then she left as quickly as she came.

WINTER

NOVEMBER

ACTION LIST

Have fun.

  Have fun.

  Try to enjoy dinner parties.

  Avoid dairy and wheat products as Anya has told me I am allergic to loads of things, but mainly dairy and wheat. I can eat lots of trout and carrots and garlic. (I live off it for two days and give up.)

  Be nice to Paul.

  Go to gym five times a week to work off aggression and frustration.

FIREWORKS

1st November

BANG. I've gone nearly a whole month without talking to John or Amanda. Or e-mailing either of them. I've been manic handling the conference on crime on the railway. Making sure all the speakers know what they are saying and stick to it and don't nick each other's thunder or sound-bites or unique selling points. That each has equal time and that their graphs and charts and pie charts are the right colour and everything is correctly spelt.

Then there is the catering. Ninety per cent of those attending are male so they want hot food which is plentiful and there on time. So lots of beef stroganoff—for two hundred. Not easy to do. Plus no gristly bits, which the Head of Publicity has told me about. Lots of bigwigs attending. The sniffer dogs will also be there. They don't want a crime conference being raided for any reason. It would look silly, somehow.

Getting back to the food. Then there is the salady stuff for the twenty or so token women who want salady stuff—unless they are trying to be macho, in which case they'll opt for the stroganoff. I almost feel like contacting them and asking them what they will want on the day. It's winter, so it could be hot for all I know. The weather has been unpredictable so far this year. Like my feelings. Up and down in emotional turmoil.

What am I doing flirting with someone at work when I have this fabulous guy at home? Or at least living fifteen miles from me. OK, we don't have sex. We haven't for years. But that's because he wants to save himself now until we are married. But he hasn't proposed, and I'm not waiting for ever. But apart from that he is fine. And, oh, yes. He's quite mean with money. But that's because he is saving for the future. Supposedly our future. So we have a future. So everything will happen soon. But not now. It's just that not now has been happening for a long time, and I'm becoming an I-want-it-now girl. And I think, if I asked John nicely, he would give it to me. Paul, alas, would not.

Perhaps the only fireworks I'll see this month will be the ones on the fifth. Hey ho.

* * *

5th November

Fireworks. Party. A friend of Paul's. All our friends were originally friends of Paul's. All my friends are still my friends. But not of Paul's. They don't like him very much and I don't think he likes them either. He likes to be around people he knows. It's just that I find them all so incredibly boring. The interesting ones don't last. The girlfriends who have some fire to them. Some substance. Don't last. Well, they last for about six months and then disappear into the never-never land of 'it wasn't meant to be'. But I liked those ones. Instead I'm always left with the boring ones who are destined to be together. Attached at the hip. Happily having charted their life and two point five children, they won't have to say much. So they don't. Fun fun fun.

Fireworks at a friend's home. This friend had wanted to build his own house and was doing so in Surrey. He'd bought a plot of land that overlooked a valley but also overlooked a motorway and railway line which on a clear day, you could hear loudly. He talked about his architect a lot. Eight to dinner. Patrick and Peter, twins; Kate, Patrick's other half; Kelly—Peter's. Then there was Connor and Shelley—who no one liked and everyone talked about when she left the room. I'd known Shelley from nursery school days, but we'd never swapped toys or anything. She'd moved away, then for some inexplicable reason my parents had moved to where her parents had moved ten years later. And we'd ended up at the same comprehensive. Paul and I had bonded through our mutual loathing of her. It had been over a dinner in Versailles.

Paul was talking about friends.

He mentioned a girl called Shelley who was going out with his best pal Connor.

For some reason I said, 'Not Shelley Beale?'

'Yes, Shelley Beale. She's horrid, isn't she?'

'Totally. Even the Sunday School teacher said she probably had three sixes on her head.'

'Match made in heaven, then.'

Mutual disappreciation society was duly formed. Everyone in the 'group' hated her, but I was the only one to be honest enough to be cold. Bullshit was never my forte. Not in personal relationships anyway. But perhaps these days I was kidding myself.

As I stood, waving my sparkler about, listening to Paul pontificate about life and love and stuff, I thought, Fuck, is this it?

Text message:
Hi, there. Are you having fireworks like me today? John

Respond:
Yes, but it's boring the fuck out of me. How you?

Message received:
1/2
Me fine. Pity you're bored. Been thinking about you a lot. Amanda has been giving me a hard time about seeing you and contacting you again and she's a good friend of Medina, so she knows if you call my office. How are your…
2/2
…nipples?

Respond:
Nipples erect and firm. Must be because I'm cold. Anything of yours erect and firm John?

Oops, perhaps I went too far. Perhaps I shouldn't have said that. Perhaps I should delete all messages received just in case

Paul happens to look through at some stage for his loving 'I am thinking about you' messages and spots a nipple one.

Message received:
Yes. When can we meet?

Respond:
What's happening with you and Amanda?

Message received:
She's moving out next month. She has found her own flat. I helped her look for one.

That was helpful of him.

Message received:
I'm feeling filthy. I wish I could stick my long hard cock in your mouth.

Christ. And I'd thought I was going too far.

Respond:
That's a bit heavy.

Message received:
Sorry Sarah, I think I've sent you a message by mistake. Pierce.

Respond:
Don't do it again.

I decided to call John rather than risk e-mailing Pierce John's messages and vice versa. I was just going to ask John how big Amanda's flat was.

'John, thought it best we speak rather than texting all the time.'

'Nice to speak to you, Sarah. When would you like to meet? This Saturday?'

'I can't do weekends.'

'Why not?'

'Oh, just busy.'

'With the boyfriend?'

'No. We've split up, actually.' (Why did I say that? That's a lie. Why did I say that?)

Bullshit. I know exactly why I said that. Deep water here, babes. Mind you, this could make me less attractive in his eyes. I'm not so unattainable any more. I read it somewhere that men who are womanisers—which I had been told reliably by at least twenty of the men and women I worked with that John was—prefer those women who are otherwise attached. Perhaps this was a good thing. Perhaps he wouldn't like me so much. That and the fact I was due to leave work soon through voluntary redundancy. So perhaps I told him this to get rid of him. Perhaps.

'Oh. Well, then, how about Friday?'

'Fine.'

'Bye, then.'

'Bye.'

It would have been almost furtive if I hadn't kept reminding myself that this guy worked for Rogerson Railways. His name was John Wayne. And the whole idea was totally ridiculous. But that was the fun of it. The sheer surrealism of doing something that everyone I knew would utterly disapprove of. After all, everyone liked Paul. Everyone. Then why didn't I? I think he'd grown dull. Controlling and dull. He wanted a square and I'm a circle and you can't change a circle into a square and he was trying really hard. So I wanted a bit of freedom. No marriage vows on the horizon, so, hey, why not. Even if it was with a guy called John Wayne who was a renowned womaniser with a fetish for chocolate cake, cats and English beer.

6th November

Call from Amanda. Could she take me to supper as a thank you for helping her out? OK. When? How about Friday? Er, couldn't make Friday. How about Thursday, then? Fine. Fine. Bye.

10th November

Thursday. Supper with Amanda. Meeting at Victoria Station. I am five minutes late.

'John says you're always late,' she says as I tap her on the shoulder and say hi.

'Yes, I am. But at least I'm consistent.'

'John suggested this restaurant in Victoria. Have you been there?'

'No.'

I was bemused by her continual references to John this and John that. I wondered if she was going to suggest things to eat that John recommended. Fuck John. Well, not tonight anyway.

The restaurant was romantic and intimate and not really suitable for two girls together, but, hey, John had recommended it. Perhaps he got some perverse kick out of his girlfriend, soon to be ex, having dinner with his perhaps soon to be next lover. Anyway, we sat down and ordered. And.

'John says the sole here is good.'

'I'll have the chicken, then.' I smiled.

Thank God. So did she.

'Me too.'

Amanda talked about herself. How much she loved John.

How she had met him. She omitted the chocolate cake bit and I hadn't drunk anything so didn't ask about it. Alas, there was no chocolate cake on the dessert menu, so I couldn't even ask if she fancied any. She talked about John a lot, and told me that he highly respected me. Really? I thought. Respected me. That's nice. She told me she's moving out because she needs her own space and that John has bought her a TV and that he is very generous. I said that was nice. I said that I was pleased he respected me, because I'd thought he only made time for me because he liked my legs. She smiled.

'No, he likes you for your mind, Sarah.'

She paid. I offered, but she paid. As we left the restaurant I felt rather sorry for her. I don't know if she really loved John but I wanted to tell her that he wasn't worth her time, her love or her sympathy. That any man who could treat her so badly didn't deserve such a sweet, gracious girl. That he was much more deserving of someone who could be as emotionally ruthless as say…me. Anyway, she kissed me on both cheeks and said it had been really fun and turned round towards Victoria Station.

I never saw her again after that. John told me months later that she had thrown a few plates when he told her that we were seeing each other, and that she had cut her wrists and threatened on numerous occasions to kill herself. And that she had started to write a letter to me but had never finished it. Somehow wish she had.

11th November

The Friday.

Message received:
Hi there. Love you. P
xxxxx

Respond:
Love you too.xxxxx

Message received:
What are you doing today?

Respond:
On a training course. In Sussex.

Message received:
Have fun. Love you.xx

Respond:
Will do.

What am I doing? Betraying the sweet guy I've known for five years with someone I know to be both devil and deep blue sea entwined. Perhaps it's the danger and immorality of it all that attracts me. I've never done anything very wrong in my life. But surely this is morally wrong? Well, no, I'm not married, am I? And Paul hasn't proposed, has he? And we're not having sex, are we? And we haven't for years, have we? So why not? Amazing how you can logic things out so quickly when you want to. Even when you're wrong.

I think that's what men do with their logic. Men automatically think they are right all the time. It's their mothers. They bring them up to think they can do no wrong. Firstborn are the worst. I can understand why Herod wanted to get rid of them. It was nothing to do with Christianity. It was probably the fact he got so pissed off with men who were first sons being boorish and phenomenally arrogant all the time. I blame the mothers. Anyway, when Paul does something wrong he makes me think it's my fault. Somehow my behaviour leads to him behaving the way he does. So it's nothing to do with him. It's natural. It's nature. It's excusable. No, not even that. It's right, and validated, and therefore I must be in the wrong.

Problem is, this screwed-up logic is catching, so now I validate actions which really are morally wrong. Like the phone call. Like the meeting with John. It's wrong. But, hey, I haven't had sex with Paul for years. He isn't treating me well. We haven't been getting on recently. But I love him. But he doesn't understand. So be discreet. And flirt with someone else who makes you feel sexy and wanted and womanly. But that's not wrong. That's just being natural. It's nature. It's right.

Woke up at eight a.m., knowing I was doing the right thing. Full of the joys of spring despite it being November. Speak to Karen about how I feel. Karen listens. Says nothing. Says it's natural and it's nature and I'm right and Paul should treat me better. I tell her what I want her to hear so she validates my feelings and ideas. But I'm using male logic here. So I'm right and I know it.

Karen—'You're right. Go for it.'

Sarah—'I'm being logical and doing what's natural—right?'

Karen—'Go for it. Whether you're right or not. Go for it. A man in your shoes would have left years ago. No sex? No sex is ridiculous. You've tried to talk but he won't talk. You love him, you say, and he loves you, he says. But actions speak louder than words, and his words are empty. There's something wrong with him, Sarah. Deal with it. Face it. You are. Just not straight. John is a crutch. He may not be Mr Right either, but at least he's Mr Right Now and he'll sleep with you.'

John's asked me over to his little yellow cottage in Redhill. For a drink. After work. I tell Paul I'll be late home. He's already working late, so he won't miss me. He says he will and makes me feel guilty by saying he was thinking of cancelling his night out with the boys. I say, no. You enjoy it. You have fun. I'll be OK. Some boring course about customer focus and how you can get more by giving more. The irony is wasted on him.

I speak to newspapers about editorial. Meet advertising company in Kings Cross with posh offices. Fantasising about John and his little yellow cottage. He has told me about his cats, Hannah and Jessica. Hannah is fluffy and scatty and lovely. Jessica is beautiful and proud and arrogant. He loves both of them. His tone softens when he talks about them. He talks in the same tone as when he talks about English beer…and my legs. I feel honoured.

I go out at lunchtime and buy a short red skirt. I never wear short red skirts, but for some reason, in November, I consider this to be a practical buy I believe I will get lots of wear from.

We are having a dinner party tomorrow. The day after I visit John's cottage. Paul has invited some of his friends.

Smoked salmon with avocado? Or fresh figs with parma ham? Decisions, decisions, always decisions. Then chicken in white wine, or coq au vin? Same thing but one has more mushrooms than the other. Fruit salad, cheese and biscuits. Marks & Spencer chocolate sponge pudding. Individual portions with cream or ice cream or crème fraiche? Port, choccies and more port and cigars. Big fat ones for his big fat broker friends. U2, AC/DC and Led Zeppelin. I like Paul's musical taste much more than I like his taste in friends.

J Day. Seeing John tonight at his place. John at his cottage. Wonder if he has a blue room in his yellow cottage. I've seen Nicole Kidman in *The Blue Room*, and wonder if the yellow cottage will be anything like that. Will he jump on me? Will he try to seduce me? Or will he be cool, in his yellow cottage, with his two cats purring at me?

What shall I wear? What do you wear for someone who looks right through your clothes anyway? What's the value of buying clothes when they don't notice what you've got on? Knickers are another complete waste of time and material. If the sex is good they're ripped off—even if they are La Perla—so it's best just to go with the M&S thong. Or something rippable that doesn't take half your thigh with it. Stockings and suspenders are too obvious. Trying too hard. And for women with huge cellulitey thighs who have to make them look sexy somewhere. If you've got good legs you don't need to fuss and truss them up. They look great naked.

So I'm wearing trousers. Suede hipsters. Joseph, half price in the sale. With hippy belt. Local shop—Blue Lawn—where *everything* looks good on me. No sales, but ten per cent off coz I buy so much there. Blouse. Blue Lawn. Semi-translucent. Same ten per cent. No bra. Knickers M&S, soft cotton. £4.99. White. Cut across the cheek. No stockings, suspenders.

Showered with lots of oil. Aromatherapy. Mix of orange and ylang ylang and patchouli. With a touch of lavender. On all the pressure points. Behind the ears, knees, elbows, ankles. Back of shoulders, front of shoulders. In between breasts. Round belly button. Basically anywhere I want him to kiss. Touch. Stroke. I digress.

Shower. Oil. Clothes on. Send text message:

Message sent:
I will be ready for you at 6pm. Where do you want to meet?

No answer. Wait ten mins. Still no answer. Have meetings. About three—back to back. So busy. Everyone remarks how nice I smell, look. Do I fancy a drink? No, thank you. Are you meeting anyone tonight? No, why? Coz you smell, look nice. Etc etc.

Still no answer.

Message received:
Got message. Have been very busy. Can meet at
6.30pm at Victoria Station. OK with you?

Message sent:
Yes, fine. Where at Victoria?

Message received:
Platform 13. What are you wearing?

Message sent:
Trousers.

Message received:
Not meeting you then.

Message sent:
But they're sexy.

Message received:
Top?

Message sent:
Translucent. No bra.

Message received:
Will meet you at 6pm. BE ON TIME. xx

Ahhh. Two xx. Is xx a snog or a kiss on both cheeks? Or
just a friendly xx flirtation or something more? I thought
x was a kiss on both cheeks. Surely xx is a snog?

Message sent:
U2 xx

Nothing. But I'm seeing him half an hour earlier, thanks to the top and lack of bra.

Time is dragging in the afternoon. Go out for something to eat as am feeling faint with excitement and anticipation. Paul hasn't phoned again and is definitely going out with the boys tonight. The 'boys' being three guys he has known for five years, all of whom work in banking, all of whom are marginally less materialistic than him, but getting there. And all of whom think women should be seen and not heard, unless they are coming, and preferably very loudly, and with them underneath (but this is their favourite position because they have all told me at one time or another in the kitchen when they have been drunk at the end of one of Paul's pissy pretentious dinner parties). They also like the idea of two girls together, perhaps twins, and always me and some other girl, possibly even their girlfriend. I think they are all wankers.

They go to a local pub or club and drink and get drunk and don't chat up girls. I go out with my friend Catherine to pubs and clubs and drink Diet Coke. Two glasses. Then dance for two hours. Then another Diet Coke. Then another two hours' dancing. We never chat to guys, just dance. If we get surrounded by about four or five males, which sometimes happens, we stop dancing. Move to another spot and dance there. It works. We lose about four pounds in body fluid and probable fat and have a good time, with ears buzzing, knowing we've frustrated a few egos if not broken hearts.

Anyway, Catherine is with her yoga instructor tonight. Bonking in the back of a car outside Pizza Hut. In a remote place where neither her boyfriend or any of his label-conscious friends would be so low as to go. She has been going out with Freddie for seven years. He is in sales. He looks as if he is in sales. He drives a big shiny BMW. Last year he drove a big shiny Porsche. Next year he will drive a big shiny Ferrari if sales are good. He treats Catherine like

an appendage. Pretty thing on his arm. She's bored and likes
the yoga instructor because he has a fabulous body and is
very flexible. The aerobics instructor is called Liam. He
lives in Basildon but wants to move to Leigh-on-Sea, which
I think is silly. Liam in Leigh. Sort of naff. Or perhaps it's a
marketing ploy. Anyway, he's ambitious, and I think he
thinks Catherine has money as well as a fab body—which
she doesn't, but I keep telling her to tell him she has.

Liam has a squeaky voice, a bronzed body, which is
usually oiled or looks oiled, and a long blond ponytail
which she likes to pull. She is very much in lust and is walking on air and not thinking straight at the moment. Women
who are in lust are interesting as girlfriends. They talk about
sex as though it's food. Women who are in love are dull as
dirt. They don't talk at all. They just smile and stare occasionally into the air and you want to poke their eyes out
for being so self-satisfied. And dull.

I have told Catherine about John.

'Have you done anything yet?'

'No.'

'Are you going to?'

'I don't know.'

'Think about Paul, Sarah.'

'I have. That's why I'm seeing John.'

'Aren't you happy?'

'No.'

'But he's nice.'

'He's also very controlling and an emotional bully and
he doesn't want me to be me. He wants me to be what he
wants me to be, which isn't me. Do you understand?'

'Yes. Same with Freddie.'

'Exactly. Well, I can't be that. He wants his mother. A nice
Irish Catholic who dotes on her children and her husband
and is the matriarch and the peacekeeper. I don't want to

be that. I want to be a travel journalist and have fun, and lots and lots of wonderful sex in very sexy places with someone who loves and lusts after me. And stimulates me mentally and is on a spiritual keel with me, and smells nice. And has nice eyes. And big hands. And a nice bum. And good pullable hair. And says all the right things at the right time to the right people. I know it's asking a lot.'

'It is. He doesn't exist.'

'He does. Just not in Chelmsford. How is Liam?'

'Vigorous. He came round to the house last week. Freddie was away on business. He just ripped off my clothes on the doorstep and took me in the hallway. And then on the stairs—hurt the back a bit—and then in the bedroom. Then we fell asleep for a few hours. Then he woke me up by going down on me. Then we had a shower and I went down on him. Then we went into the kitchen and did some *9½ Weeks* things with cucumbers and yoghurt and honey. Then we had another shower again and did it there. He's very strong...'

'OK OK. So you had a good time.'

'I'm coming to the good bit.'

'The good bit?!'

'Yeah, well, he gave me a sweet as a small token of love. And I didn't have the heart to eat it. And when Freddie came back, you know what the bugger did? He saw it on the kitchen table and ate it. Greedy pig. And, do you know, that night I noticed scratch marks on his back, and he couldn't explain them away, and he eventually admitted that he'd been with a girl and she was rather forceful, but that he was sorry and wouldn't do it again? And, do you know, Sarah, I don't give a fuck?'

'Did you say that?'

'Of course not. I played upset. He got upset. We went out for dinner and had a kiss and cuddle and went back to bed and made love. But it's not the same any more. All I could think about was Liam. I hate being in the same bed with Freddie now.'

'This is what I'm concerned about, Catherine. If I take the plunge with John, how will it make me feel about Paul?'

'Has Paul promised you commitment. A ring?'

'No.'

'Then why are you holding on? It's five years. You don't have a sex life. You love him, that's why you are with him, but what future do you have? Go for it, Sarah.'

So Sarah did.

Six p.m. On the dot. Platform 13. Victoria Station. Biting lip. And index fingernails. Stop it. Stop it.

Message received:
I'm behind you.

Turn around. 'Hello, John.'

'Hello, Sarah.'

Kiss. Kiss. Both cheeks. Not a snog. Xx was right, then.

'We can catch the 6:10. Do you have to be back home early tonight or do you have a pink ticket?'

'I can be back late, but I must be back. OK?'

'OK. I can drive you home. Just round the M25 and A12—right?'

'Yeah, that's right.'

Train journey conversation:

John—'Had a good day?'

Sarah—'OK. Busy. Meetings.'

John—'Me too. You look nice. Like your nipples.'

Three people in the carriage look up from their papers. One *Daily Mail*. Two *Telegraph*.

Sarah blushes.

Sarah—'Thank you. I can't see your nipples, but I'm sure they look great too.'

John—'Erect. Like yours. It's the nipples that do it for most men. It's not the breast size. It's the nipples. The pertness of them. I'm a bum man. You have a lovely bottom, Ms Giles. Looked disgusting, of course, in those culottes, but I could see it was pert. I'm intrigued to find out if you have cellulite at the top of those long legs or if they're as good as they look from the knee down. With lots of women they look as though they have lovely legs and then you get the skirt off and, hey presto, like two sacks filled with lumpy porridge. I'm sure you're gazelle-like. Lean right to the top. Well, are you, Ms Giles?'

Ms Giles says nothing.

Three people in the carriage look up again. Smile. Then back to papers.

Seven stops. Past Croydon. Redhill.

John—'I've parked the car in a car park just a few minutes from here. Would you fancy some dinner first?'

Sarah—'Fine.' Fine? I'm nervous. Why nervous now? I can back out now. I can turn round and say, Hey, I have a boyfriend, whom I love but doesn't treat me well, and you are fun and sexy but I don't want to get involved coz it will hurt you and me and him and all be a dreadful mess.

But I don't.

Sarah—'Sounds great.'

He has a black Golf GTI.

John—'My other car's in the garage. It's red and called Charlotte and it's an old Sunbeam and is my pride and joy. After my cats.'

We drive to a small Italian place where they seem to know John by face if not by name. Tables are intimate. In booths. I order sole. With something tomatoey on it but I'm not really hungry. He orders fish, but he's not hungry either. Neither of us touch our food.

We quickly get onto the subject of sex, as you do when it's on your mind and you want to have it at some stage during the evening.

John—'You look good. Much better than at the pizza place. And Santini's.'

Sarah—'Thank you. So do you.'

John—'You have very pert nipples.'

Sarah—'It's cold in here. I'm not pleased to see you.'

He smiles.

'So, how you getting on with Paul?'

'I think we are just good friends now. How about you and Amanda?'

'She's moving out.'

Two uneaten starters, main course and desserts later, we head out.

In the car, music. Something classical. Radio Four. Mozart.

Little yellow cottage. Just as I imagined. Very small, very intimate. Very cosy. No black or chrome or mirrored ceilings, as per most bachelors living alone. The kitchen seemed to be the most lived-in room.

I like to cook.

Open cupboards full of spices and herbs. Fresh variety, not the 'dried muck', for curries and stews which he concocts.

'I would like to cook for you, Sarah.'

'I don't think you will be able to. I'm fussy with food. No dairy, no wheat, no red meat.'

'I could cook you a chicken curry with coconut. Or don't you eat coconut milk either?'

'I don't eat that either.'

'Well, I'm sure I can think of something. Would you like a tour of the house?'

'Er, yes, that would be lovely.'

The front door entered into the kitchen. Then the kitchen led into the dining room and this led into the sitting room. It was then I realised the front door was actually the back door, but it was at the side. The front door was in the sitting room at the bottom of the stairs, but John never used it. Up the stairs was a large landing, on which was a sofa, so it was sort of another sitting room.

'It could be the second bedroom, but I've kept it as a sitting room-cum-dressing room. It's got more light than the downstairs.'

Then into the bathroom, and lastly the bedroom. Black duvet, black sheets. The bed took up the whole room. Except one wardrobe.

'That's it. I've had it for five years and love it. Bought it with my girlfriend, but bought it off her, and am now quite happy living by myself, or soon to be by myself—when Amanda moves out completely.'

'I can't see any of her stuff,' I say, looking around for female stuff. Knickers, bottles and potions in the bathroom. That sort of thing.

'No, she's moved most of it out, and some of it is in boxes. She says she's going to come round for the rest at some stage. I've bought her a TV for her new flat,' he says, pointing to a big brown box in the corner of the bedroom.

'Wondered what that was.'

Some sort of sex toy, perhaps?

Perhaps.

I leave the bedroom quickly. Where has my nerve gone? I should have drunk more wine.

'Do you have any wine?' I say as I go down the stairs.

'Why, yes. Red or white? Dry or full-bodied?'

'Red and full-bodied.'

'OK.'

Bottle of Australian Shiraz. Very large wine glasses. The sort you like to hold and play with. Which I do. Sitting on the sofa in the downstairs sitting room. He has a range of music. What would I like? I try to pick something I doubt he has or likes. Sweet. 1970s. 'Love is Like Oxygen.' Does he have that? He does. Single vinyl. He plays it. Always did make me feel, well, slightly icky inside.

Another glass of red wine. Head going fuzzy and feeling flirty and relaxed. Glazed. He's not drunk.

'I do a mean massage.'

'OK, then.'

He takes his shirt off. 'Massage the shoulders, please.'

OK, then. I slip my shoes off and ask him to sit on the floor in front of the sofa. I sit on the sofa behind him, legs either side. Skirt hitched up ever so slightly. I've come prepared. Aromatherapy oil in pocket. Patchouli, ylang ylang and lavender with a dash of orange. Massage round the shoulders. Then the neck. Then through the hair.

'You don't mind getting oil in your hair, do you?'

'Don't have much say, do I?'

Not really. John's hair is dark and curly and soft and good to run fingers through. Notice my nails are badly bitten. Must do something about this.

He starts to touch my ankles and I remember I haven't remembered to wax for weeks. Shit. Oh well. First impressions.

After ten minutes of ankle tickling and hair massaging I ask if that's enough.

'Fine.'

I sit by the fire. Unwaxed legs on show. John leans over and starts to blow—yes, *blow*—on my calves. I initially think this is weird and I don't like it. Then think it a bit kinky. Perhaps it's an erogenous zone I haven't heard of. Anyway, it's working and I have this desire to rip his clothes off and force myself on him.

He gets there first.

I'm naked with John Wayne.

I'm naked with John Wayne.

I can't believe I'm actually, sort of, almost having sex with this man. For once in my life someone I've lusted over I've now, er, got. I've never got anyone I really, *really* fancied. Only ones who were nice and I thought would grow on me, but for one reason or another never did because they had bad breath, or no personality, or an eating disorder, or combination of all three. I want to cry because I haven't been touched for such a long time like this, and it's wonderful and I'm angry with Paul for withholding sex but I don't want to cry because it's a turn-off for John and it's unfair on him. So I hold it back. And swallow the pain with the pleasure.

But here I was, with a man I was in lust with, and he was actually wanting to have sex with me. Lucky, huh? I kept looking at him, and he had his eyes open too. He kissed hard and held me very tightly, almost crushing my ribcage at times. Then stroking my back, from the top to the bottom of my spine. Caressing my cheeks (on bottom). Gently persuading me to move this way and that without telling me or forcing me, and making it seem natural, as if it was my idea. It wasn't, but every time he did it I thought, I wish I'd thought of that.

'I can't close my eyes, Sarah. Every time I look at you I think, Hey, I'm kissing Sarah Giles. I'm naked with Sarah Giles.'

I smiled. 'I'm thinking that about you, but didn't want to tell you. You've slept with *sooo* many women. They must all tell you the same things and I would like to be original and keep my own counsel.' I stroked his hair and started kissing him again and closed my eyes.

We were completely naked, lying side by side, but hadn't (as they say at school) 'done anything'.

John—'I don't want to sleep with you tonight. I want to wait.'

Sarah—'What for? Do you respect me?' I said half jokingly.

John—'Yes.'

This made me feel uneasy. It was much easier to think John a hardened womaniser rather than a man with feelings and sensibilities who actually cares about the women he sleeps with rather than just uses them. I reassured myself this was just part of his spiel, and the real, tough John would come out later—if not tonight, at some stage during the next month. At least I would have some time with the lust of my life—albeit brief. And anyway that's what lust is all about. Brief liaisons, furtive, forbidden and above all short. And dangerous and anything goes.

Sarah—'OK, then. Are you going to take me home?'

John—'Yes. I think so. I'll get dressed.'

And with that my dark prince withdrew, and put on his Next underpants.

He drove fast back along the M25. The journey was quiet. We listened to Dido—'All You Want'. He had one hand on the wheel, the other between my legs. Making me come every ten minutes with the fingers of an expert who knows what he's doing without looking. This was a little disconcerting, but my body didn't seem to mind. And my mind was somewhere else completely.

Through the tunnel. He stopped to get the pound coin, pay, and then resumed his position as I resumed my composure, smiling at the attendant as though nothing was happening and I wasn't having orgasms as regularly as most tourists ask for directions in London.

It took just over an hour to get home. By the time we arrived I had arrived so many times I was dazed and confused and wanted urgently to take all my clothes off again. And his. But he kissed me on both cheeks (on the face) and said that I should go in and he had an early-morning meeting and he would call me. With one last sweep of the hand he undid a button, pushed my blouse aside and kissed and sucked my left nipple. Then he did up my blouse and left me standing there. In the middle of the road, with one nipple erect and the other jealous.

12th November

Dinner party at Paul's home. I don't want to be there. I'm not there, actually. I'm somewhere else altogether. I am with six of his friends. They are his friends. But because I am going out with Paul they are now my friends. They are nice enough people. Interesting and genuine and some kind. But they're not my friends. Paul doesn't like me mixing with my friends. He says he wants to meet them and then passes judgement that he doesn't like them. These are not my friends. That sounds harsher than it is meant. I wouldn't choose them in a crowded room to talk to. And I'm sure they feel the same way about me. It's just that they have known Paul for x amount of years, and he likes them, and so they are here.

I get the feeling with Paul that even if someone doesn't want to be his friend he will somehow make them be his friend. Controlling. As a trader, he negotiates every day, and I think he takes this into his personal life. His relationships. He always negotiates to get the better deal. We always end up going somewhere he wants to go, and so much the better if I genuinely want to go there too. But in the end I wonder if I wanted to go there genuinely or am being so mind-fucked that I don't know what I really want any more. But I know he wouldn't want me to see John, so it's nothing to do with him. But it has everything to do with him. So perhaps he's still controlling me. See what I mean?

Anyway. Dinner party for six. Two ask themselves unexpectedly. Paul is cooking boeuf en croûte. Never done it before and likes cooking. Not washing up. He doesn't have a dishwasher. I wash up. Then we have sex. Which is good and wonderful and worth it. Paul has an earthy quality. Knowing what to do, when to do it. He's quite selfish without being rough. He's a wonderful caring lover and it's sad we don't make love now...since the abortion.

It affected him quite badly. Worse than I thought at the time. We agreed it was the right thing to do at the time. That it had happened and that I should have told him, but these things did happen. But Paul was traumatised and from then on we didn't make love. Or hardly ever. And when we did afterwards there would be silence and he would, he tells me, be overcome with guilt. Guilt is something Catholics do well, it seems. It is part of their creed. *I believe in the Holy Ghost, the Holy Catholic Church, the Communion of Saints, the Resurrection of the Body and the Power of Guilt. Amen.* I would cry because it would be beautiful, but so rare these days that it upset me that now I couldn't make love to this man. With all his controlling ways, I felt this was just another opportunity to control a situation. The problem was it wasn't controlling it. It was stifling it. Hiding it. Not dealing with it.

I tried to talk to him about it, but he wouldn't listen. I didn't want to create an argument as I knew he was extremely sensitive and would burst into floods of tears, just like a young child who's had his toys broken. And I loved him. Not just lust. A spiritual love. A love that comes when you first meet someone and know from the onset that you will marry them and that he is your soulmate. That it doesn't matter about the fact he picks his nose and eats his bogeys (which he does) and doesn't do any of the washing up and is selfish in so many ways. You know that you love him, and that is all you know. Or all that I knew. I was sad, but happy to be with the man I loved. Happy I had found my soulmate in life. Chemistry was there, but communication wasn't, and I knew that would have to do for now. For now.

But over five years I became resentful of the no sex policy and started feeling angry. Hence when I met John I was primed for a fling. Ripe for the picking. Full of anger, pride and above all a sexual imagination which hadn't been used in years.

Dinner party was fine. There was the usual crowd. Patrick and Kate, Peter and Kelly, Connor and Shelley. These were his schoolfriends. Peter and Patrick he had known for many years. Connor even longer. Connor had been going out with Shelley for six years.

Kelly had been going out with Peter since school. She was blonde and cute and, I felt, very tough. Tougher than she came across. She wanted to marry Peter, and I think he was OK about marrying her. But both Peter and Patrick had a love greater than that for any woman. Rugby. It came first. Women came second. They would play it at every opportunity. Patrick was county standard. Paul who was just under six foot (he lied about his height always) would use them as bouncers. Both over six foot three, with hands as big as cauliflowers and ears that resembled them, they were gentle giants and both, especially Patrick, were rather lazy and selfish, but kind and generous at the same time. I blame the mother.

Kate, whom Patrick had only recently started dating, was a beauty therapist. She was loud and funny and called a spade a fucking shovel and I loved her to bits. She was genuine and kind and you knew where you stood and she said she put up with Patrick because he had a big dick and nice arse. But you knew she was genuinely fond of him and wanted to marry him.

Connor had tight curly blond hair and looked like one of the Marx brothers. The one that couldn't say anything— just squeaked a horn. He was kind and thoughtful and the least selfish out of the schoolfriends, and I had a soft spot for him because it was he who had suggested Paul call me and pursue me to France and meet me in Monte Carlo and start the relationship all those years ago.

They all arrived at the same time. In convoy. Despite the fact that they all lived in different towns—all the men were Virgos and therefore punctual.

Menu for the evening:

Champagne and handmade vegetable crisps (from Marks & Spencer)
Olives—black and green, marinated in garlic (my favourite)
First course:
Parma Ham (Paul's favourite)
Fresh figs
Second course:
Boeuf en croûte (aka Wellington)
Carrots (cut lengthways not across—Paul tells me he read somewhere that across is common)
French beans
New potatoes
Potatoes Dauphinois

All from Marks & Spencer except B en C which Paul wanted to cook himself. Even the pastry.

I cooked chicken in white wine with garlic for those who don't eat beef. That's Kate and myself.

Dessert:

Profiteroles
Sticky toffee pudding and custard
Häagen Dazs ice-cream—three varieties
Cheese (nine sorts)
Four sorts of biscuits

Cape gooseberries, grapes—black, apples—green, celery—hard
Filter coffee and chocolates (not Ferrero Rocher, ever)
Port (Paul's favourite)

And so it was for most dinner parties. The same. Everybody disliked Shelley but no one told her to her face, or told Connor. She was insecure and put everyone and everything down. Everyone else's achievement could be bettered in some way. First time she came round to a dinner party at Paul's house she kissed him full on the lips and groped at his groin. Just for me. That was nice. Anyway, I wanted to tell her to her face, but no one else seemed to want to rock the boat with Connor, so it was the conversation piece before and after she left the room. A sort of bonding amongst the others. As I had known her from the past I was an honorary Shelley-hater, despite the fact that I actually felt sorry for the girl. Everyone 'put up' with her and she didn't even know it. Made me wonder if they did the same with me. Paul assured me not.

En croûte was undercooked. So everyone wanted my chicken. Conversation revolved around music, sex, drugs and Shelley—and not in that order. I did the washing up. Kelly helped. Kate talked a lot and told Paul he was boorish and I was an angel to put up with him. Shelley sulked a lot. Paul drank the most port, but got least drunk out of all the men. Then we watched *Highlander* (Paul's favourite film), then Paul in a rally car race (Paul's favourite video), then played Led Zeppelin at full blast and the men played air guitar till three in the morning while the women talked about fluff. They then left, women driving home.

Paul went to bed.

Sarah finished washing up (I would have to do it in the morning anyway), then came to bed to snoring, farty boyfriend. He slept till two the next afternoon. Then got up. Had something to eat and then back to bed again.

It was the same every time there was a dinner party. Occasionally we would get up at one and go to the Punch Bowl. I still loved the restaurant because it was romantic and it had good memories and it reminded me how much I loved Paul, which made me as melancholy these days as it did happy in years past.

I remember when we had lunch the first time, returning from France. We couldn't eat anything. We then went to the cricket ground and watched them play and kissed in the hope that a ball wouldn't knock us out or kill us. I have never been happier in my life than those first nine months of meeting Paul.

At the end of dinner party evenings, if I had drunk a little too much champagne or wine or a combination, I would try to think of people I was indifferent to. Who made me numb with their blandness. It was a sort of mental anorexia. Think of people who starve you of feeling about them and with them, and there is no chance for sadness or any emotion. It worked. Usually. Sometimes I would sit in the downstairs toilet and sob. Then wait while the flush died from my cheeks and I could go out into the dinner party crowd once again and face even the sulking Shelley.

We had about ten of these a year. Sometimes Paul would invite his broker friends. Once, my friends were invited, but he didn't like them, so they weren't invited again.

13th November

Two p.m.

Message received:
Thinking of you. Jx

Message sent:
Thinking of you too. S xx

Message received:
XXXXXXoXOXOXOXOX

14th November

Still in bed eight-thirty a.m.

Message received:
Still thinking of you. Can I call?

Message sent:
Yes.

Phone rings.

'How are you? Been thinking about you all weekend. Amanda was here and she kept asking if I was OK I was so distracted. We're supposed to be going on holiday for a week, but I don't want to go.'

Sarah—'You must. It will do you good. Anyway, you can still contact me. Where are you going?'

John—'The Caribbean. St Thomas. Got it at that travel agent at Liverpool Street Station, ironically. It's the most built-up but it's a cheap deal. They are renovating and the water sports are supposed to be good. Hiring a car and touring the island.'

Sarah—'Have fun.'

John—'I won't.'

DECEMBER

ACTION LIST

Buy presents which are meaningful for friends and family but are also cheap.

Don't eat everything at parties.

Don't drink too much at parties—makes me too honest.

Be nice to Paul.

Be nice to me.

Go to gym six times a week, two hours on Saturday morning.

Enjoy work.

1st December

I am miserable. John has not called. He was back over a week ago but Medina, his PA, says he is out of the office and can't be contacted. He hasn't texted or phoned or left a message on my machine or anything. Karen says he hasn't left a message and I trust her. Haven't told her about him, that I like him, but I think she guesses.

★ ★ ★

2nd December

Still miserable. Still hasn't phoned. Paul asks why I'm distracted. I just say pressure of work and that I may be made redundant and that I'm looking for a new job. I've had about fifteen since I've been going out with him, but that includes temporary work. I want to be a travel journalist and get paid for travelling but don't know how to do it. So far my jobs have been in every conceivable field bar the one I want.

I got a week on the *Mail on Sunday* once, as a junior reporter at the start of the Gulf crisis. Told them I'd worked on the *South China Morning Post* and on regionals. They gave me a break. I got them a scoop (first British family to escape). Made page three (only beaten to front page by torpedoes being sent off). But second week they discovered I was just a wannabe so gave me the push. Ironic that when I'd managed to prove myself in one week they didn't give me another chance. But that was life. And it proved that I could do it—given the chance. But here I was, working for Rogerson Railways, hoping to become a travel writer.

3rd December

John still hasn't phoned. He has forgotten about me, obviously. Am getting the *Guardian* and UK *Press Gazette*. Must focus on something positive. Plus have lots of parma ham and port dinner parties to prepare for. And go to. The dinner parties Paul's friends organise obviously sing from the same cookery book. Some are Delia. Some are Nigella. Some are Oliver. All taste the same. All finish with some sort of chocolate decadence and all finish with men as pissed as farts. And the women drive home. And the conversation is always the same.

4th December

I've given up on him. He's not going to phone. He blew on my calves and rolled about with me half naked and didn't even get to second base, but that was it. My wet dream has to stop at that point. I have to wake up and smell the roses. I love Paul. Forget John. He's an unknown. The deep blue sea. Better the devil and all that.

5th December

He phones. Back to the deep blue sea.

John—'Sorry I haven't called.'

Keep cool.

Sarah—'Don't worry. I've been very busy.'

John—'Really? Medina said you phoned quite a bit. Six times in three days, in fact.'

Sarah—'Must have been another Sarah.'

John—'No, she said it was you. The one she overheard calling me a rude wanker. Anyway, I was in a stream of meetings, so very busy.'

Sarah—'How was the holiday?'

John—'Fine. Lots of sunshine.'

Sarah—'And sex?'

John—'Some.'

I shouldn't have asked. It made me feel sick to think of him with Amanda. But why should I worry? He wasn't mine. We'd just had a grope after all.

Sarah—'That's nice.'

John—'No, it wasn't actually. It was quite disconcerting. I thought about you all the time. I kept seeing your face in my head.'

That's nice, I thought.

Sarah—'That's nice. I've been thinking about you too.'

John—'When do you want to meet next? Tomorrow?'

Sarah—'I can't do tomorrow. Have a date I can't break—' (true) '—with Paul and friends.' False—just friends, but didn't want to break it.

John—'When can we meet, then? Can you do a weekend?'

Sarah—'How will you explain that to Amanda?'

John—'She's moving out of the cottage soon. She doesn't know about you but suspects. I've told her it's nothing. Which of course it is, isn't it Sarah?'

Sarah—'Of course. I'm just a bit on the side, John.'

John—'Quite.'

Sarah—'I can't do a weekend, but I may be able to manage an evening. Can you come over to my flat and stay the night?'

John—'I should think so.'

Sarah—'Fine. Next week.'

6th December

Called into the boss's office. Edward Benjamin. In his forties. Bright, drinks too much, ruddy-faced. Likes me, but not sexually. Level-headed. Worked with John lots.

Nine a.m. I'm being made redundant. Nothing personal. Culling at Central Office pre-privatisation. I'm a good one; they want to keep me. But I can take redundancy and cheque if I want it. Either that or I can move to a new department. Do I want to move to one of the regions? Rogerson Railways Southern? John Wayne has suggested that he needs a good PR. Would I like to work for him?

I think hard.

Sarah—'No. I would rather take the money. Next question.'

Edward—'Are you having an affair with John Wayne?'

Stunned silence.

Sarah—'No, er, isn't that personal?'

Edward—'It's been noted you've been talking to him a lot recently and calling his office.'

Sarah—'That was just on business.'

Edward—'I understand, Sarah. But remember John is amoral. He doesn't know right from wrong. He's a womaniser and plays with the minds of young ladies, as he does their bodies.'

For some strange reason this turns me on. I smile. Edward sees it.

Edward—'Just be careful, Sarah. I like John, but he's no good for you and no good for women. OK?'

Sarah—'OK, Edward. Thank you for your concern but I think I can look after myself.'

15th December

Last day in the office. Huge bunch of flowers. John due to meet me at Liverpool Street Station. He's staying at the flat. Karen has decided she will stay with her boyfriend tonight. I've asked her to. Train journey takes for ever. We don't say anything. Just look at each other through the foliage. He asks who the flowers came from. I say an admirer. In reality they came from a PR company that wants me to work for them.

Six-thirty p.m. we arrive at my flat. Only thing I have in the fridge is vodka and fresh orange juice. I fix two drinks. Then order pizza. I don't eat pizza, but John does and I'm not hungry. For food anyway. I want him to blow on my calves again. This time I've waxed.

Six thirty-five p.m. TV on. Clothes off. He rips my knickers. La Perla, £55. Why do I bother? I tell him he can buy me more. He says he will. Rolling around. Trying to tease one another into submission but neither gives up. He doesn't want to 'take me', he wants to save the moment until Amanda has moved out. Do I understand? Yes, I do. But that doesn't stop me trying to tease him into submission. It doesn't work. He is controlled and in control, and it's wonderful and illicit and dangerous and I'm high on him and his touch and just being with him for the moment.

Seven thirty-five p.m. Pizza boy arrives. I pay him. Dressed in dressing gown. He smiles. Takes money and leaves.

One a.m. Still rolling around. Naked. John says he will sleep in Karen's bed. If he sleeps with me, he may be tempted. He tells me Karen keeps all her underwear under her pillow. She is a size 12-14 and likes M&S cotton.

One-twenty a.m. Watch bedroom door, wondering if he will come in and 'take me'.

One twenty-five a.m. He doesn't. Fall asleep.

16th December

Eight a.m. John goes. Very cool. Make him toast. He says it's slightly burnt. I apologise. No kiss on cheek. Seems too clichéd. I'm not going into work today, but don't want to wish him a 'nice day'. He tells me he is having dinner with his work colleagues. I ask him not to mention that he's seen me naked or that my cuffs and collar don't match. He says he will.

Eight-thirty a.m. I'm daydreaming and call Catherine. Catherine tells me she is in lust and love with yoga teacher and wants to come round and talk about him and how wonderful he is at sex. I tell her about John. She understands why (she knows about abortion and no sex and stuff).

Nine-thirty a.m. Catherine comes round and talks about Liam. Solidly for three hours.

Twelve-thirty p.m. We go to Pizza Express and get a salade niçoise and Diet Coke (me) and cheese pizza with extra mushrooms and apple juice (her). She tells me more about Liam and then I start to talk about John.

Two-thirty p.m. Still talking. People on surrounding tables stop talking and listen to our conversation. Far more interesting.

Catherine—'When I'm with him I just want to rip his clothes off.'

Sarah—'It's lust, not love, then.'

Catherine—'But I think about him all the time.'

Sarah—'What about Freddie?'

Catherine—'I can't bear for him to touch me. And anyway I know he has seen other women. Once I found scratch marks on his back and he admitted there was someone else, but only a one-night stand.'

Sarah—'Why are you still with him?'

Catherine—'There was no one else and he said he would never do it again.'

Sarah—'Do you believe him?'

Catherine—'No, but I don't care now.'

Sarah—'What are you going to do?'

Catherine—'Freddie wants to move to Richmond. I want to stay put, for obvious reasons. He's buying a place there. Think he's almost completed.'

Sarah—'Have you seen it or had any say on where in Richmond?'

Catherine—'Freddie never asks, Sarah. He just does something and expects me to follow his lead.'

Sarah—'And you're not going to this time?'

Catherine—'Right. All I can think about is Liam. When I'm with him, the next time I'm going to be with him. It's nearly Christmas and I'm wearing skirts up to my bottom and don't care. He makes me feel sexy and wanted and it's wonderful. He's also experimental.'

Sarah—'In what way? With sex?'

Catherine—'Fruit and chocolate, and he does things Freddie would have never considered.'

Sarah—'Like what?'

Catherine—'I wouldn't like to say.'

Then she spends the next hour saying what she wouldn't like to say. How flexible, focused, fun and fuckable Liam is, and how she never gets to bed but he doesn't want her to stay the night at his place ever or stay over at her place ever. And how the oral sex is good. And the anal sex is good. And how well-endowed he is and how size matters. Which disturbs me, but I say nothing.

Catherine—'He keeps asking about my parents. He seems concerned that they are both dead and asks if they left me OK financially.'

Sarah—'Does he think you're loaded, then?'

Scowl.

Catherine—'No.' More upbeat. 'But perhaps I should tell him I am and then he'll ask me to marry him.'

Sarah—'Do you want to marry him?'

Catherine—'At the moment I want to spend the rest of my life with him. All I can think about is being with him. Smelling him. Touching him. When I go to his classes all the other girls lust after him. When he stretches our inner thighs he steps over us, and the girls try to look up his shorts and he looks at me and I look at him and we know what we will be doing in two hours' time and that this exercise is just the warm-up.'

The conversation continues. The surrounding tables are silent. The closest ones have had three cups of coffee and are phoning their offices, telling their bosses or secretaries that the meeting has overrun. I suggest she tries Pilates instead.

17th December

Seven a.m.

Message received:
Thinking of you. Can I call?

Message sent:
Yes, call me.

Phone rings.

'Hi. Where are you?'

Sarah—'Still in bed.'

John—'What wearing?'

Sarah—'Nothing.'

John—'Pity. Much sexier with something on. Put something on.'

Sarah—'When I have something on, knickers for example, you rip them off. So why bother? And I'll wear or won't wear what I like, OK?'

John—'Sarah, I would really like you to put some lacy knickers on. Do you have lacy knickers?'

Sarah—'Yes.'

John—'Could you please put them on for me?'

Sarah—'Yes.'

Sarah gets lacy knickers and thinks, This is stupid, but, hey, it's seven a.m.

John—'Have you got them on?'

Sarah—'Yes.'

John—'Where are your hands?'

Sarah—'Where would you like them to be?'

John—'In between your legs.'

Sarah—'Where are *your* hands?'

John—'I'm in the office. I'm not going to start wanking off in my office.'

Sarah—'Why not? You're asking me to do it.'

John—'OK, then.'

I hear fumbling.

Sarah—'You're pretending.'

John—'Suppose I could fake it, but it's got to be quick. I've got a 7.30 meeting and I've got to be on time.'

Sarah—'Then start talking and turn me on.'

John—'You've got to turn yourself on, but I'll talk you through it. We're in a restaurant. Late lunch. Midsummer. You're wearing a skirt. Silk. Just below the knees. Tight white top and cardigan. Lacy knickers.'

Sarah—'How can you tell?'

John—'I can tell. It's my story so I can tell. Shut up and listen. You're wearing lacy knickers.'

Sarah—'You've already said that.'

John—'Shut up. Do you want to come or not?'

Sarah—'Yes.'

John—'You sit down on the other side of the table. I ask if you can sit by me. I ask you to go and take your knickers off and return and give them to me.'

Sarah—'Mmm. But that's not exactly original. Didn't Sharon Stone or someone do something like that in a film?'

John—'She nicked the idea from me. Don't interrupt. You do it. You go and take your knickers off and return, hiding them in your hand. You hand them to me as the waiter appears for our order. He sees what you are doing and you're embarrassed, but he says nothing. You sit down opposite me. We order. Something light.'

Sarah—'What do I have?'

John—'It doesn't matter.'

Sarah—'It does matter. Can I have sushi?'

John—'It's not a Japanese restaurant, but if you want sushi you can have it. Shh, just listen and come. I ask if I can see you. See between your legs. You agree. I drop my napkin.'

Sarah—'Bit obvious, isn't it?'

John—'That's the sex in it. Stop interrupting. I bend down to pick it up. As I do so, I move your legs apart and watch you. I move my hands slowly up your thighs and almost reach you, but stop short. I pick up the napkin and call the waiter to order some wine and water. When the waiter has gone I ask you to put your hand down your skirt and to gently start playing with yourself. Move yourself closer to the table so people cannot see. You're starting to get wet.

'I ask you to move to my side and sit by me to read some papers I have brought with me. As you do so, I move closer to you and lift your skirt and move my fingers into you, which makes you flushed and vulnerable and nervous the waiter might return at any moment. Apart from the table-cloth you are on show. The restaurant is half full and you're on show and starting to feel very turned on, and can't stop yourself. You're so wet now, Sarah.

'The waiter returns. I take my fingers from you and ask you to move back to your seat. He delivers the food. He returns with the wine. Asks me to try it. I say it will be fine. Then the water. I eat the food and feed you some of mine and you feed me some of yours. We drink the wine. I dip my fingers into my glass and ask you to come to my side of the table again. You do. Once again I put my hand down your skirt. This time my fingers are moist and I gently stroke you. I'm talking to you all the while about business and asking you questions which you are increasingly not able to answer. You are more aware that people are looking at us, but you can't help yourself. You can't help yourself, Sarah, and I'm stroking you more urgently and you want to open your...'

Sarah—'Aghhhhhhhhhhhh...'

John—'And you come.'

Sarah—'Have a nice meeting.'

John—'I will. I also need a tissue now.'

Sarah—'Sure Medina will get one for you.'

John—'Er, no. She does most things, but this I think I will do by myself.'

Sarah—'Thank you. Lovely wake-up call.'

John—'Next time I see you. I want to do it for real.'

18th December

Seven a.m.

> *Message received:*
> Been thinking of you. Can I call?

> *Message sent:*
> Yes.

Five past seven to seven twenty-five a.m.—phone sex.
This time a crowded beach. Sand gets everywhere. Make myself come thinking of him...

> *Message sent:*
> 7.30
> Just have.

19th December

Seven a.m.

> *Message received:*
> Been thinking of you. Can I call?

> *Message sent:*
> Yes.

Five past seven till seven twenty-five a.m.—phone sex.
This time a board meeting. On the table. In front of all the directors. Purpose of meeting: a lesson in customer

focus. How to give and receive it. How to manage expectations. Benefits and concerns—

20th December

Seven a.m.

> *Message received:*
> Been thinking of you. Can I call?

> *Message sent:*
> Only if you make me come.

Five past seven to seven fifty-five a.m.—phone sex.
In cinema. Matinée. A comedy. Back row. Semi-crowded. Coming at an inappropriate moment. Having to be quiet. No screaming. Difficult for me. Very wet. Very turned on.

21st December

Seven a.m.

> *Message received:*
> With Amanda this week. Will be difficult to call. Hope you have a good Christmas. Will call after Christmas. Big kiss. Keep wet and wild.

> *Message sent:*
> You too. I will.

24th December

I don't feel Christmassy. I feel lustful and in party mode but not for and with my boyfriend of five years. I go to church more times in a week than I do all year. With my family, his family, friends. We sing carols and say prayers. But Paul's not in my head or my understanding. Not in my eyes or in my looking. Not in my mouth or in my speaking. He's still in my prayers and in my thinking. But not the way he was— five years ago. I'm thinking of John. I'm thinking of what John will be like. If I will see him again. If he will decide to stay with Amanda or if he will decide to give me a try. Or if he will find another squeeze to be festive with this season.

I wonder how I can break it to Paul that we should per-haps give each other space. The 'I need space' line. You know—the one that precedes 'I've found someone else' if you're pressed. I can't do it before Christmas. It will ruin his holiday. He's doing well at work, expecting a large bonus, going to buy a new house and seems happy. I haven't been asking or hinting about marriage because, hey, my mind's been on something and someone else—so I'm cooler but also more energised with Paul, because I'm thinking of John and Paul gets the benefit of John's influ-ence. Win win win situation, methinks.

Spending Christmas with cousins. Paul picking me up from my flat. Karen staying with her on–off boyfriend and his family. Exchange gifts. Leave flat at five p.m. and drive to Weston Turvill. Paul says he wants to stop off at a pub on the way. We pull into the car park. Six-thirty p.m. Paul hands me a little black box.

Paul—'Will you be my wife?'

Stunned. Have been thinking about John all day and on the journey, and thinking about breaking up with Paul. Now he proposes. He hasn't gone down on one knee. He is proposing to me in a car park. Of a pub. On Christmas Eve. Do I say no and ruin his Christmas so he has to spend it with my parents and cousins knowing that I don't want to marry him? He's bought the ring. I open the box. It's lovely. Diamonds. Four. He's chosen it without consultation, but he's chosen well.

Paul—'I chose it. I hope you like it.'

I don't look at him. I think fuck. What the fuck shall I do? Devil or deep blue sea? John is lust. I know that. I've just met him. I know that. It's sex. I know that. Paul is my love, my soulmate, but there's a problem. I know that. What the fuck do I do? Can I call a friend? No, I cannot. I choose.

Sarah—'I would love to be your wife, Paul.'

I lie.

He kisses me. I kiss him back. We go to the pub and order champagne and look into the log fire and tell the girl serving us that we've just got engaged and she's happy for us. Happier than I am for us. I look at Paul and know I love him, but also want to tell him stuff that I can't tell him. I love him but can't talk to him any more. I can't open up to him any more. I can't tell him I resent him. Not now. Not now, as he has just proposed and given me this ring, which he proceeds to tell me cost more than £1500, which somehow takes the magic out of it.

After an hour drinking champagne we return to the car. Holding hands. Arrive at my cousins'. He tells me he hasn't asked my father. He goes to the house first. He goes to my father, who is sitting by himself in the sitting room. My mother and cousins are in the kitchen. I go into the kitchen and make small talk with my cousins and try to ignore my mother.

When Paul returns I go in to see my father while Paul breaks the news to my mum. As I walk to the sitting room I can hear silence, then screams of delight coming from the kitchen. I hope they don't follow me in. I want to be with my dad at this moment. He smiles at me as I enter the room.

Dad—'I'm very happy for you, Sarah.'

Sarah—'Thank you, Dad. He's lovely, isn't he?'

Dad—'I hope he will make you very happy. Are you happy, Sarah?'

I look at him as though he can read my mind or my face or see through me that I'm not quite sure. But I think it's just the way it's come out. No. I look at his face and it's a genuine question. He asks it again.

Dad—'Are you happy, Sarah?'

Sarah—'Yes, Dad. He's a very good man. He loves me very much.'

Dad—'Do you love him? Will he make you happy?'

Sarah—'Yes, I think so. Yes, I do.'

Dad—'Good, Sarah.'

He looks at me and says nothing. As if he knows but will let me lie in my own bed and sleep in it and learn from it.

Mother comes in with cousins. Hugging me and kissing me. Mother cries. It's for herself. She's got her daughter off her hands to a well-off young man. She has something to tell her friends. Her coterie of Hyacinth Bucket ladies who lunch. I can see in her eyes she is planning the big white wedding. Boasting about how wonderful the groom is. What a nice family they are. The church. Who she will invite. Who she will tell. What dress she will wear. All the things that are not important. How it will be her day. And I don't want her there. For fuck's sake, I don't know if *I* want to be there.

Dad—'When are you going to get married?'

Paul—'Well, probably in about nine months. We were thinking September. Why wait? We've been going out for over five years.'

Dad—'The weather will still be good then. Good idea.'

I'm given a glass of champagne and drink it quickly. Then another. And another. We drink until four a.m. the following morning. Christmas Day. And then make our way to the bedrooms. I cuddle up to my fiancé. I feel good and comforted but disturbed. I should be ecstatic but I'm not. I should feel secure but I'm not. I love Paul. There is no doubt. But until this moment in time, this very moment in time, he's been far from my thoughts and my dreams. And I think of John and how I shall tell him and how I shall broach the subject.

Sarah—Hi, John, did you have a good Christmas?

John—Yes, Sarah. Did you? Get anything nice?

Sarah—Well, yes, actually. I got a really lovely diamond ring and I'm going to marry Paul. OK? In September. Big white wedding. Would you like to come?

Yes, I can see it now.

25th December

Blur. Turkey went in late so we ate at six in the evening. Lots of laughter, tears and dirty jokes. Feeling numb. Holding Paul's hand a lot. Dad keeps looking at me as though he knows. He smiles and stares at me. And then at Paul. Mother totally oblivious of everything. I wonder if she really is my mother or if I was swapped in the hospital. I am so unlike her. She is horrible. Like Hyacinth without the humour.

26th December

Early start. We set off to Paul's parents. Back to Chelmsford. Paul rang his parents on Christmas Day to tell them the news. He tells me they are delighted. When we arrive at their home the only one there is his brother Mark. His parents and younger brother are at church. They are Catholics and Irish and Mark doesn't believe and is the rebel and is the one out of all the family (including Paul) I most like and respect. He's honest with his anger. He's the black sheep and talks to his parents, whereas Paul and his other brother Andrew don't. They are economical with information. Don't think it's an

Irish thing. Or an Irish Catholic thing. Or a son–parent thing. Perhaps it's a combination of the lot. Anyway. They don't talk.

Mark hugs me and says, 'Hello, sis.' And I cry. It's a genuine hug and I think he's genuinely happy to be having a sister and I'm genuinely happy to be having him as a brother. Only children miss out on that. Got to play with all the toys, but would have liked a brother. Preferably an older one who would invite his friends round. Potential boyfriend material.

The others arrive about ten a.m. Hugs all round. More champagne. More turkey—this time at a reasonable time. No TV allowed. Just games. Mark likes to win. Even with his new sister-in-law. I like being part of this family. They are nice people. I prefer them to my own family. They seem to like each other. There's always a tension with mine. Sort of dysfunctional but I love them all. As individuals. Just not together in one room for any given period.

I should forget John. This is what I want. A proper family. Nice people. People who will accept me for what I am. Er—hold on one minute there. They won't accept me for who I am. They don't know who I am. I've been seeing someone else. They don't know about the abortion. They would be devastated if they knew. Paul has not told them. They don't know about our problems. Paul won't tell them and neither will I. They won't accept me for who I am. They accept me for what they perceive me to be. Which isn't me. *Which isn't me.*

Boxing Day afternoon I find myself for a few minutes alone. Sitting on the toilet. Contemplating life. And finding space. I think, Shall I go through with this? I'm deceiving everyone, but especially myself. Do I come clean with Paul? Do I say, By the way, I've met someone else, but it's just a sexual thing? A fling? Or do I keep my big mouth shut. After all, John is a womaniser. He'll get bored of me—

right? He's amoral and I'll grow to hate him as he'll treat me badly, and Paul, despite the fact he won't sleep with me, is a nice guy. He's a lovely guy and I love him. But I'm sleeping with someone else. Well, not exactly sleeping with. We haven't actually done *it* yet. Phone sex? Does that count? It's not even oral sex. Does rolling round naked count? Or snogging? Or thinking about it? According to the church if you think about it, it's as good as doing it. Then again, it may all fizzle out with John anyway, so why rock the boat and tell Paul? He'll be upset and I love him.

Keep it to yourself, Sarah.

So I do. For Christmas. I smile and drink and get drunk and get a headache and a fucking migraine which bangs away at my head. And I fall asleep and Paul tells me that despite the fact we are engaged it would be nice to wait. And that we can hug naked and would that be all right? Wait for the wedding day before we make love properly? Wait nine months. Nine fucking months to make love. Do I understand?

No, I don't, but I will have to *try* to understand. Yes, I understand.

He tells me he proposed because we had been long enough going out, and that we had had our ups and downs, but now that I had left the Situation Manager's role at the railways I would be getting a job locally, and that he had done well in the City and was expecting a big bonus and that it was the right time to do it.

So, nothing to do with spontaneous romance, then, or an undying urge to want to spend the rest of his life with me. Nice. But practical, I suppose. Practical. I don't think I will ever be poor with this man, or feel insecure. I may feel unloved and unwanted and stifled and controlled and aching for affection. But I will never want for food or clothing or material comforts. All things that matter to my mother and which I don't give a fuck about. But perhaps this is what marriage is all about. Compromise and seeing a sense of what is and isn't important. After all, romantic love dies, doesn't it? And marriage evolves into friendship. It's just that I thought that happened when you were in your sixties, not *just* getting married. And perhaps waiting will increase the excitement. After all, Paul is wonderful and I love him and he loves me. Or what he wants me to be or what he thinks is me. Which isn't the same thing—but does that matter?

New Year's Eve

I haven't contacted John. I haven't answered his calls. I haven't answered his text messages. What can I say to the man? I've got to do it at some stage, right? He'll get bored with me and I won't need to chuck him—he will chuck me. Right? At some stage, before September. It's nine months, after all. He'll get bored with me in nine months. And I live in Chelmsford and he lives in Surrey and I don't work for the railways any more. So it will be difficult.

JANUARY

ACTION LIST

To be loved and feel loveable.
   To become a yoga instructor.
   To be as fit as I possibly can.
   To have fun.
   To win an award.
   To present a TV series.
   To present a radio series.
   To write a bestseller.
   To cherish my friends and build upon their friendship.
   To be lovely to Paul.
   To kick-box with style.
   To avoid all dairy and wheat products.
   To go to the gym every day of the week.
   How many ticks this year? Last year I got two out of ten,
but, hey, some of them were impossible. Like: Have orgasm
with penetrative sex.
   Don't think it happens. Especially when you're not hav-
ing sex.
   Spend New Year's Eve with Mike and Gemma. Mike is

a schoolfriend of Paul's. He is nothing like any of Paul's other friends. He is not rich. He is not from the City. He is genuine and kind and loving. He is also a karate black belt, so few people argue with him. Both twenty-eight. He doesn't have to bully or emotionally manipulate because he can kick you in the neck and kill you as quick as you can blink (probably quicker). He knows it. Gemma knows it. The pets know it. Other people know it. The only interesting times are when people don't know it and they find out. But he hasn't killed anyone yet. Fabulous body, lethal and loving disposition. What more could a woman ask? I don't fancy him, have never had fantasies about him, so despite his many and wonderful qualities, he remains unsexy to me. And anyway, I am newly engaged and my thoughts are for two men—my husband-to-be and my lover-to-be.

Mike and Gemma live in Reading—Caversham, which is supposed to be the nice part according to Paul, who lived there ten years ago before moving to Chelmsford. They are preparing the main course. We are given the starter and dessert. Paul brings port, which he loves and Mike hates. So more for Paul, then. I bring avocados and melon and parma ham and figs and various cheeses and green apples and grapes and biscuits and pre-prepared chocolate sponge puddings from Marks & Spencer and luxury extra creamy custard. Something different.

Their house is Victorian and messy and loved. Good vibes about it. Sort of smiles at you as you enter the door. They've got a black cat called Cherish and a retriever called Harry who get on and take over the house and their hairs are everywhere. Paul is allergic to cats. Perhaps over the years it's why I've grown to love the place and visiting Mike and Gemma.

New Year's dinner is in their kitchen. They're happy for us. We drink ten bottles of champagne between us. Mike is almost unconscious by two a.m. He doesn't usually drink. Paul is telling bad jokes and playing air guitar to Led Zeppelin. Mike does a party trick of breaking a walnut shell between his buttocks. Paul doesn't try. I keep getting text messages from John.

Gemma to Sarah—'So, when's the happy day?'

Message received:
Hope you have a wonderful New Year. Where are you?
I haven't been able to get in touch. What's happened?

Sarah to Gemma—'I think sometime in September. We don't want to wait too long.'

Message received:
Don't you lust after me any more? Amanda is driving me nuts. She's asking if anything is wrong and I can't tell her anything of course. Very distracted and distressed you haven't called. Why not?

Mike to Sarah—'There's a lot of arranging to be done. If we get married we don't want any fuss. Where are you planning to do it?'

Message received:
Thinking of you. Wanting you. Wanting to kiss and touch and make you squeal. Wanting to watch you as you come.

Sarah to Mike—'Um, probably the local church.'

Message received:
I've booked a weekend in Bath in January. Something to look forward to. Aching to see you.

Mike—'Toast. To the happy couple.'
All up-standing. Glasses clink. Big smiles.
Methinks perhaps not a good time to tell Paul that I'm

not sure about marrying him and why. Perhaps not. Wait till later in the year. John will be sick of me by then…

5th January

Nine a.m.

> *Message received:*
> I have a surprise for you. Call me, darling.

I check the sender. It's Paul. This type of message is usually from John. I call.

Sarah—'Hi, lover. What's the surprise?'

Paul—'I've bought a house. Well, almost. I will only buy it if you like it. Are you doing anything today?'

So much for respecting my opinion.

Sarah—'Well, I think this might take priority.'

I cancel my lunch and cinema with friends. I tell them why. They think it's wonderful and inconsiderate at the same time.

I drive over from my little flat. Karen tells me it's not right that he should buy a house and expect me to just lump the idea. My mind's not really on the house or Paul. It's on John. I'm due to see him this weekend.

The house. Large. Four bedrooms. Victorian. Large garden. Lots and lots of heavy wooden panelling which people older than fifty absolutely love. I hate it. Next door to park. High ceilings. Some rooms nicer than others. Small kitchen which needs gutting. If Paul says, 'It has incredible potential,' once more I will thump him.

Paul—'The family who lived here before were the Godlys. Mr Godly has now moved into an old people's home and that's why it's being sold. I got it only because I was able to strike the deal really quickly. Working in a bank helps. Some of Mum's friends wanted it, so we're very lucky.'

Sarah—'It's a family home.'

Paul—'I know.'

Sarah—'But I don't want a family. Not yet, anyway. I

want to have fun. This is not a fun house. This is a dinner party, stuffy, formal entertaining and children running all over the place sort of house.'

Paul—'You don't like it, then?'

Sarah—'Well, no. It also needs lots of work doing to it. It will need lots of cleaning. And it's too near your parents. Electrics and everything probably come from the Dark Ages. Don't think you should buy it.'

Paul—'Well, I have.'

Sarah—'Well, it's your house, then.'

Paul—'But we're getting married, so you're living here as well.'

Sarah—'Perhaps you should have thought of that when you bought it without asking my opinion first.'

Paul—'It's a beautiful home. You're very ungrateful. You're lucky I'm marrying you. Your mother seemed very happy to get you off her hands. You're marrying above your class, you know. This is a wonderful house. Worth nearly half a million and you're turning your nose up at it.'

Sarah—'You shouldn't have bought it without asking me. I don't like it. It's an old person's home.'

Paul—'I thought you would like it.'

Sarah—'You thought wrong. But it's done now. I suppose we can always funk it up a bit.'

Paul—'It will be our home. We will make it wonderful.' (Hugging me and looking into my eyes with his big doe eyes and fluttering his long dark eyelashes. But it doesn't work any more.)

Sarah—'Yes, perhaps.'

I pull away and say that I need to see the rooms again.

Message received:
How are you my love? I haven't seen you for ages. Are you still gorgeous?

Message sent:
I'm OK. Miss you. Want you. Still gorgeous and hungry.

Message received:
Sorry you don't like the house.

Paul's just downstairs, but obviously texting me.

Message sent:
It will grow on me. We can personalise it. It's an investment.

What the fuck am I doing? I'm now getting married to a man I'm not sure about at all. I've gone out with him for years, but we don't have sex, we increasingly can't communicate, I'm fantasising about someone else and there's no one I can talk to really. Catherine is smitten with Liam, and feels the same way about her boyfriend Freddie as I do about Paul. So she's telling me to go for it. My mother is the last person I could speak to about anything. She still doesn't know about the abortion. Only other person I can tell is Anya.

Anya is a reflexologist, a masseuse, a nutritionist, a qualified alternative therapist. She knows her stuff. She is half-Portuguese and half-Iranian. She is beautiful and fifty and looks about thirty. Bright, multi-lingual, with two gorgeous and brilliant children and Boris, Belgian husband she finds boring.

I confide in her.

Anya—'Don't go through with the marriage, Sarah. Postpone it. It's not right. You wouldn't want to do this with John, let alone actually do it, if you felt OK about the wedding and being Paul's wife.'

Sarah—'But couldn't it be the last fling? I haven't had sex for such a long time. Couldn't that be it? I love Paul.'

Anya—'If you loved Paul you wouldn't be doing this, Sarah. As for the sex, Paul has an issue he has got to deal with, but he hasn't and you've been stuck with it not for months but years. Now, could you lie down and take your clothes off?'

Going to a reflexologist and masseuse has been a lifesaver for me. Did you know that animals, if they don't have sex, end up biting one another? Well, I haven't had an affair with anyone since I met Paul, and one of the reasons, I'm sure, is because I've gone to the gym so much and started—only recently—to have a massage. Once a month, then once every two weeks and now once a week. I need it. I need to be stroked and pummelled and caressed. And even if it is painful it's doing me good, which is more than you can say for some men when they supposedly make love to you.

Anya—'I'm too old to change now. I'm fifty. I'm going to massage your shoulders. This may hurt as you're very tense today, Sarah.'

Anya pushes her fingers into my shoulders and I emit a loud yell.

Sarah—'Ugh. Fucking hell, that hurt. Anya, you don't look it. And Boris loves you.'

Another pummel. Other shoulder. Another yell.

Anya—'Don't do what I did and wait. And have children and get trapped, Sarah. You don't want that. You are young and have a life to lead. Paul is not the one for you if he can do this to you and if you want to see and be with and sleep with John. Learn from this. Take my word for it. I know what will happen. Don't get trapped in a sexless marriage. Sex isn't everything, but when you don't have it, it becomes the most important thing. What's John like?'

Anya works fingers down spine. Down to sciatic nerve. It kills me.

Sarah—'Ugh. You bitch. You're enjoying this. John is dangerous. Potent. He has more sexuality in his little finger than most men have in their whole bodies. But I think he's ugly. He used to be a research chemist. I'm sure he injected himself with pheromones. He has the most amazing smell. Doesn't that sound weird, that I'm attracted to his smell?'

Anya—'Not at all. Smell is a very basic instinct. It's just

that we hide our smells with perfume and aftershave and crap so that we don't smell how we should any more. Amazing we find the right mate at all. This may hurt.'

Anya starts reflexology on my feet and touches the bit which is supposed to represent my knees. I want to die.

Sarah—'It hurts. *It hurts.* I'm in absolute agony. Anyway, I love his smell. But his eyes are too close together. He has jet-black curly hair—you know, tight curls—and a small, almost mean mouth.'

Anya—'He sounds disgusting. And you like him?'

She pushes the part of my foot which is my heart. I inadvertently start to cry.

Sarah—'I'm crying coz it hurts, not because of the conversation, Anya. OK?'

Anya—'OK.'

Sarah—'Yes, first time I met him I thought he was ugly, and I still look at him occasionally and think yuck. But, hey, there must be something. Chemistry. I love being with him. And find him fascinating to talk to—or perhaps it's just the illicitness of it all. Perhaps that is why I am excited.'

Anya stops working on the feet and starts the nice stuff. Oils—patchouli, ylang ylang, lavender and other stuff which she keeps a secret and will sell off one day and make millions.

Anya—'That's why you've got to give yourself a break from Paul and see if it's for real or not. Plus you're not being fair to Paul either.'

Sarah—'I can't very well say to Paul, Hey, there, can we not see each other for a year while I get my head straight and see if the man I want to sleep with is my love or just some last-minute nerves before I swear eternal love to you in the eyes of God. Don't think that will wash, Anya.'

Anya—'You can't have your cake and eat it, Sarah. It won't work. It will screw you up and John and Paul. Just think about it. What happens if you get more involved with John? What then?'

Sarah—'He'll get bored. He's a womaniser. You just wait and see. He will dump me long before September.'

Anya—'Perhaps.'

We don't talk for about ten minutes. Massage is wonderful and I think I'm falling asleep. Then:

Anya—'Would you marry John?'

Sarah—'No.'

Anya—'Everyone is brought to our lives for a reason. Perhaps he's just a catalyst to make you re-evaluate your life.'

Sarah—'Perhaps. But I think it's just bad timing. He is sexy, and I haven't had sex for years. I've been faithful and celibate and now feel resentful. I don't want Paul's children, or any children for that matter. I may in the future, but not now. And now he's bought a big fuck-off family house five minutes from his parents and I feel trapped and confused and unhappy.'

Anya stops massaging and asks me to turn over so she can work on my face and scalp. She does the most fabulous scalp massages.

Anya—'Don't do it, Sarah. I've been there, seen it, done it. Got the T-shirt. I see so many women who've been through this. You don't want to go there. John may not be the right one, but you don't want to waste your life. You are young and beautiful and intelligent and Paul is a nice guy. I've met him, but he's not for you. He is a rock. Yes. Perhaps *your* rock. Problem with rocks is that they are stabilising but they also hold you down. Hold you back. There is an element where he may be protecting you from yourself. This is good. But it can also be bad, because, Sarah, you've got a lot of life to live and he's an old man before his time. The house sounds like an old family home. He's into drinking port and dinner parties and, yes, he likes going to the Grand Prix and, yes, he can afford to go, but these are all fast cars and show-offy things. He likes cigars, for goodness' sake. He's not even thirty and he has all the trappings of someone twenty years older than himself. And you're a young girl. You're not for him. You like the security he brings, and, yes, you may love him, but you've got to see with better eyes and see it for what it is. It may be love. It may not. The only way you can find out is to let go now and see for sure. But do you have the balls to do that, Sarah? Do you?'

Sarah doesn't have the balls, I thought. She doesn't. She will get married in September to someone who is sensible and spiritual but just a little screwed up at the moment. Someone who won't change but who may mellow over time. Who may start to realise money isn't everything. It can buy security but not happiness. It may happen. It may not. But only time will tell. And I love him. And I think he's sexy. And I will be safe with him. And I have faith in him and believe him to be a good, honest person. Unlike the person he is marrying...

Sarah—'Yes, I have the balls. I will tell him, Anya.'

Anya—'Good girl. It's the best way, Sarah. And then you can have fun with John without a guilty conscience. And try a different cake. One a little spicier if not as rich.'

I left Anya's feeling like a fraud. I knew she was right, but didn't have the confidence to tell either of them what was going on and how I felt. So I let it lie. And I lied.

10th January

Have started new job in Chelmsford after being made redundant from the railways. Got pay-off and now in new family home (allowed to sleep with fiancé although still no-sex rule). Job is five minutes' drive from home. Fifteen mins if I walk. Paul is pleased. He is pleased because they give good maternity leave.

I liked the guy who interviewed me. He was almost as mad and quirky as I would like to be. He liked me. Think he could tell I wanted to be almost as mad and quirky as he was. He likes my body language (very open—not legs, of course). But not crossed arms (think this is a silly rule as I cross my arms to hide my bitten nails, not because I feel negative towards the person I am speaking to or listening to).

The job has dull title. It's as Communications Manager for a local firm in Chelmsford. Communications Manager means sweet FA. I tell him that I won't communicate for the whole company, but that I will facilitate communication. Put in place a process which will do so. Does he understand this? He does. He tells me the problem. Departments don't communicate with one another because Boss A doesn't like or trust or respect Boss B. So nothing gets done, or it takes a lot of money and time to get done. So Sarah at vast expense (£34k plus perks) has been hired to hand-hold and get them to sit in the same room for half an hour and talk sense.

I will not have my own office, because it's open plan. I will have a team of twenty who write letters to customers. Responding to complaints. They need to improve their letter-writing. So it's external communication as well as internal communication then. Plus the company is spending £300,000 on management consultants who are telling them how to communicate and who have so far not been able to succeed. They have used up two-thirds of the budget already.

I have no faith in management consultants. I had my fill of them at the railway. They tell you what you already know, and show you a way to deal with the situation, but it rarely works. Bit like them asking for your watch, telling you the time and then keeping your watch. Sort of win-lose situation. They win. You lose. Anyway, it sounds a challenge so I'm going for it and today, on the tenth I start.

Bad start. Am told that I am doing someone else's job and that several board members didn't know I had been hired. Tell my boss this is not my problem and that they should do something about it. Have first department meeting and meet all team on one-to-one basis and then as a group. They are all from Chelmsford. All doing it for the money. All friendly without aspiration.

I set up meeting with other departments and get briefing from Number Two, Jennifer, on who likes who, who doesn't like who, who would like to sleep with who, who is sleeping with who and who she likes, would like to sleep with and is sleeping with. We talk a bit about letter-writing.

11th January

I have a call from the Personnel Director, Mr Harry, who is based in London. He says can he see me? I say fine. He says he is coming to Chelmsford and would like to have lunch. Is this OK? I say fine. I book the local eaterie, which is half decent.

12th January

I meet Mr Harry. Place called the Wine Cellar which does OK food. I order smoked salmon as a main course. Something light that I can eat with my fingers. I like eating with my fingers. Even salad and soup (chunky variety). There's something very sensual and reassuring about it. And something very unnatural and rigid about using knives and forks. Especially forks. I heard back in Elizabethan times everyone used to eat with knives, and forks came much later. I eat with fingers.

He orders steak with new potatoes and uses his knife and fork with precision and focus and it annoys the shit out of me. He also puts his mobile phone on the table by his fork as though it's another utensil he is going to use to eat his food. Every five minutes it goes off and he answers it, saying yes or no or I'll call you back. Why can't he switch the fucking thing off?

He orders a bottle of the house red. I say I don't drink. He says more for him. I have to keep reminding myself Harry is his surname and not his first name. I ask him what his first name is. He tells me it is Harry. He says his middle name is Richard, so people call him HRH. I ask him if his parents had a sense of humour. He tells me they did. And fortunately so does he. And that in the past the name has got him interviews when perhaps his credentials might not have.

Harry Harry—'Believe it or not, Sarah, everyone needs a unique selling point and that is mine. Now, the reason I've asked to meet you is because you are causing problems—'

Phone rings.

Harry Harry—'Hi. Yes. No, not yet. I'm doing it now. Bye. Yes, I will. Bye.'

Sarah—'Er, I've only been here two days. What have I done?'

Harry Harry—'Well, it's not a case of what you have done. It's more a case of you being hired in the first place. No one knew you were being hired. The man who hired you didn't clear it at the top. And because of what you do, and the way you've been doing it, everyone is talking about you. And saying how good you are. And how it should have been done a long time ago. And why weren't you hired before? But it's not your job. And so it's political, you see. Your job. The job. You have become untenable. We are going to have to let you go.'

Sarah—'But I've only been here two days.'

Phone rings.

Harry Harry—'Hi. Yes. No, not yet. I'm doing it now. Bye. Yes, I will. Bye. Sarah, if you had been a little quieter, hadn't made such an impact within forty-eight hours, then it would have been fine. But you wanted to make an impression and you have. The management consultants don't like you. They think you are obnoxious. Did you tell them they were a waste of space and that all they do is tell us what we already know?'

Sarah—'Yes, but they do and they are.'

Harry Harry—'The MD hired them. The CEO of the company is his golfing partner. Been friends since school.'

Phone rings.

Harry Harry—'Hi. Yes, I have. Yes, now. Yes, I'm with her now. Bye. Yes, I will. Bye.'

Sarah—'So that has an impact on business decisions, does it?'

Harry Harry—'You are very naïve, Sarah. You have a lot

to learn. Secondly, you've got departments to speak to one another, haven't you?'

Phone rings.

Sarah—'Can you turn that off, please? Most of the board must know by now you are telling me or have told me. Can't they wait?'

Harry Harry turns off his mobile. Begrudgingly.

Sarah—'It's a good thing. It was needed. They didn't talk to one another. It was ridiculous. Now things are progressing and they know where they can improve and what still needs work. How can that be a problem?'

Harry Harry—'It is a problem. They've decided that they don't like the way it's being done and want to change everything. And that there are not enough people in either department. They have asked for more people and have produced a strategy and plan. Problem is, the board likes to clear and create this sort of thing. They don't like initiatives coming from the staff. They may say they do, but in reality this is a very top-led company and they like to keep it that way. Unintentionally you've rocked the boat, Ms Giles.'

Sarah—'So they're going to sack me because I've helped to make the company more efficient?'

Harry Harry—'You've come from the railways. What do you know about efficiency?'

Sarah—'Cheap shot. Anyway, just because you're making money doesn't mean a thing. What I'm trying to do is make you *more*. And your staff have taken the initiative. They should be praised. I should be praised. Not sacked.'

Harry Harry—'This is the way it is. I am offering you a deal. If you go willingly we will pay you four months' salary and you can retain your company car for four months—whether you find a new job or not. If you refuse to go we can find a reason to sack you and you go away with nothing.'

My first thought is, How am I going to explain this to Paul? He will not believe me. I ask Harry Harry if he can put it in writing. He says he will. I ask if he wants me to work out the week. He says no. That I can leave after lunch if I want. I say I have left my stuff in the office. He says I can collect it. But that I shouldn't mention anything to the staff. He asks me if I am OK. I say no, I'm not. But that I won't cry (I probably will later on). That I think I could have done good. That this is incredible. Why was I hired in the first place? Harry Harry tells me I shouldn't have been hired and that I did do good but that I stepped on too many toes and was not politically astute enough to realise when to keep my mouth shut and when to speak. That this is business and a fact of life and a good lesson to learn. That I should be happy with my green Golf GTI and enjoy the first four months of the year because I had a good start.

I think about this. Be philosophical. It may all be for a reason. At this moment in time I can't think what reason. He says they will give me a good reference. For two days? Yes, for two days.

Harry Harry—'You've managed to create an impact. That is a skill few have.'

Sarah—'Yeah. I've also managed to lose a job in two days.'

The lunch lasts an hour and a half. Harry Harry switches on his phone. As I get up to go (wine untouched, my fingers smelling of smoked salmon), I hear him say, 'Yes, all done. Yes, fairly well. We may have made a mistake but that's life. Nice nipples, though.'

I call Paul.

Sarah—'Hi, darling. Got something to tell you. I've been sacked, but I haven't done anything wrong. I've done good, actually, but stepped on toes. They're giving me a letter of recommendation and four months' salary and the Golf for four months.'

Silence.

Sarah—'Are you still there?'

Paul—'Yes. I'm still here. You are incredible, you know. I can't think of anyone else who would be like this.'

Sarah—'Yes, I know. Well, at least there is some money and I have time to look around.'

Paul—'So you do. See you tonight.'

Sarah—'See you tonight.'

I collect my stuff from the office. This is very surreal. I say goodbye to Jennifer, and say that she should speak to HRH and he will tell her what is going on. She looks confused. I say, 'You'll find out.'

Driving back home to the house I don't like, jobless, to a man I'm not sure about, I wonder what life is all about. Then I get a text message from John.

Message received:
Missing you. Thinking of you. Wanting and needing you. We're the right people at the right time at the right place.

If only.

FEBRUARY AND MARCH

ACTION LIST

Be nice to Paul.
   Be faithful to Paul.
   Think only of Paul.
   Forget fun.
   Be responsible.
   Go to gym to work off naughty thoughts.
   Avoid dairy and wheat products.
   Avoid alcohol, which makes me a) tearful, b) honest.

INVITATION TO A DIRTY WEEKEND

January went in a blink. I haven't managed to see John. I've
been concentrating on finding another job. Which I have.
As Marketing Manager for the Mightlight Group—an ad-

vertising company. They need someone to help promote their advertising campaign with some PR support. The main one being a tourism initiative and travel seminars to promote England overseas.

I think God is playing a trick on me. I hate England. Weather sucks. People reticent and rude. Dirty and anal. I wanted to be the skirt on the board—but not like this thank you very much. Plus the Mightlight office is in Hammersmith. And there's nothing mighty about it. I live the other side of London, for goodness' sake. It takes two hours to get there and two hours back. I will spend most of my time travelling and the rest knackered. This leaves little time for one man—let alone two.

But the role means I may get time to travel—overseas and in this country—and it may keep me out of trouble. Plus there are the wedding preparations—which take time. The little wedding with only a few friends has grown into a big FO wedding for one hundred and fifty. His parents are paying a third, as are mine, as are we. I don't know *any* of his extended family. They are all from Ireland and all seem to be cousins of some sort. Then there are 'our' friends. All of whom work in his office and are on average about twenty years older than him and very important and influential and probably worth inviting for the wedding presents alone. My family don't talk to one another so have to be put on separate tables. My friends have been restricted to ten. I have more than ten friends but they are not good enough to invite to my wedding. Obviously not wedding present good enough.

We are having the reception in a priory that is costing a fortune and was used by various celebrities from *Eastenders* for their weddings. This does nothing to sell it to me. In fact it's more a black mark, but Paul says this is OK and we won't tell anyone. They are charging us ten pence per olive. I have worked it out. We take a leap of faith. Starters are melon and parma ham. There is the option of smoked salmon and avocado. With a balsamic vinegar dressing. I suggest something different for a change. Paul says best to stick to what people like. At his dinner parties anyway. Main course is beef or chicken, with new potatoes and mange tout and sugar snap peas and carrots. Followed by miniature chocolate sponge puddings and custard. Port to finish, with truffles. Cheese was too expensive. They hadn't heard of physallis— even when I said they were cape gooseberries and M&S sold them.

Wedding cake being done by someone in Basildon. Flowers by someone in Southend. Dress by someone in Colchester. Catherine to be the bridesmaid. She to wear green, I to wear oyster. With a hat, not a veil. Paul is to choose the honeymoon. I had had, and wanted, nothing to do with it. The whole situation bored and depressed me. But by the beginning of February most was getting sorted. Church, invitations, dress, cake, menu, and flowers had been decided. That left car, honeymoon (which Paul wouldn't tell me about, but told my and his parents) and band to be confirmed. Plus I had a hen weekend to arrange.

In the midst of all this I had kept in touch with John only by text message. We hadn't seen each other or touched each other. For goodness' sake, we hadn't even fucked each other, but I felt more close to him just by texting him and talking to him. Work was interesting and fun, and the journey was horrendous, and it left little time for anything other than work and sleep and organising wedding plans.

I told John I didn't have time to see him at the moment, but he arranged for us to meet in April, at a hotel called the Plumtree at Peerton. Where he took all his women, he told me. I felt reassured by this. The fact he was flippant about me being just another of his women made me feel that I was an insignificant lay to him. Just one of many. He would tire of me soon. Plus I was sure that I wouldn't live up to expectations. The phone sex was good, and became more imaginative and outrageous—but always possible. So, we could do it in a stable, but not in space.

Paul was worried about this year's bonus. I was worried about keeping my job for more than two days. We had more dinner parties. More parma ham and port and chicken suppers. And air guitar and *Highlander* and his friends and occasionally mine, none of whom he liked and was pleased they weren't coming to the wedding. The priory didn't have a large enough room to seat all the guests, so there were two adjoining rooms. Most of my friends were in the 'other' room because, quote, 'they will understand about being in the other room'. His friends and family and his work colleagues would not. I thought this was a cheek, but had given up trying to express an opinion.

The house I didn't like was taking shape slowly. Because Paul was a trader in the City his negotiating skills showed in everything he did. He would prefer to work with one-man bands who had been recommended. He would negotiate a deal for a lot of work and money up-front and most on completion and strip costings down to the bare bone. I never had any doubt he had got a good deal on anything. But the builders never returned after doing one job. They never came back and somehow they were always busy when Paul asked them to quote again. I became the good cop and he the bad. He bought pictures that reminded me of Old Masters, but they weren't. It was an old man's house and my fiancé was turning into an old man before his time. He even liked gardening.

So I was aching to get February out of the way—and March. Yearning for April showers and the weekend at the Plumtree. I researched it on the internet and got pictures of the room we would be staying in. Work took me around the UK and overseas—so I would occasionally be away—one weekend in every four—so it would be easy to say I would be away for a weekend in April. I would just tell Paul he could contact me on my mobile, and that I would be in meetings so not to disturb me too much. Plus, when I was away he would be away with his work colleagues on a golfing weekend in Ireland. So he would be busy too.

The last remaining bits to be done for the wedding were sorted throughout March. Band was chosen. Something funky. No disco. Car chosen. A black Sunbeam. John's red Sunbeam Lottie kept coming to mind, but this one was older. Wedding list chosen and sent out. Paul and I had spent two hours looking round Peter Jones in Sloane Square for gifts—prices ranging from £10 to £200. Lots of glasses (port, of course), Villeroy & Boch—which were so delicate I would be scared to use them. A dishwasher (woman's best friend—forget the diamonds), washing machine, fish kettles, Le Creuset. We couldn't agree on cutlery so we didn't put that on. He wanted formal. I wanted something modern. For some reason I wouldn't budge on this. I conceded (gave in) on everything else, and in light of the fact I rarely used cutlery (fingers instead) I didn't understand why I was so fussy about this. Probably out of principle I said no. Invites were coming back. Mostly acceptances. A few of my friends out of the country in September. Hopefully sun would shine. Hopefully.

I had bought myself a self-help book, *Feel the Fear and Do It Anyway*, which I thought strangely appropriate. Then *Embracing Uncertainty*, which taught me that everything happens for a purpose—even the bad. That I should not hope for things, just wonder if they will happen. It amused me that I considered marrying Paul to be a bad thing, but it served a purpose and obviously I was doing it for a reason. But I didn't think I should think that way. I talked to no one. Not even Anya. Not even Catherine. Anya thought I had told Paul that I was finished with him and was seeing John. And Catherine thought I had finished with John and was devoted to Paul. And I was juggling both balls in the air and waiting in anticipation of the weekend in April, which would help me make my decision.

Paul does not believe in Valentines, so there was no dinner or card. John sent me one. I got to it before Paul did. It was a picture by Monet with dancers. And said 'I want you' inside. I presume it was from him. I had no other admirers at the time.

In March, I went on a course in Cookham. The Mightlight Group had sponsored a marketing diploma. And this was a week-long residential course. There were twenty others on the course and we were divided into groups. My group consisted of four very self-opinionated men. All in their late twenties. One American, one Liverpudlian, one Londoner and one Scot. And me. They argued about everything and I was very much the cement that stopped them from killing each other. The American—Tony—said I was very maternal and caring and could he take me to lunch? I said fine. For some reason I didn't mention I was engaged. I didn't feel engaged or in love or excited, so why should I?

13th March

Lunch with American Tony. At Andrew Edmunds.

Tony was prompt. I was ten minutes late. After all, I had come from Hammersmith and the Piccadilly Line on the underground was stopping and starting due to a person underneath the rails. Always amazed me how inconsiderate people were. 'Why the fuck couldn't he have killed himself some other time? Why did it have to be now?' was the most common comment. Screw the fact the guy was someone's son or dad or brother and was probably feeling like shit or nothing when he did it, and the last thing he was thinking was I want to screw up everyone else's day. Or perhaps it was. But I always gave suicide cases the benefit of the doubt.

I explained when I got to the restaurant. For those who don't know Andrew Edmunds, it is unashamedly romantic. The lighting is so dimmed you can't see your plate, let alone the food on which it is daintily placed. The chef can't make up his mind whether he is into vegetarianism, or French or Italian, rustic or nouvelle cuisine. So there's a combination of everything and it just about works. There are candles to play with, and the tables are close enough to each other that you can listen to other people's conversation if yours becomes dull. Lovers talk to each other and don't eat. Marrieds eat and don't talk to each other. The evenings and lunchtimes work when the owner positions the tables marrieds/lovers/marrieds. Whole groups of lovers together unbalance the boat, as you have one side buzzing and the other dead. The owner has been known to ask customers if they are coming with their wives or associates for this very reason.

Tony and I were neither, but we were seated between two marrieds. I could tell. None of them said a word to each other during the time we were there.

Tony stood up as I came in to take my seat.

We chatted and chose food. I chose something I could use my fingers to eat. So did he. It was a mutual bonding thing without us knowing it.

Tony—'I had an accident yesterday. I nearly died.'

Wow. Good opening line. He had my attention.

Sarah—'God, Tony. How? Where? When?'

Tony—'Someone crashed into me from the side. It was a getaway car from a robbery. Police were chasing it and he went straight into me. Police say I'm lucky to be alive.'

I automatically leant over the table and gave him a hug. He hugged me back. Seemed a bit intimate for someone I had met only a week ago, but the week had been intensive and I knew he would take it the right way.

Tony—'Well, Sarah, it made me think. About life. About what's important in life and what isn't. And why so many people wait for something good to happen to them and don't just take it. It made me re-evaluate life and, well... Will you marry me?'

Silence. Brain working overtime. Does not compute. Man known one week proposes after near-death experience. He could see I was confused.

Tony—'I can see you are confused. Sarah, I know this sounds strange, but I think we have a connection. A chemistry. You are a caring, lovely person and I know that, and you're special, and I think we would work well together. And this has taught me that when you have a chance at happiness you should go for it. And I'm going for it. I don't know if I love you, but I think I do, and we have a connection. A spiritual connection.'

Silence. Brain working double overtime. Still didn't compute. Other than the finger food stuff and the fact I laughed at his jokes I couldn't see the connection. I didn't feel any of the sexual or sensual urges I had for John, nor the deep loving ones I had for Paul. Nothing. Friend, yes. Lover, no. Husband. Forget it. I speak.

Sarah—'I am very flattered, Tony. Very. But I don't think this is a good time for me.' (You bet, and for more reasons than you think). 'I'm not into relationships at the moment. I don't want to settle down. There is nothing wrong with you.' (Notice his face becoming stiff. Verging on the grim.) 'You are wonderful and handsome and kind, but I don't want a relationship at the moment.'

I smile and put my hand on his. Hoping he will think it's just for friendship. He doesn't.

Tony—'You are wonderful. Perhaps if we could start with a physical relationship. Sex isn't everything, and if you are a virgin then it doesn't matter. I can teach you.'

Arrogant eat-shit-and-die wanker. Do I look like a virgin? Do I act like a virgin? Patronising arsehole. Don't care if he's had a near-death experience. If he wants another one, he's coming close to it. I bite.

Sarah—'What makes you think I'm a virgin, or that I'm afraid of sex?'

Tony—'Nothing. Only that you seem a bit awkward about being touched.'

Sarah—'Perhaps its just about being touched by you. I'm sorry, Tony, but we can be friends and that's it. This is completely out of the blue. I'm not a virgin. Sorry about that. And I don't fancy you and don't find you in any way sexually attractive. There is nothing attractive about you on a physical level. I'm sure other women find you attractive, sexy even, but I don't. I don't think I could ever find you physically attractive and that's the way it is.'

I wanted to nail this coffin and bury the box with flowers on then and there. I wanted him to leave without any doubt at all. There was absolutely no chance of a return lunch. I had experienced lunches like this in the past. An insurance salesman from Cobham, a Jewish banker from Loughton, an Essex young farmer from Colchester, a Turkish hotel-owner from Bodrum. I'd tried to be nice and say no thank you nicely, but they'd never got the message. I wanted to be cruel to be kind on this occasion. I knew he had had one near-death experience and wouldn't go for another, so had no doubts he wouldn't try the 'I'm going to kill myself' scam, which I'd had once before and it scared the shit out of me. I might have damaged the ego, but it would be short lived and he would hate me. He did.

Tony—(scowling)—'Fine. I get the message. You could have been a bit more subtle about the way you told me. After all, being proposed to doesn't happen every day. Especially to someone who looks like you. You're not exactly Cameron Diaz, you know. You're not that special. Nice arse, but small tits. Nothing there. And your conversation sucks. And I bet you do in bed as well. You're just a prick-tease, aren't you? Met your type before. Pathetic little cow. You should be grateful for what you get.'

The prick-teasing pathetic little cow with small tits and nice arse realised she'd gone too far in an attempt to kill any suggestion of romance. So to get rid of the psycho for good I conceded graciously that I was and would always be the ugliest most ungrateful thing on the planet but that I still wouldn't sleep with him or entertain him as anything other than an acquaintance—which was obviously out of the question now. Because I didn't want to know of him, let alone be with him.

He decided that lunch was too much and left. He stood up, chest out, stomach in, chin erect, gave me an I-could-strangle-you-bitch look, took out his wallet and threw a couple of fifty-pound notes on the table, saying that I could finish my lunch on him. And that I should take five pounds for myself, because that was what my company was worth. That he would take the ring back (what ring?) and wouldn't contact me again. That I was a sad bitch and would doubtless die a lonely wrinkled spinster without friends or memories to lighten my days.

The marrieds on either side of our table hadn't touched their food, nor their drinks, and were now overtly staring at me and then at him and then at me again.

Sarah—'Thank you, Tony. You are probably right. And thank you for the money.'

He left like a drama queen should. In a flurry of anger and bruised ego. His black cashmere coat brushing against the tables and knocking a few Badoit bottles over in the process. The fact he was balding meant he couldn't swish back his hair. Instead he swept his scarf round his neck. Dunno if it was cashmere.

I sat there. On table twenty-five. With my fifty-pound notes and smoked salmon starter untouched. A bottle of finest something untouched. I didn't know whether to laugh or cry as I felt completely numb with indifference. I started to laugh into my hands. One of the marrieds leant over and asked if I was OK and would I like a glass of champagne?

'Some Americans are wankers, darling. All marketing, no substance. Shitty little man.'

I finished the salmon and offered to pay for it. The waiter said he had heard everything and I could have it on the house. So I took the one hundred pounds, went to Agent Provocateur, bought several sexy pairs of almost-there knickers. Cut across the cheek, just the way I know he likes them. Thank you so much, Tony. John would be oh, so very happy with these.

And he was.

SPRING

APRIL

ACTION LIST

Get legs, armpits, moustache and bikini line waxed. Try
Brazilian if not too painful.
  Go to gym every day. Twice on Saturdays and Sundays.
  Practise box splits.
  Get roots done.
  Have fun.
  Be extra nice to Paul.

THE YELLOW LOTUS

7th April

D Day. Dirty weekend. Told Paul was at a business seminar.
Assertiveness training. Not contactable most of the weekend. Was he OK with this? Yes, he would be in Ireland, with
the boys, playing golf. Was fine with it.

  I would meet John at Reading Station at eight p.m. on
Friday. He would then drive to the hotel. We hadn't spo-

ken or even texted each other for several weeks. I had been up to armpits in organising nonsensical functions for regional journalists who for some inexplicable reason wanted to promote Year of the Pier. Why this year should be the Year of the Pier I didn't know. I continued to ask but, having never received a sensible answer, promoted it for all it was worth. Which wasn't much. All the journalists I spoke to asked why this year should be the Year of the Pier, and I told them because it commemorated the first ever pier going up. Forty years ago. This was complete and utter bollocks, but they bought into it and we received good coverage, albeit a little inaccurate in parts.

So I was nervous about meeting John. Would I still fancy him? Why was I doing this? I was starting to get on marginally better with Paul. I had almost resigned myself to a life of domesticity, but perhaps the four-hour journey in and out of work was wearing me down, as well as Paul's consistent nagging about having the house decorated this way and not that. That being my way and my suggestions. I gave in. We had the panelling polished to its natural finish. We had wallpaper instead of plaster and paint. We had watercolour paintings and Old Masters and black and white architectural drawings of churches. Granite tops in the kitchen. Fitted bedroom furniture that was made not to look fitted. I didn't even flinch when he suggested gold and green curtains for the dining room. Hey, why not go the whole hog and turn the house into a fucking mausoleum for old folk?

The train journey to Reading took about an hour. It was on time. I was on time. I carried one light overnight bag. Had all the latest skincare products. Aromatherapy oils. Wearing red. Stockings for the first time in ten years. Last time I had worn them they ended up round my ankles at the end of the evening. Not because of any wanted or unwanted advances. But because I have slim legs and they slipped over them. There I was, walking down the steps to Liverpool Street Station, and ping they went. Bankers I'm sure still talk about it to this day. Bright purple they were too, so not even subtle.

So, black stockings, black suspenders. Little red dress. Slut. Slut. Slut. I hadn't had anything to eat that day. Only black coffee and buzz gums so was feeling flying and hyper. Work had been difficult. I'd been in front of the manager, who was querying some of the excellent, albeit untruthful copy we had been getting about Year of the Pier and asking me how she would explain to the Travel Editor of the *Times* this was complete fabrication. She told me one more instance like this and I would be out on a leg. I didn't care. I had lasted more than two days—so what? Two months was long for me.

John was on time. He was waiting at the station. He hadn't changed. I kissed him on the cheek. He looked at me.

John—'You look tired.'

Great. Hadn't seen him for months and first thing he says is that. Not, I want to fuck you. Or, You look gorgeous. Just, 'You look tired.'

Sarah—'Thanks. So do you.'

John—'Touché. I've got the car just round the corner. Can I take your bag?'

Better.

Sarah—'Thank you. There's not much in it.'

The coffee is making me jittery. Wish I hadn't drunk so many pots of it that morning. What with being shouted at, nearly fired and the coffee, and not being able to take solids that day, I was almost faint with stress.

We reached the car and he opened my door.

John—'Like the stockings.'

Sarah—'How do you know I am wearing them?'

John—'I can tell.'

Better. I smiled at him. He just looked at me as if I wasn't wearing anything. Perhaps just the stockings and suspenders. But then he always looked at me that way. Just I'd forgotten over the past few months.

As we drove out of the station he put his hand between my legs and started to stroke my right inner thigh.

John—'So, have you had a good day? You look stressed.'

Sarah—'I am stressed. But this is relaxing me.'

I nodded to his hand. The hand that seemed to be having so much fun with my suspender top.

John—'I've had a bad day too. Had to fire two men. Plus make a presentation to a group of students, some of whom were good, others of whom were complete wasters. We should be at the hotel in an hour. It's not close to anything. Very quiet. Ideal for us. If you want to go out we can. But you may just want to sleep. You look as though you need it.'

Sarah—'You look haggard too.'

John—'I'm not saying you look haggard. Just tired.'

Sarah—'I'm fine.'

John—'As long as you are. I don't want to overtire you.'

His hand was moving further up the thigh. I was starting to wake up. He only took his hand from me when he changed gear.

John—'Wish this car was automatic sometimes.'

Sarah—'That was my suggestion. Perhaps the next car will be.'

By the time we arrived at the hotel I had come once and was close to coming again. I felt the bed was superfluous. The front seat of a car would be fine.

As we drove into the car park I did up my suspenders and brushed down my dress. Looked in the car mirror to see if I looked ruffled or had that 'I've just come' look on my face. I looked flushed but nothing that too much caffeine wouldn't do. Plus hair was thankfully unruffled, which is what usually happens with me post-sex.

The Plumtree at Peerton is a boutique hotel. With twelve rooms. And three four-posters. John had booked a four-poster. Actually Medina had booked a four-poster. With views over the surrounding fields. The receptionist greeted us and asked us to sign the book. John signed his name. I signed as Sarah Smith. Original, huh? Credit card details and then shown the room. The girl first. I followed. John led from the rear.

Up two flights of stairs. It seemed to take an eternity. Room Number Four. Byron. Would we like Byron? Yes, we would.

Girl—'Tea served at four in the afternoons. Breakfast from seven a.m. till ten-thirty, lunch from twelve till two p.m. and supper from seven until ten-thirty. If you would like anything, please call Reception.'

John—'Thank you.'

Sarah—'Thank you.'

Door closed. We looked at each other. He walked towards me. Knock on door. Bags.

Door open. Bellboy with bags, looked nervous. John took them. Thanked nervous bellboy and closed the door. Turned round. Put bags on floor in front of door. And walked towards me.

I stood there motionless. He didn't say anything. He didn't kiss me. He undid the front of my dress, having some difficulty with the buttons. I took over and undid the ones he couldn't. Neither of us said anything. I felt nervous and not quite sure why I was there or what I was doing. I could walk out now and say, Hey, I'm getting married in five months' time. This is my last fling, do you understand? I'm sure you do. But I didn't. I just walked round the bed and slowly undressed, leaving the suspenders and stockings he had been so eager to play with. He undressed himself. Black shirt that all men who are slightly overweight wear because it makes them look cool. And thinner. Or they think so. John was in OK shape. Not great. But he was manly compared to Paul. Broader.

Stripped down to his underpants he looked much more vulnerable than I had seen him before. Gone the arrogance, the power of the boardroom. He looked nervous. Perhaps he was unsure too. Perhaps he knew. Perhaps I was seeing too much in something and should *feel the fear and do it anyway.* I walked over to the end of the bed and pulled down his briefs. Valentino. Black. Stroking him, I leant over and began to move my hand over him.

I sort of thought myself an expert at oral sex. Had had loads of practice with first boyfriend David, then lots with Paul when the no-sex kicked in. And, as Clinton knows, oral sex isn't sex, really, is it? Plus the porno magazines Paul bought had taught me even more. Like most men he had a stash of porno magazines under his bed which he showed me when we first started going out. He had the good idea, methinks, of getting me to read the words—something I don't think anyone who buys them ever does or anyone who writes in them ever expects to happen. They were hilarious. Sexy, filthy and funny. And it worked. They were a turn-on in a funny sort of way. Word most used: Cum. And phrase most used: Fuck me, baby. Fuck me, baby, up the arse. Fuck me, baby. Kept thinking of Britney Spears but sure they weren't the lyrics. Perhaps Suck. Anyway, I forget.

Girls were always called Britney and boys Tony. I never read about a Sarah, which was strangely reassuring. Perhaps disconcerting. Perhaps Sarahs weren't thought of as slutty but Britneys were, and I didn't know any Anthonys. Probably for the best. Paul said there were probably a lot of Sarahs but they changed their names to remain anonymous. *Anonymous!*

Anyway, learnt a lot from those magazines. Mostly about oral sex and the fixation men have with it. And that they don't get it enough and would like it all the time. And that some men are really into big tits and others into pussies and others into bums. Really big bums. And some men like to be peed on and some men like to be sat on and some even like to have nappies put on them, but they are mostly MDs and CEOs of the larger multinationals. Mostly in media. And, oh, yes, they would quite like an intelligent woman. Yes, it helps keep the relationship ticking over. That and the ability to cook their favourite meal. They are pluses. Depending on the intellect of the man.

According to the magazines, oral was tops. Beat penetrative, anal and bondage hands down. Cut across all classes, professions, nationalities and religions and men have one thing in common. Men love women who love going down on them. Fortunately I had had a lot of practice with David. In the back of his BMW Five Series convertible, blue, I would try to make him come, sometimes counting up to five thousand up and down by the time I succeeded. It was easier when he had some good music, coz at least then I could get a rhythm going. U2 was probably best. Good fast rhythm and he liked it as well and I usually made it to five hundred and then he came. Some, Whitney Houston or Sting, were no good at all. Sometimes I would be there for hours and have to give in to just using my hand and kissing him slowly up to his belly button or trying some new manoeuvre.

I was usually covered in sweat and on the verge of fainting, but felt a genuine sense of achievement and also lost a few pounds in the process. Something that is always a plus point for girls of an anorexic disposition. Plus I'm sure this is why I now have very prominent cheekbones. All that mouth-work makes you ache, but it does have its plus points. One of my friends recently told me spunk is full of a lot of calories. As many as one double vodka. But saltier. I felt that I could handle the calories because by four thousand five hundred I needed them.

I didn't know what to expect with John. Would he be a two hundred or a two thousand? However, as I started I felt his hand on my hair, stopping me.

'This doesn't usually happen to me. It's never happened before. I'm very sorry.'

And, with that, he came.

Wow. Two. Record for me. I didn't know whether to feel an incredible sense of achievement or disappointment. This man was the stud. A man who'd slept with hundreds of women and I'd made him prematurely ejaculate. Surely men like this don't do *that*. I stood up and said, 'That's OK.' Then swallowed.

'Don't worry. Shall we have a bath now? Or go down to dinner as it's quite late?'

'Yeah, let's have a bath. I'll run it.'

He seemed shy and unsure of himself. I liked it. I felt more in control and better able to handle the situation. Perhaps he was like a little boy after all. I had this theory that men, no matter how mature they seemed, were still all mummy's boys. No matter if they hated them, had been bullied by them, abandoned by them, spoilt or unspoilt by them, they were still all wanting to be nurtured till their last breath. And, quite frankly, I didn't want to do that. I didn't want to nurture in a maternal way. I wanted a partner in life and crime, and despite the fact men had told me that was what they wanted too, they didn't. They wanted a mother. Perhaps not their mother. But a mother. I thought there were enough women to go around who were happy to mother and nurture their men. Just I wasn't one of them. Perhaps a mistress, then. But never a wife. That was until I met Paul. I wanted to be with him for ever because he made me feel like an angel. I was an angel when I was with him. But not now. And anyway, now I was with John, in a boutique hotel room, almost having oral sex.

John—'I'll run the bath.'

Sarah—'OK.'

As we were both half naked perhaps it wasn't such a bad idea. Taking all our clothes off made me feel more vulnerable again. Sitting opposite him, he said I looked like Chrissie Hynde from the Pretenders. As she was fifteen years older than me I didn't think this was such a good thing.

John—'I've never done that before—ever.'

Sarah—'Done what?'

John—'Come as early as I did.'

Sarah—'I just seduced you so much that you couldn't help yourself. It's natural.' I said it half self-mockingly.

He smiled.

John—'Perhaps.'

We got out of the bath. I said I wanted to wash my hair. He said he would do it for me. I bent over the bath as he shampooed and rinsed and conditioned and rinsed my hair, massaging in between. I found it very sensual. Rather than sexual. By the time he had finished I felt as though he had taken back all the power he had just lost. I think so did he. He wrapped a towel around my head and then started to dry my body, then his. Led me back to the bed and started to kiss me. First on the lips. Then the neck. Then the breasts, then to the belly button. He hovered around there for a long time before making his way down.

Twenty minutes later I still hadn't come.

John—'What's wrong with you?'

Sarah—'Could it be, perhaps, something that you aren't doing to me that isn't turning me on?'

John looked completely bewildered at this. A premature ejaculation and a woman who wasn't turned on by his tongue in one hour? Surely not.

John—'Perhaps you're frigid.'

Sarah—'Perhaps you just don't turn me on.'

John—'Perhaps you're right.'

Shouldn't have said that. He obviously thought twice about it too, because he started to kiss my body and pushed himself inside me.

First thought: He's big. As in Can I get him inside me without crying 'ouch'? big. Deep breathing. I know how women feel when they are giving birth. But in reverse. Breathe deeply and relax those pelvic floor muscles. Just relax. Relax. Relax. The words repeated in my head over and over again. Relax. Relax. Relax.

Ummm. I'm starting to enjoy this.

John stopped kissing me and looked into my eyes.

John—'You're really enjoying this aren't you?'

Sarah—'Can't you tell?'

One hour later. Tired. Happy. I started to leave the bed to go to the toilet.

John—'Where are you going?'

Sarah—'I want to go to the toilet.'

John—'What for?'

Sarah—'A pee if you must know.'

John—'Stay.'

Sarah—'John, I want to go.'

John—'I have a thing about women who are desperate to go for a pee. I told you. Their orgasms are heightened. Much more powerful.'

Sarah—'Do they also pee over you as they come?'

John—'Doesn't matter. It's an incredible turn-on for both the woman and the man. She feels vulnerable, he knows it, she knows it, but it still happens.'

Sarah—'Well, not this woman. I want to go.'

I pushed myself away, slithering out of his reach down the bed and running for the toilet before he was able to grab me and I peed myself at the Plumtree in Peerton.

Dinner late. He wore a suit. I wore a cocktail dress. Chiffon. Chine. Belgian designer who specialises in floaty feminine stuff which is also sexy. Wonderful stuff. Lovely to put on, quick to take off. Men love it.

Avocado and parma ham were on the menu and for some inexplicable reason I didn't choose it.

Smoked salmon with capers. Simple and difficult to screw up.

Followed by Dover sole. Expensive for what it is, but good, and plain grilled is simple and doesn't repeat on me or hang in the stomach, which is a big turn-off for after-dinner sex.

Dessert? Don't have to choose yet.

John ordered soup. Something cream of. Then a steak. Simple. Medium to rare. That means some blood but not too much.

We ate in silence. Just looking at each other. I lost my shoes. I always lose my shoes when I eat. I fiddle with them. My toes are long. I can pick up a cup and saucer with them. Cup full. Only tried it once. Got a bit scalded, but not badly. Anyway, I can tick box for that challenge. Alas, with shoes, they tend to end up by my partner's feet or, worse, escape from underneath the tablecloth and end up for some inexplicable reason under someone else's table. I usually have to apologise, embarrassed, and retrieve them at the end of the evening.

I start a conversation as the main course is taken away.

Sarah—'When did you discover you liked women with full bladders?'

John—'When I was a boy.'

Sarah—'How old were you at the time?'

John—'About eight.'

Sarah—'Don't you think that is a little perverted?'

John—'No. Just forward thinking. Would still like you to experience the sensation.'

Sarah—'Sure you would.'

End of conversation. Then he speaks.

John—'So it's all over with Paul?'

Sarah—'Yes. Where is Amanda?'

John—'At home, I think. I don't know. She called me and asked what I was doing this weekend and I told her I was out with a friend.'

Sarah—'So you haven't told her yet?'

John—'No. She's not ready to hear it so I won't tell her.'

Sarah—'Does she still hate me?'

John—'Yes. But I've told her it won't do her any good or me. It's best she doesn't know for now.'

Sarah—'I agree.'

John—'And Paul. Does he know you have a new lover?'

Sarah—'Er. No.'

I keep forgetting what I have told John and what I haven't. Lies beget lies and I forget what I have told to whom and why and hope the people I have told some things to never meet up with those I have told other things to. Half of my friends don't even know I am going out with someone, let alone getting married in five months to someone. It helped with the guest list. Good way of culling. I feel more like Walter Mitty every day. Living a lie. To them and myself.

Sarah says—'Paul is oblivious and I think it best that way. He still loves me.'

Sarah thinks—And is getting married to me and would go nuts if he knew.

Coffee in the lounge. I manage to find my shoes after searching for five minutes. I apologise to the elderly couple on the next table. The old man smiles; the old woman doesn't.

John suggests an early night. I say it's midnight already so not that early. He says it is for him.

We go to Byron. We make love until five a.m. and sleep for three hours. I wake up at eight. He is still sleeping. I go to the toilet and cleanse, tone and moisturise, and puff myself up with aromatherapy oils so that when he wakes up I look OK to wake up to. I return to bed.

At eight-fifteen he wakes up. I am just dozing. He kisses me on the forehead.

John—'You are lovely to wake up to. So many women I wake up to and I think, Ugh, I slept with that last night. And, Why? And, How could I have? And, I wish I could get out of bed quick. They look like shit. You look wonderful in the morning, Sarah. Fresh and beautiful.'

Trick works, then.

8th April

Trip to Bath. Drive for an hour. Visit vegetarian restaurant. Play with food. Lose shoes. Cuddle and kiss in public. Feel furtive and look furtive. Notice other couples not talking to one another who must be married. John buys me a pair of leather trousers. I try on lots. He stands in the changing room watching me try on lots. We go into Agent Provocateur. He wants to see me try on lots but the girl behind the counter says he will have to wait until I get home. He says he is buying them for himself, not me. She smiles and says all the men say that. And it's not funny or clever any more. I get two pairs of almost-there knickers. One black. One blue.

We go back to hotel. Black and blue knickers get torn off. Waste of eighty pounds. John says it was worth it. I think so too.

Get dressed for dinner. John says he wants me for dinner. I show him dress. He takes it off me, saying it doesn't look good and I should wear another one. Then admits he just wants to undress me to have sex with me. I tell him I know, but it's OK. We have another bath. We stay there so long I get chapped fingertips. He finds this a turn-off and suggests we don't do it again. We splash like children and have a mini-waterfight with sponges. Laugh loudly and dry each other very slowly, making sure all the crevices are dry as well. Start kissing. Then into the bedroom, just reach the bed, and make love again for two hours. Realise it's nine p.m. Put dress on and ask John not to take it off me. He says he won't. Just kneels and puts his hand up my skirt and rips off my last pair of lacy knickers for the weekend. I ask him if he is going to replace them. He says that he likes the idea of me not wearing any knickers to dinner. And asks if that is OK with me. I say fine and that I have little choice unless I wear some of his briefs. He says that won't be a turn-on. And anyway it would give me a horrid panty line.

He makes me come.

Four times. On the bed. In the *en suite* by the bath. In front of the window. Facing out towards the coming traffic. No one crashes. And over the dressing table. Facing the mirror. From behind.

We are very late for dinner. He rings to apologise and says we have been held up. Thankfully, they don't ask what has held us up. They probably know. John leaves two of his ties attached to the posts of the four-poster, as though he had tied me up in some sex game. I say it's a pity he has to pretend to tie me up and that I like the idea of being tied up by him. He says he will when we get back from dinner.

Dinner at ten.

John—'Sorry we're late. Sarah got tied up.'

* * *

9th April

On way back home. By train. It's on time. I'm depressed. Last kiss was wonderful and unexpected and romantic, considering John is not romantic or unexpected or wonderful in a conventional sense.

John—'I'm not what people make me out to be, Sarah.'

Sarah—'You're not amoral, then?'

John—'No. I know what I'm doing. And I want to be with you. Not Amanda.'

Sarah—'I know. Just kiss me.'

He does as he's told and then sees me onto the train. He's recognised by some of the station staff and says hi. I sit on the train as though I never met the guy.

Coming home. Opening the door in Chelmsford, I feel such a fraud. Why am I here? What the fuck am I doing? Why am I playing this game? It's exciting. Christ. I'm getting married in five months. I've just had a wonderful weekend with a very sexy man who's given me little sleep, who I've kept up (literally and metaphorically speaking) all night. Who's fed, watered and made love to me, and who wants me sexually if not emotionally right now. And it was wonderful and exciting and unexpected. And yet I love Paul, whom I obviously don't respect. Whom I trust. But don't respect. So can this be love?

Message received:
You are wonderful, J xx

Message sent:
So r u S xx

I check my e-mails.

One from Amanda. My friend. Not John's ex. Confusing, this. Columnist for *Telegraph*. Fun, funky, London.

How you doing darling? How is the bride to be? Nervous? Happy? Are you sure about him? Bit square. Met him at a formal bash at the Bank of England. You have a bit too much fire for him. Perhaps that is what he likes.

I return:

Fine. Love him, but yes he is a bit solid. I need a rock. Butterflies need rocks. But feel a bit unsure at the moment. Last-minute nerves. Plus no sex which always helps, doesn't it?

She returns:

Don't tell me about sex. I haven't had it in weeks. Feeling very ratty. Hey ho. Shit happens. Night-night.

Paul home at eight p.m. Tanned. Tired. Smiling. With golf bag. Can I help him with them? Yes, I can. Hugs and looking into the eyes.

Paul—'Did you have a nice weekend, Sarah?'

Sarah—'Lovely, thanks.'

Paul—'Did you achieve much? What was the course like?'

Sarah—'Good. Interesting. Unexpected. And the golf?'

Paul—'Fabulous. We all played well. The sixteenth was a bit difficult, and most of us came unstuck on the third, which is always a bit of a bummer with the water being so close, and then on the fifth Richard decided…'

The conversation drifted away. I wasn't there any more. I wasn't with Paul. I was with John. Body may have been there. But mind was elsewhere.

10th April

I've arranged to have girlie meet with Catherine. Plus Karen, old flatmate. I miss her. I miss our girlie chats. Our fornication talks. Me talking about Pierce and the latest 'fuck-and-suck-me-hard' text message I'd received that week. He seemed to have so many sex kittens on the go, all of whom were called Sarah, it wasn't surprising he got confused sometimes. But every week? I kept a list of them in the end. Sort of something for my old age, to read when my eighteen-year-old son shouts at me and says I don't understand. And I can say I do. OK, they're not for me...allegedly...but they can make lots of girls happy, albeit not in the way Pierce intended.

> *Message received:*
> 1/3
> When I came round that time and saw you in those jeans and they were so tight and I couldn't keep my eyes off you. And I had to go to the...
> 2/3
> Loo to wank myself off because you make me feel so fucking horny. And I wanted to rip them off you and push you over the fridge and ruck you senseless.

I'm sure that was meant to be fuck, but perhaps ruck is a new derivation of it.

> 3/3
> And I could c yr nipples and they wre soo erect and I wanted to rp that top off u 2. God I've got to go now.

Karen—'I didn't think people still talked like that any more. Or wrote like that any more. Is he nuts or something?'

Sarah—'Just think he has issues. Paul tells me he's had relationships in the past and none have worked out, but he's a bit of an expert on relationships coz he's been to so many counsellors he knows all the spiel and why people behave the way they do and why he behaves the way he does. And he has about fifty books on how to improve and understand women. You know—*Girls from Venus, Men Mars, Women Who Love Too Much*. But Paul tells me he has those next to books on erotica and how to fuck a woman up the bum and get maximum impact. Plus he spends lots of time in Soho, checking out the bondage places. I think he's into dildos—not just giving but receiving. Strange thing is, he's very bright, talented, comes across as quite sensitive, albeit intense when you first meet him.'

Karen—'What do you mean?'

Sarah—'You know the sort. Stares at you in the eyes without blinking. Not so much imagining you naked but more a bent over a fridge, fucking you from behind stare.' (Methinks of John.)

Karen—'Er, right. And this is common knowledge? The fact he's a bit, well, extreme?'

Sarah—'Think so. But he's also good-looking, rich. Sort of an English Psycho. I've read *American Psycho* and I could imagine Pierce having the potential to do similar. He's not so interested in labels. More music equipment, and his CD collection is fabulous. But he also has an incredible DVD collection—everything from *Once Upon a Time in America* to *Bambi*. And he cries at *Bambi*. And the bit in *ET* when ET is dying. You know, he's a real sensitive guy.'

Karen—'Sounds completely fucked up to me.'

Sarah—'Well, a lot of people are fucked up these days. What's normal? What's abnormal? I don't know. I remember as a little girl knowing children who had divorced parents and feeling very sorry for them, but that was the odd person. Now there must be a decent percentage in every nursery and school. What the fuck's going on? I'm not traditional or conventional by any stretch of the imagination—' (perhaps at this point I should mention I'm sleeping with someone else…but I don't) '—people don't get married for life. You've got men marrying men, women marrying women. People not marrying at all. Children not knowing where the fuck they are. Emotionally, mentally or spiritually, not to mention physically sometimes. Divorce is being made easy, though I'm sure it's actually in many ways much harder emotionally. Infidelity is OK sometimes, in some circumstances, and sometimes not in others. Everything's OK and nothing's OK. You get judged if you're judgemental and judged if you're too liberal. Women are accused of loving too much. Men not loving enough. Selfishness is in turn good and bad.'

I listened to what I was saying. Why couldn't I take my own advice? What was I doing? I couldn't marry Paul. I was sleeping with someone else. How can you agree to marry someone and sleep with someone else during the engagement? OK, if you're going out with them and there's no commitment and there's no sex, then, hey, that's understandable. But Paul's proposed, so why have I started a relationship while I'm engaged to be married? What am I playing at? Is it the fun of it? The immorality? The fact that Paul doesn't know about it because he's so controlling and John's my secret and he can't change it or do anything about it and when Paul's shitty with me I can deal with it because I can think of John and it's all OK? And I know that someone will hold and kiss me and make love to me. And when John's cold and shitty I have Paul who I know is like a rock and will hold and kiss me, and will perhaps make love to me. One day in the future.

Perhaps I should read one of Pierce's books. They don't seem to have helped him much. He seems to hate women, despite the fact he wants to fuck them so much. He says it's due to his mother being such an emotional bully, and I identify with that, but I told him that not all women should be judged like his mother and not to treat them the same way. He said that he was treated as an inconvenience when he was little and he's sure his mother used to drug him to make him sleep longer. I identify with this. I felt my parents put me in a little box and brought me out only when it suited them and then, hey presto, back in the box again. I didn't need a counsellor or spiritual healer or tarot card reader or feng shui expert to tell me that. It's just a pity that I went from one emotional bully to another emotional bully and I've got stuck in the pattern. But perhaps I'm meant to break it. Perhaps I'll break it with Paul. Perhaps.

Don't need women's magazines when you have friends you can sit round and chat to. Be sort-of honest with. No, I didn't want to tell all about the Dark Prince. Well, I did, but I didn't think it appropriate. Catherine and Anya knew about it. But I wanted to keep it simple. Too many people knowing wasn't a good idea. Plus, they'd all start to give me their views. Their opinions on whether I should do it, why I was doing it, how I could have gone out with Paul for such a long time putting up with no sex, and him putting up with me. Loyalty or love?

Karen was a fervent believer in star signs. And feng shui. And tarot cards. And spiritual healing. She said that as I was a Gemini and he was a Taurus we were incompatible. That he was a home-lover and stubborn as a—well, bull, and I was an air sign and up with the butterflies and I couldn't be caught. Bit like trying to catch a flame. You can't. You just get your fingers burnt. She said our Chinese signs were also incompatible. I was a dragon, wood and fire. And he was a horse, fire and metal. Incompatible again. Well, almost. We got on okay. Better as friends than lovers or partners or spouses. She said that when we moved here it meant that I would have lots of children—become very fertile, but that was all it would be good for. I told her this was complete bullocks. She said I should hang crystals in windows and keep goldfish and buy lots of mobiles.

Karen—'Are you OK? You seem somewhere else, Sarah?'

Sarah—'I'm fine. Lots on my mind at the moment. Plans and all that.'

Karen—pause, staring at me, looking through me—'You sure you're doing the right thing?'

Sarah—longer pause, staring down—'Yes, Karen. Think so. Sure as can ever be.'

Karen—'Mmm. Still think he's not the one for you. He's a bit too conventional. You're not conventional, Sarah. Not saying you're a boho chick or a complete free spirit and up with the fairies, but he's quite, well, square, and he might make you go more one way and you'll make him get more set in his ways. That's all I'm saying. I saw it with my parents. You know mine are divorced? I was three when they divorced, and they said it was a good age for me and that I would get over it. They said it would be better that they'd divorced at that age than when I was older. I say they shouldn't have got married in the first place or should have stuck it out and worked at it. It did affect me. Don't care what the counsellors and books say.

'I went all through this, Sarah. It's bloody horrible and scary and weird and I didn't really understand what was happening. Everyone was listening to me. You know, that active listening to everything you say bit, and it's disconcerting when no one's ever done that before. You sort of get used to it in the end, and start to speak as though you're full of the Holy Spirit and know everything there is to know about relationships and try to act how you're supposed to react in situations like this. I got the full works when I was eight and started to rebel, and they thought it was because of this, but it wasn't. It was just my age.'

Karen pauses, then looks at me again.

Karen—'What I'm saying is that if you're not sure, Sarah, don't do it. Coz if you have a child you don't want to put that child through it, do you? It's not fair. It's not fair on the child, nor on Paul—though I don't like the git—and nor on you. Think about it.'

Someone knocked on the door. Catherine with bottle of Sauvignon from Tesco. New Zealand.

Catherine—'Hi there, sweetie. How you?'

Sarah—'Me fine. Karen's just telling me I shouldn't get married.'

Catherine—'Oh.' Pause. 'Paul's lovely, Sarah. You know that. You love him.'

Sarah—'I know I do. I know I do. But you know the situation.'

Catherine—'I know. But I still think it's the last fling, excitement, illicit thing. It's not real. It's not the real thing. You have the real thing with Paul.'

Sarah—'Perhaps I don't want it, Catherine. Perhaps I'm not ready to have it. And Karen made a point about children.'

Catherine—'You don't want children, do you?' (Catherine didn't want children. She wasn't child-catcher-I-hate-children material, but she didn't like the idea of having to look after more children as well as her husband. Strong believer that all men are babies or at least toddlers and that looking after them was enough.)

Sarah—'I don't mind. I know Paul would love children, and I think I will one day, and I think he would make a great dad and I would make an unconventional mum, but a good one, and hopefully my kids will think I'm fun and I'll be there for them. May forget to feed them, but never forget to tell them they're fabulous and love them to bits.'

Maternal instinct surprised me as much as it did Catherine. But we went in as we'd been gabbing on the doorstep and Karen was wondering where we were.

DVD. *Moulin Rouge.* Nicole Kidman dying of consumption. Torn between duty and genuine passion and love. Horny music. Made me think of both Paul and John in turn. Paul was a wonderful dancer. John was better horizontal. We sat and drank and got slowly merry. Text from Paul:

Message received:
What you doing sweetheart?

Message sent:
With girls, getting pissed and watching film.

Message received:
What one?

Message sent:
Moulin Rouge. Nicole is just about to die.

Message received:
Don't cry. I love you. Just remember that. Love is all that matters.

Eyes glazed over at the right time. Nicole was just dying. The other girls thought they understood.

Message received:
How is my wonderful lover?

Message sent:
Fine. How is my wonderful lover?

Message received:
1/2
Missing you. Your touch. Your smell. Your taste. I get so low when you're not here. I just mope and then kick myself out of it and think how bloody soppy I am. I've never been like this.
2/2
With any other woman.

Message sent:
Don't believe you.

Message received:
It's true Sarah. This is different. This is different. Xxxxxxxxxxx

Message sent:
Xxxxxxxx U2

This is different, all right? Women dream about changing men from womanisers into lap dogs and supposedly it seemed I'd done it when I'd had no intention nor wanting to do it. It was extremely inconvenient. As the credits rolled we had a pissy conversation about love. With a capital L.

Karen—'Do you think the only important thing is to learn how to love and be loved in return?'

Sarah—'Yes. I think it's one of those phrases that gets misquoted a lot. You know, like Chaucer's "the love of money is the root of all evil". Lot of people say "money is the root of all evil". Then they go on to say but who creates money? Therefore Man is the root of all evil. But that wasn't the original quote. It's desiring it that's wrong, not having it.'

Karen—'So learning to love. What is love?'

Sarah—'Million-dollar question, that. I think most people say it's when you feel more pain being apart from them than you do being with them, and that you can't bear to live without them.'

Catherine—'Yeah, I would say that's true. But what's the difference with lust and love?'

Sarah—'Don't know. I loved Paul when I first met him. Knew instinctively he was the one for me. Just wanted to be with him. Around him. Wanted only him. Was totally and completely in love with him. Just wanted to be there for him. Be what he wanted me to be. But perhaps that was just lust. Because lust is fleeting. Love's eternal, or should be. Dunno. I think both of them are like diseases. Like viruses. Uncontrollable. Inconvenient.' (I was thinking of John.) 'Happen when you don't want them to or least expect them to.' (Definitely thinking of John.)

Karen—'Think it's different for men. When I'm in love or lust I can't focus on anything other than wanting to be with them. Near them. Thinking of them.'

Catherine—'Most of the men I know say when they're in love or lust they do better at work, have better focus and achieve more. It's like their love is more selfish. Perhaps it's true that men love in a different way to women. Hey, I don't know. Don't know on that one.'

Sarah—'There are sooo many books and sonnets and films on love. I'm deep-down romantic. English teacher said I was romantic coz I used to turn up in flowing flirty dresses in the sixth form and think I was a bit sort of boho chick even then. Flowers in the hair. Loved Keats. Learnt most of the *Odes* by heart. Bloody difficult. Got them all mixed up. Use to start off with *Ode to a Nightingale*, move onto *Autumn* somewhere and end up with the *Grecian Urn*. He was a miserable bugger, though. He wrote reams on the bloody stuff. Most of it bloody depressing.

'There's this poem about this lover who cuts his girl-friend's head off—after she's dead, of course. Can't remember what she dies of, but think it's to do with another guy or unrequited love or something. Anyway—' (slurping more Sauvignon) '—for some reason he puts it in a pot and the pot sprouts a tree. And the tree grows big and strong. Think it was a basil pot or something. Now I can never buy basil without thinking about this bloody woman's head. And as Paul sometimes forsakes parma ham and melon and goes for mozzarella and tomato salad with fresh basil I often have this subconscious urge to throw up. And then the other guy finds out that the tree sprouted from this girl's head—and cuts the tree down. And I always visualise the tree sprouting from her head and wonder if it sprouted from her neck or her hair—and think of that film *The Thing*, where there was that alien that takes over and kills people in this camp one by one and the hand—or was it a head that had legs? and I think it destroyed the whole beauty of the poem for me at the time.'

Catherine—'Think I remember that poem. Was it *Lamia?*'

Sarah—'No, that was about the girl that was a snake, or something, and turned into a girl. Or was it the other way round? But that was a long one too. Wasn't it?'

Catherine—'No, no. It was called—think it was called two things, *The Pot of Basil.* And *Isabella.* That was it. *Isabella.* Remember there was this line in it which read…oh, bugger. Forgotten. May have the book somewhere.'

Sarah—'I don't think I've got it. I loved Keats. I remember there's this line which when I'm feeling really shitty just about sums up how I feel. "My heart aches, and a drowsy numbness pains My sense as though of hemlock I had drunk". Real sort of slit-wrist time, that. And there's this other line. What is it now? Oh, yeah. "Darkling I listen; and for many a time I have been half in love with easeful Death". Forgotten the rest. But anyway, it's very good to say out loud when you really want to have a good wail and total emotional meltdown. Keats knew how to be miserable.'

Catherine—'Don't you think most poets and creative types are miserable? I remember my English teacher telling me T S Eliot produced his best work when he was having a horrible time in his personal life. And then he married his secretary or something, and got all happy, and couldn't write a bloody word after that.'

Sarah—'Perhaps that's the secret of it, then. I can marry Paul, be miserable, get creative and make money writing. Knew there was a reason. Must find that book of poems, or at least buy one.'

Karen—'Can we talk about something else? Didn't study Keats. He sounds fucking boring and a complete manic depressive. Just watched a film about a beautiful girl dying of consumption and the guy being heartbroken and I want to have a giggle and I'm feeling like shit.'

Sarah—'Group hug. Group hug.'

We all hugged each other and looked through the DVDs to see if there was anything superficial and fluffy. *Sleepy Hollow.* Too depressing apart from Johnny Depp looking achingly fuckable. *ET.* No. *Jean de Florette.* You must be joking. *Big.* Reminds me of Paul. *Four Weddings and a Funeral.* No. Obvious reasons. He soooo marries the wrong woman. *What Lies Beneath.* Too close to home. *Casablanca.* Too romantic. Decided on *Ferris Bueller's Day Off.* Decide that girls should live life to the full as well as boys.

Then sex conversation. Topic: masturbation. I start it. All extremely drunk (three bottles of Sauvignon. No food).

Sarah—'Have you ever been out with a guy who gets really turned on by watching you masturbate?'

Catherine—'They all do, don't they?'

Sarah—'Do they?'

Catherine—'Well, think about it. They get turned on by

watching you come. They don't have to do anything to make it happen but can actually see everything. Then they can please themselves.'

Sarah—'Oh. Remember I did that once with Paul but didn't let him do anything afterwards. I didn't really look to see if he was enjoying it much. I was enjoying myself so much. Then when I'd finished he went to approach me and I said no. And he seemed really pissed off. Almost in pain.'

Karen—'Probably was.'

Sarah—'Really?'

Karen—'Oh, yeah. I dunno if it's true, but you know they have to relieve themselves after a certain time if they've gone, you know, toooooo far. They just have to come.'

Sarah—'Oh, well, he did. But not in me, over me or looking at me. He just went to another room and had a strop on for the whole day.'

Catherine—'So next time you did it you let him?'

Sarah—'Fuck that. No. Don't like men who sulk. Act like children. Treat them like children. Told him to say please. Not much to ask.'

Catherine—'Did he?'

Sarah—'Yes. With cherries on top. And lots of whipped cream.'

Eleven p.m. Catherine gone home. Karen gone to her room. Sarah goes home.

Message received:
Love you. Xxxx P

Message received:
Want you. Xxx J

15th April

I'm in bed and I don't want to get up. My head is yo-yoing backwards and forwards. Do I tell Paul? Do I tell John? Do I tell Paul? Do I tell John? I work out case scenarios of how they will react or how I think they will react. Most end up in lots of tears and blood. All mine. So block out honesty. Not best policy here. Policy here is to stay alive and have fun and not hurt anyone.

Message received:
Can I call you? J

I'm still in bed with Paul.
Paul—'Who's that at this time in the morning?'
Sarah—'No one, just work.'
Paul—'It's early.'
My mobile rings. It's John. Got to answer it. Looks strange if I don't.
Sarah—'Hi.'
John—'Hello there, sexy. How are you?'
Sarah—'I'm fine. How are you?'
John—'Fine. Very formal, this. What, no kisses and underwear talk? What are you wearing? Are you wearing anything?'
Sarah—'Yes.' (Pause coz I think I'm blushing and Paul is looking at me, which is making me blush more.) 'Can I call you back later on that one.'
John—'On what one? On you wearing underwear?'
Sarah—'Yes. I need to do something about that.'
John—'Are you OK? Got your brain in gear?'
Sarah—'Yes, had heavy night last night. Can't really talk now. Have to go. Byee.'
John—'Er, are you sure you're OK?'

Sarah—'Yes, I'll speak to you tomorrow, OK?'

John—'You don't sound OK.'

Sarah—'I'm fine. Bye for now.'

Click. Turn mobile off so he can't ring again. Paul looks puzzled.

Paul—'Very strange phone call. Why do they need to call you at seven-thirty in the morning on a Saturday, Sarah?'

Sarah—'Oh, you know what it's like. These PRs think they own you. Work, work, work all the time. Not good.'

Paul—'No, and I want them to leave my fiancée alone.'

He gives me a cuddle which he hasn't done for months and I involuntarily flinch. He notices.

Paul—'Don't you love me any more?'

Sarah—'Of course I do. Just that we haven't touched for such a long time. It's lovely to be cuddled by you again.' (Strange but true.) 'I've missed it.' (True.)

He cuddles me again and I snuggle up into his arms and remember how it used to be in the beginning. How I felt protected and loved by him and how now when he does it I just feel trapped and suffocated and it's not the same person he's cuddling. So it doesn't feel the same. And she misses the old Paul. Not this one. And she's not the same Sarah any more. She's ever so slightly resentful and is getting her own back, though he doesn't know it and hopefully never will. But for now I allow myself to be snuggled and stifled and I've got the excuse that I've got to go to the gym in an hour, despite the fact I desperately need to put on weight rather than lose it at the moment.

At the club, my instructor, Jeff, says, 'You look ill. You OK?'

'Yes, I'm fine.'

'Well, you've lost weight and it's not through training. That would make you put it on, if anything. But you're losing. What's happening?'

'Getting married.'

'Congratulations.'

'Thank you.'

'You don't look glowing.'

'Don't feel glowing.'

'Then you're not marrying the right man.'

'I think I am. Just a bit under the weather.'

We do five minutes warm-up to 'You Are My Fantasy', then kick and twist and do some step—up and down, up and down, up and down to Liberty X and Misteeq and lots of J Lo and some old Spice Girls and some Geri and some Posh. And my mind is not on the jump kicks, or the splits or the pushing the legs to the limit—it's on John. And on Paul and on how to leave both with good grace.

At the end of the class, I turn on my mobile.

Message received:
You OK? You sounded strange. Call me.

Message received:
Call me. Can't get through to you.

Message received:
Have I done something wrong?

Message received:
I'm gonna call your home. Think I've got that number.

Which home? Call home when Paul is there? Please God he hasn't answered the phone. He can't have the house number. Perhaps he means the flat number.

Race back in the car.

Open door.

Sarah—'Hi—Paul?'

No answer. Answer-machine beeping. Two calls while out.

First: 'Hi, Sarah. Just popped out. Be back in half an hour. Hope the workout was good. Big kiss.'

Second: 'Hi, Sarah. You OK? Can't seem to get hold of you. Will try later.'

Must call John back. Run up to study.

Sarah—'Hi, John.'

John—'Hi, Sarah. What happened? Why couldn't you speak this morning?'

Sarah—'It was a bit inconvenient.'

John—'Why? Were you in bed with someone or something?' (Getting a bit annoyed.)

Sarah—'No, of course not. But Paul had come round. He's getting married.'

John—'Didn't know that.'

Sarah—'No, neither did I, actually.'

John—'Do you know the girl?'

Sarah—'Er, no. But I'm told she's very nice. A bit scatty. Erm. Short. Very short. Big boobs and big bum and, er, reddish brown hair. Name Tina, I think.'

John—'Oh, right. Well, what did he want?'

Sarah—'Just to tell me he was getting married. He didn't want me to find out another way. Wanted to tell me directly and all that.'

John—'But doesn't want you to come to the wedding?'

Sarah—'Well, ex-girlfriend and all that.'

John—'I've been to a lot of my exes' weddings. Don't think the grooms either knew who I was or liked the fact I was there, but I still went anyway. Interesting to see how exes choose their husbands. Sometimes it's surprising; sometimes I can guess exactly who they would choose.'

Sarah—'And who would I choose, then, oh wise one?'

John—'You? You wouldn't marry anyone. You're not the marrying type. You're too independent. No ties. No commitments. Don't think anyone could tie you down, Sarah.

And you don't need a man either. You don't need one. You'd like one and want one, but I think you like your own space. Positively enjoy it. There are women out there who don't. They have to be with someone. They need someone. They need a man in their life. I think you enjoy male company but that's different. Don't know why. Perhaps that's why I find you so interesting.'

Sarah—'Perhaps I do need a man. But I don't like to show you my vulnerable side. Perhaps I do need that emotional crutch. That love. Need to give and receive love, and perhaps this coolness is all just a ruse.'

John—'Perhaps. Could be. Could be wrong. But don't think so. You seem too independent. You're an only child, like me. And you've got used to your own company. People who've influenced you. Think you said there was David, your first, right?'

Sarah—'Yes.'

John—'Well, he sounds like a right pretentious prat. But then he worked in a bank. Not all bankers are prats. Just sounds as though he was.'

Sarah—'He wasn't. He was lovely. Bit confused, but lovely.'

John—'And then there was Paul. Right? He's another banker and he sounds very confused. Wouldn't sleep with you or something. Honestly, how can a man sleep with you and not sleep with you? He should have got help. Think he probably needs help. He'll probably do the same to the next girl he meets and the next. He sounds like a control freak, but, hey, lot of them about.'

Sarah—'So you think you're Mr Right.'

John—'Could be. But you know two Mr Wrongs don't make a Mr Right.'

Sarah—'Very droll.'

Methinks relationship with John is getting more exciting. Taking more risks. John has told me he is falling in love with me. I do not believe him. I tell him I am falling in love with him too. But do I? How can I fall for someone I'm treating this way? He doesn't know I'm getting married. Or even still have another boyfriend. So how can I love someone I blatantly don't respect? I love Paul. But I don't act as though I love him either. I'm fucking someone else, for fuck's sake. But men do it. I know they do. My male friends tell me they do. At the stag do, they usually bonk the stripper, don't they? One of Paul's friends had one come into his room after the evening was supposedly over and give him a blow job. Pressie from his mates. Everyone sworn not to tell the wife. Someone did. Tears on wedding night. From groom, after bride went down on him to prove her bite was worse than her bark. Didn't need stitches.

Do any of Paul's friends live in Surrey? Get real, Sarah, what's the chance of being spotted by one of Paul's friends in Tesco with John buying bananas and whipped cream? How do I explain?

Sarah—(walking down dairy aisle with John, in search of low-fat cream I can spread and lick off him, John tells me cottage cheese won't work the same way. Hand in hand. Pre- and post-coital) spots Peter—Hi, Peter, hi, Kelly. Just happen to be in Surrey and thought I'd do some shopping. With friend John. (Introduce John. John will look as though he has just gone down on me or just about to and game will be up.)

Peter—Hi. (Looks confused.) Spoke to Paul this morning. He said you were on a course in Lincoln.

Sarah—(flushing violently)—yes, but I came back early and popped in to see some friends. (Turning to John.) This is John. He came on the course as well.

Peter—still looking confused. Kelly looking…knowing. John looking very confused and angry.

John—Paul?

Don't go there, Sarah. Scenario won't work. No, can't let

it happen. Plus won't go shopping with John in Tesco. Bad move. Plus too domesticated. This is the last fling, surely? So it's all about being in bed as much as possible. Or wherever will support two naked/near naked/soon to be naked bodies.

I've discovered I have a thing for al fresco. Preferably olive grove somewhere remote in Tuscany. Doubt if there is anywhere remote left in Tuscany, but in my dreams there is. I'm outside with John. Walking through the olive grove just before lunch. Very hot. Midday. He turns me to him. I'm wearing white Ghost top, with laces down the front. The air is heavy with the smell of olives. He has to very slowly undo the laces in order to get to me. I don't allow him to take the top off immediately. Too soon. Too easy. Then the skirt. Silk. Flowers. Floaty. Easier. Just unties and falls down around my feet. Then he kisses me on the lips. For ages. He's still fully clothed in white shirt. Crisp, half open. And I'm near naked and can feel the heat on my back and bum and hair. He hasn't touched me other than kissing me on my lips and cupping my head in his hands. And I'm becoming frustrated and start to pull away and want him to do more. And then he moves his hands down from my belly button to my thighs. Very slowly. Almost painfully slowly so I move my body as though I want him to feel my urgency and my... Then he kneels and kisses me on my...

Message received:
1/2
I'm on the underground and I can taste you. Am licking my lips and the guy next to me says he knows what I'm...
2/2
...thinking of. And then he spoils it by saying supper. I can still taste you. J xx

Message sent:
What do I taste like?

Message received:
Parma Ham. Have you got it for next week's dinner party? P.

Message sent:
Yes I'll get it this evening at Tesco.

Message received:
1/2
Of you. The smell and taste of you drives me wild. You've a unique taste. I could say like sunshine or...

Message received:
Cod. We need cod for the fish pie. Trying something different from Delia's book. I don't like the taste of fish but everyone we're inviting seems happy with it. Do you like cod?

Message received:
2/2
...bluebells. Most girls taste salty. Fishy. Those that don't wash. Like prawns or cod gone off. Like some sort of botched fish pie.

Message sent:
I'm happy with fish. Something plain grilled. I can get something fresh from Tesco.

Message received:
You taste fresh and clean. Not fishy at all. And your taste gets stronger as you're due to come. If you like

the taste is more of a good thing. If you don't best to steer clear.

21st April

I haven't kept up with my diary for fear Paul will read and find it, and also I can't express what I'm feeling. It's lust. It can't be love. John is potent. Sexed. Not over-sexed. Just sexed. The only word for it. I'm walking on air. Nothing matters other than being with him. Work, friends, family, health, nothing. I can't concentrate on even the dinner parties I'm supposed to be preparing. I want the avocados to stuff themselves. I go to aerobics classes and practise pelvic thrusts thinking about him. My instructor (Jeff) seems to know what I'm thinking.

'You're getting good at those. Had a lot of practice recently, have you, Sarah?'

I'm more flexible and toned. Sex is soo good for the bum.

When Paul is away I drive my new yellow Lotus from Chelmsford to Redhill and park it in the car park by John's road. It takes me forty minutes. I get excited from the moment I get in the car to the moment I arrive at his door. It's the anticipation of knowing at the end of the journey there is going to be him waiting for me in his yellow cottage. We manage to make love in every room of his house. I complain I wish it were bigger. He says so does he. We make love on Box Hill in his car (with difficulty). Choose hotels from brochures, all of which are designed for lovers, not businessmen or newly weds. He takes me to see where he was born. Where he grew up. I say I don't want to meet his parents. This is too eerie. Too eerie for words.

SARAH, YOU ARE GETTING MARRIED IN FOUR MONTHS.

I don't hear this.

Catherine realises I'm getting in deep and says I should cool it.

'Tell him you're getting married. Just say you want to cool it as it's getting too intense,' she says.

I say I will. I drive in the yellow Lotus to his yellow cottage and start to tell him and then he touches me and kisses me and undresses me and seduces me into silence. Well, almost. He tells me all women are different when they come. He says some are moaners from the word go. You don't have to touch them. Just the thought of you being near them makes them start to moan. He tells me again that he went out with one woman who all he had to do was brush past her nipple and she would come. He says he has to work more on me. I tell him I'm pleased. Very antisocial behaviour. Good party trick, though. He tells me that I'm quite quiet. That I just breathe deeply but that he can tell when I'm about to come. I'm a sort of air raid siren. I say this is very unsexy. He says a siren is sexy. Air raid perhaps not so. But that it's very reassuring for a man, any man, to feel he has satisfied a woman so much. Some men are more interested in their own pleasure, but John tells me they are missing a trick. They will get as much from giving pleasure as receiving it. I say this is what God tells us in the Bible. He says he doesn't think God was thinking about sex at the time. I tell John he doesn't know this for sure. He says he doesn't but would average a guess that He wasn't.

22nd April

In bed with Paul.

> *Message received:*
> Couldn't sleep. Thinking about you. Coming over your face. J xx

Paul—'Who's that?'
Sarah—'No one.'

Message sent:
Was I smiling? S xx

Message received:
Of course.

Wedding. Paul and I have been invited to the wedding of one of his broker friends. Paul tells me he is a friend who happens to be his broker. I tell him I think he's a wanker, but if he is good for business that is fine. He is marrying Eleanor and his name is Nicholas Gravestone. Handsome rogue-type marries Sloane. I don't know if she's a bitch because I haven't met her enough. Think once. I know more about him. He went to public school. A lesser one. His father sailed him round the Caribbean Islands for his eighteenth birthday present. He always talks about it.

I've known him since going out with Paul. He's had fifteen girlfriends during the five years. This excludes the one-night fucks. One dinner party, he got his dick out and nodded at it arrogantly, exclaiming, 'Do you know how many cunts this has been inside?' Some of the men guessed, others applauded. I made tea. Plus, he's only got one ball as he tried to kiss Kevin Spacey and a bouncer kneed him so hard he had to be taken to hospital. They settled out of court.

She is a headhunter and settled for his one ball. Size six, five foot nothing, and allegedly wants to become triple-barrelled with her Bavely-Hunterdon surname. But doesn't like the idea of her initials (GBH).

Wedding in Surrey. Near where John lives. Have bought new Chine, Ghost, sexy knickers. Not that Paul cares. But he notices. And kisses me as we're changing and says how much he loves me and how beautiful I look. And I don't care. But I smile and say thank you. I'm looking and feeling good for John. Not Paul. We drive in yellow Lotus. Top off. It's a sunny day. Warm for spring. Hair is fucked.

Sarah—'My hair is getting fucked.'

Paul—'Brush it when you get there. It's lovely today.'

On arrival, hair is so matted I just shove it under hat. Drive the car the same path that I take to John's house. I try very hard to not look as though I know every turn of the road and where to buy papers and cards and confetti. I suggest the High Street would be good as they usually have a shop that sells such things and, hey presto, they do.

Wedding is in twee church. Eighteenth century. Neither bride nor groom are churchgoers. Over half work in the City. Over half cars outside church are Porsches, Beemers, Bentleys, four red Ferraris and even a silver Aston Martin—which all the men ogle. Girlies all wearing very short skirts. Cream. With long navy jackets. Next to nothing blouses. Big black hats. Tall if they're short, wide if they're emaciated. Thin if they have a metabolic disorder. Groom's parents look disappointed.

Groom's father—'I preferred Jessica. She was nice. She went off to Australia.'

Kept thinking of John's cat Jessica.

Groom's mother—'I know. But this one is fine. Bit quiet. But she's fine. Has he got her pregnant, do you think?'

Groom's father—'He wouldn't tell us, darling. Last to know. You know that. Plus, with only one ball, do you think we'll get a grandchild?'

I'm not meant to hear the conversation. But as no one is approaching me (not wearing obligatory cream and navy garb), I'm being a wallflower, taking in the conversations and realising how much I don't fit in and don't want to. I text John.

Message sent:
How are you? At wedding. Boring. Full of stiffs.

No answer.

Bride's father, shape of a pot-bellied-pig, I overhear saying, 'I haven't been in a fucking church since I was christened.'

Congregation of over two hundred. Church full. No one sings. Choir get extra time. Bride enters to Vivaldi's *Gloria*. Broker friend of GBH reads *The Song of Solomon* with as much gravitas as he can muster post-two Bloody Marys. *Ave Maria* sung beautifully. 'Toccata', *Symphony No 5*, by Widor stirs everything it should, and somehow the service comes and goes without it looking too superficially meant to impress.

Reception held in old manor house owned by Earl or Duke of something. No one could tell me. Everyone says how pretty and thin the bride looks. Groom has two best men. They don't say what went on at the stag party. Paul and I sit on a table of Nicholas's friends. They all work in the City. They all ignore their partners and wives. They all talk about car size and who the fuck owns the Aston Martin. And who's got cigars and does anyone want a spliff? No, wait till later. And wager on how long the marriage will last. If at all. And who will dump who. And the fact Nick hasn't invited any ex-girlfriends and that's a pity coz some of them were rather a laugh and good shags. And I don't want to be there. Guy on right introduces himself.

Guy—'Hi, I'm Guy.'

Sarah—'Hi, I'm Sarah.'

Guy—'Who do you know? Bride or groom?'

Sarah—'Groom via a friend.'

I'm doing it again. Why the fuck didn't I just say, I'm here because my fiancé knows the groom?

Guy—'Oh. I don't know either of them very well. Her

not at all, him coz of work, but couldn't really call him a friend. More a sort of acquaintance. Business.'

Sarah—'Oh. I think I'm the only non-banker here. Everyone seems to work in the financial markets.'

Guy—'I don't. Work in TV.'

Sarah—'That's interesting. Some people have an idea about people who work in TV. I think the word is "flaky".'

Guy—'Yeah, a lot of them are. I do the creative stuff. Very frustrating. Have all these wonderful ideas which are fun and funky and educational and interesting and people will actually learn from and, for fuck's sake, the station will make money from—which is what it's all about. And all they want is game shows and snide TV which makes the general public look like fucking idiots. It's cheap in every way, but that's what they want. They say with TV, the presenters have either got to be funny or fuckable. Now all they want is presenters who are happy to be laughed at, and/or fucked on screen—preferably live. It's sick.'

Sarah—'Why are you still in it?'

Guy—'Pays the mortgage. And there is a creative side. Occasionally you get the odd gem through. It's always someone else's idea. But, hey, shit happens. There are more important things in life. What do you do?'

Sarah—'Well, I used to work in a bank. Then PR and marketing. Now I work in advertising. On the marketing side.'

Guy—'Is it interesting?'

Sarah—'Yes, but I would like to write a book one day. Think I've got some living to do.'

Guy—'Why don't you start now?'

Sarah—'I think I am.'

Guy looked at me again as though he was looking right through me.

Guy—'Mmm. Change subject. I've got two kids. Do you plan to have kids yourself?'

Don't plan to get married, let alone have kids.

Sarah—'Haven't thought of that. Not really. Not ready yet.'

Guy—'Married?'

Sarah—'Actually getting married.'

Guy—'Congratulations. When are you getting married?'

Sarah—'September.'

Guy—'Everything planned?'

Sarah—'Well, yes. Fiancé's doing a lot of it.'

Guy—'That's unusual. Know my wife wanted to do the lot. I didn't mind. Less work for me. I chose the honeymoon.'

Sarah—'Fiancé asks my opinion on stuff, but basically he's choosing what happens. It's mushroomed a bit. We've got a third my friends, a third his and a third family. We're sharing the cost.'

Guy—'Sounds fucking confusing to me.'

Sarah—'It is.'

Guy—'Obviously not if you've got a Catholic priest with a mass. I was Catholic, but don't believe now. Got married in Leeds Castle. Fabulous. Friends, no family. My family's a bit dysfunctional. Divorced parents. Father buggered off when I was three. Left my mum for a younger model. Ten years younger. Albeit a woman with the same name as my mum. So that confused me a bit. The new woman came from a divorced family too. She reassured my dad that she was OK, and that I would be OK too if my mum and her could handle it maturely. Now I think back and realise what an arrogant self-serving shit he was and how badly he treated my mum and how it knocked me for six. It took me a long time for Fiona, my wife—' (he nods to the girl sitting at the other end of the table and smiles at the brown-eyed beauty) '—to make me think marriage was OK. God, I want it to work. I don't want to do that to my kids. They always say kids are tougher than you think, so it's best to part, but I think that's a cop-out. Don't get married in the first place, or have kids, if you can't make the commitment. That's what I say.'

I liked Guy. He wasn't the usual full-of-shit banker Paul usually introduced me to. The fact that Paul didn't know Guy was probably why.

Sarah—'Did Fiona invite her family to the wedding?'

Guy—'She has divorced parents too. Actually, not strictly true. Her parents are still married, but four months before our wedding date her father went off with her mum's best friend. They didn't want us to put off the wedding. Thought they'd be mature about it. So there we were, all dancing at the reception. They had all been going to salsa classes together. Remember them strutting their stuff round the dance floor. And Fiona's mum looking on and trying not to cry and trying to look as though she didn't care. And her father telling me it was great that Katie—that's the wife's mum— was being so mature about it. And me thinking, What's fucking mature about that. This is sick. If I'd been Fiona's mum I would have kicked both their arses into touch.'

Sarah—'So, what about the wedding?'

Guy—'Well, Fiona's dad didn't want to take her down the aisle as there's a bit of a history between the two of them, so I took her down the aisle. And though she was brought up a Catholic too, she doesn't believe in it. But we did have a Catholic priest—albeit one we'd both known since we were kids. And he performed a really short twenty-minute service. And no one had to sing hymns, and the choir was fabulous and our ten-year-old nephew read the reading, and it was lovely. And there were friends there and they had a great time. And I come to weddings like this and I think this is bollocks. Coz it's false and I can tell you for a start over half this lot are clients of hers and the other half are clients of his.

And they've become "friends". I know Nick coz he does business with me. And he wants to do more business with me. But I've never been in a room with so many bullshitters in my life. And I work in TV, so that's saying something.'

Sarah—'Where are you from?'

Guy—'Southend.'

Sarah—'Essex man.'

Guy—'Yep. And you?'

Sarah—'Chelmsford. But really Gants Hill.'

Guy—'Essex, yourself. Actually, no. You're Greater London now, aren't you, really?'

Sarah—'Supposedly. Anyway I live in Chelmsford.'

Guy—'With your man?'

Sarah—'Yes.'

Guy—'Happy about getting married?'

Could he read my mind?

Sarah—'Don't know.'

Guy—'Perhaps you shouldn't do it, then.'

Sarah—'Bit late now.'

Guy—'Not too late.'

Sarah—'When is too late?'

Guy—'After you say I do. After you give birth to a child. That's when it's too late. When you fuck up not only your life but others. What does your husband-to-be do?'

Sarah—'Works in the City. Fixed Interest.'

Guy—'Trader. Mmm. Well, some of them are OK.'

He doesn't look as though he is convincing himself.

Guy—'Do you want children?'

I tell the truth.

Sarah—'No.'

Guy—'Told your man yet?'

Sarah—'Yes.'

Guy—'Did he listen?'

I looked at Guy. He looked a bit like John. Dark curly hair.

Clear complexion. Bright brown eyes. Not as close together as John's. Smiling eyes. Steady gaze. Soft voice. He reminded me of John in his questioning. Incisive. As though he could read my mind. See my discontentment. Made me wonder. Can anyone else see it? Can Paul see it? Is he ignoring it? Does he think it's just last-minute nerves? Or is he so arrogant he doesn't think anything could be wrong? Or doesn't he want to see it? Being honest I said, 'No. Probably not.'

Guy—'So he thinks he can change you, then?'

Sarah—'Probably.'

Guy—'Can he?'

Sarah—'No.'

Guy—'Then don't marry him.'

Sometimes I feel as though I have a guardian angel who tries to show me the way. Sometimes she does it subtly. Sometime she bashes me hard on the head. This was a definite head butt.

Sarah—'Sometimes it is too late.'

Guy—'It's not. Do you love him?'

Sarah—'You're getting very personal.' (Getting very defensive.)

Guy—'Well, you haven't got personal with your fiancé if you haven't talked about this. He wants kids. You don't. You don't talk about him in glowing terms. In fact you don't talk about him at all.' (In quieter voice.) 'Is he the guy to your left?'

Sarah—'No, he's sitting three seats away.'

Guy takes a sip of champagne, looking over the glass at Paul, who is now peering aggressively and intently at him because he's been talking to me for more than the recommended half-hour. Paul doesn't like me talking to any man for more than half an hour as he thinks it is rude of me not to talk to other people. I'm excluding them.

Guy—'Looks like a banker. Nice eyes. Catholic, you say?'

Sarah—'How does a banker look?'

Guy—'Smug. Tired. From time to time up their own arse. I know because people in the media are the same. Except they are usually up someone else's arse as well as their own.'

Sarah—'Yes.'

Guy—'Catholic, but not practising. Why not?'

Didn't want to tell man-I-had-just-met-and-got-more-in-common-with-than-my-intended about the abortion.

Sarah—'Things happened which made him realise that there was hypocrisy in the religion.'

Guy—'Yeah, but you're still having a church wedding?'

Sarah—'Yeah, Paul—that's my fiancé—' (realise this is the first time I've mentioned him by name) '—says the Protestants took all the best churches so he wants the best of both worlds. I don't believe in the church. Think it's just there to keep the masses in place. An establishment like any other. A meeting place. But then I've got the gym now. Worshipping of a different sort. I believe in God.'

Guy—'Do you pray?'

Sarah—'Every night.'

Guy—'What do you pray for?'

Sarah—'Wisdom, health and happiness.'

Guy—(looking me up and down)—'Well you look fit.' (He smiles.) 'Are you happy and switched on, then?'

Sarah—'Think so.' (Unconvincingly.)

Guy—'Hmm. Your man's got a good catch. Sharp your man.'

Sarah—'Yes.'

Guy—'He should know he can't change you, then. Make sure he doesn't start a trade on you, Sarah. These men can turn nasty if they don't get their own way. Men's love is very fragile. Very selfish, Sarah. They can turn their work into their pleasure, if you know what I mean.' (Looking at me

closely.) 'And you don't strike me as the marrying kind.
Women getting married are usually, well, more glowing.
Happy about it. They mention their intended usually in the
first few sentences. You're not acting like a soon-to-be-
married woman. You're acting like a single woman. It's not
that you are flirting. But you don't talk about him at all.
You're interested in me, what I do, what you do, but most
women talk about the event—especially when it's fairly
soon—like four months away.'

Sarah—'I've got more interesting stuff to talk about.'

Guy—'Expect you have.'

This Guy I'm sure can read minds.

Sarah—'Can you read minds?'

Message received:
Who is that you've been talking to for over an HOUR
NOW!

Guy notices the message received. I think he sees it.

Guy—'No. But I've met a few women like you. You're
bright. Sharp. Got lots going for you. You look good. Fit.
You're interesting and interested and I don't think your
banker, however nice or not nice he may be, is good enough
for you. Or right for you. Or will make you happy. He sounds
insecure and confused and—' (looking down at my mobile
text message) '—controlling. And that isn't a chat-up line. Coz
I'm happily married and love my wife to bits. You don't fit
in here, Sarah. Neither do I. But at least I know it and can
see it for what it is. It's one big fucking fake. Every other conversation I've had today has been about that fucking Aston
Martin and do I know who owns it? Well, I do. And it's fucking boring. It's my dream car, and it cost a fucking fortune,
and it is what it is, but the way this lot have been talking about
it you would think it's the second fucking coming.'

Message sent:
His name is Guy. He works in TV. He is happily married.
He owns the Aston Martin.

Message should have sent:
His name is Guy. He is the only real person here. Including me. He's telling me not to marry you coz you're probably a control freak and you wouldn't make me happy. And
I don't want to have your children. And I'm kidding myself. So mind your own fucking business.

Message received:
Introduce me. I want to buy one.

Best man shouted very loudly. 'Speeches about to begin.
Pray silence for the father of the bride.'
I didn't hear the speeches. The jokes by the father of the
bride. The jokes by the two best men, by the groom. The
bride wanted to say something, but it wasn't the right thing
to do, so she stayed sitting and looked pretty and thin. And,
well, sort of miserable. And the men looked happy and
drunk, or perhaps just excited with the expectation of getting drunk or stoned. And I remember looking at Guy
during the speeches and catching his eye and him looking
back at me and mouthing 'Don't do it'.
After speeches and coffee and port and cigars and the
obligatory nose powder (for the girls) and bum-licking (for
the boys) the band plays lots of Dire Straits and old rock 'n'
roll. Everyone thinks they look sexy.
In the 'powder room', which is larger than my old flat.

Message received:
I look forward to setting my eyes on you for they have
been deprived of your gaze for too long. They hope

their joy will be returned. Meanwhile my lips want a
snog. They have always been easier to please! J Xx

Message sent:
I miss you and love you and need you now. S xx

Message received:
Where are you?

Message sent:
At a wedding. It's horrible.

Message received:
Most are. Very false. Full of false comment and compliments. Do you know the people getting married?

Message sent:
Sort of. The groom.

Message received:
Well at least you can see it for what it is Sarah. At least
you won't make the same mistake. With anyone. Including me (that was a joke by the way)!!!!!!!

Message sent:
I know. Wish I was in bed with you. Miss you. Love you.
xxx

Message received:
Can I call you at ten tonight? Xxx

Message sent:
May be still at wedding.

Message received:
1/2
No matter. Am in the pub at the moment. W th friends.
At Chessley Arms. They're asking about the woman I
have in my life. I told them. They asked if I love you. I
said...
2/2
...too early to tell yet. I lied. Thanks for a lovely evening
the other evening. I love spending time with you. I
wish we could have spent the night together but there
will be other times I know. Xxx

I felt sick and elated at the same time. Elated coz it was
a wonderful message. Sick coz the Chessley Arms was the
pub we were staying in tonight.

I introduced Paul to Guy. Guy smiled and took all the
compliments Paul bestowed on his car with good grace. And
congratulated him on finding such a lovely girl as Sarah for
his wife-to-be. Paul cuddled me, pushing me to him as
though to say 'she's mine' rather than 'I'm hers' or 'I love her'.
Guy introduced Fiona, who said she had to go soon coz of
the children. Guy suggested Paul have a look at the car. Paul
was very happy and stopped squeezing me to look at the
car. Guy asked if I would like to see it. I said no. Paul said I
wasn't interested in cars. I said I was, but not at the moment.

Guy—'It was good to meet you, Sarah.'

Sarah—'Good to meet you too, Guy.'

Guy—'Good luck.'

Sarah—'You too.'

I never saw or spoke to Guy again. Paul told me in the
car on the way to the pub that he thought the Aston was
fab, and Guy seemed OK. Bit distant. But OK. Typical TV
type. Bullshitty. He told me he was complimentary about
me. We compared notes about that wedding and how ours

would be. How it would be better. More genuine. We'd have more friends there and it would be lovely. And special and just right. And he was so happy we were getting married and it would be the happiest moment of his life. And that wedding had been a bit too much ostentation. And I looked at my slightly drunk fiancé, and thought, Sometimes you say the right things at the right time.

At the Chessley Arms we didn't see John. Arrived at one a.m. No one in the bar. Paul too drunk to 'do' anything. But kissed me and told me he loved me. And how lucky he was. And how wonderful I looked today and how every-one said I looked wonderful and how he was so very proud of me and all my achievements and that we had been through some tough times together but that would make the two of us, working as one, a team, two against the world, stronger. And I didn't speak. And then he sort of spoilt it. He asked if I would consider anal sex. Just like that.

Paul—'Would you consider anal sex?'

Sarah—'Er, no.'

Paul—'Don't be so prudish.'

Sarah—'I'm not. You're drunk and I'm not drunk enough.'

Paul—'Italian—' (one of his friends) '—says it's fine. But you end up farting cum all the time afterwards.'

Sarah—'Does he say the girl enjoys it?'

Paul—'Italian doesn't give a fuck if the girl enjoys it. He does it coz he does. He once had this girl sandwiched be-tween him and another guy and they took her from both sides.'

Sarah—'Did she consent?'

Paul—'Italian didn't tell me. He said she was so loose she would have given in to anything.'

Sarah—'I don't want to do it.'

Paul—'You've become frigid.'

Sarah—'Wouldn't be surprised if I have. We don't make

love any more. And now you ask for something like this, which I don't think is exactly caring, of the face-to-face variety.'

Paul—'Why don't you try to explore, Sarah? I've taught you how to masturbate. Just think of the pleasure you had with that.'

OK. I remember the pleasure I had with that. First time I did it I almost rubbed it off completely. Paul taught me because it turned him on to watch girls getting themselves off. So even that was selfish. I remember Paul looking over me as I lay on the floor, legs apart, as though about to give birth and him saying—'Do it there. Try it there. Do it that way. Try it that way. No, not that way. Faster. Slower. How does that feel? Too harsh? Getting anything there? Let me have a go.' Twat. Got there eventually, and gradually it became less and less painful. At the beginning, thinking about Paul helped, and over the years, as I had sex with Paul less and less and made love to myself more and more, I didn't think about him any more. Well, not as much. I found that when I did I would cry after I came. If I thought about someone else it was somehow less emotional. Less meaningful. But the pleasure was still there. Anyway, it had kept me sane since Paul had decided celibacy was the best policy.

Sarah—'Yes, you taught me. Very grateful I am, too. It's come in handy when you haven't been there or didn't want to make love over the years. And occasionally you've wanted to watch, or have mutual masturbation sessions, which are fine. But it's not really enough for me, Paul. I want more.'

Paul—'Well, this is more, darling.' (Taking me in his arms and making me look into his big blue doe-eyes.) 'Why don't you try? Oh, go on.'

Sometimes I don't just think I despise Paul. I know I do. He asks me as if he's asking me to iron one of his shirts. Not that I would want to do that either these days. How can the wonderful, romantic man I first met have turned into this arrogant, boorish prat? Perhaps it's the port talking. The finest vintage. Perhaps.

Sarah—'No.'

Paul—'Please.'

I think, Shall I do this? After all, I know girls who have. They say they have. I think it sounds degrading, especially the way Italian talks about it (his name is not Italian—it's Terry—but he's half Italian, and Italian is sexier-sounding than Terry so everyone calls him Italian. Or rather he makes everyone call him Italian). Wonder if John has done it. We haven't talked about anal sex yet. Perhaps I should have talked to him about it. Asked if he would do it. What he would think of it. If it would be natural, or is unnatural, or whether it's just something men like and women have to put up with. Am told men enjoy it coz it's tighter. And that women love it. But none have said they do. Just that they get turned on coz their men get turned on by it. It wasn't on my action list for the month. 'Have anal sex with Paul.' Nope. Not there. But perhaps if I do it just this once he won't ask again. And he will know that it's not that great anyway. So I do.

I tell him I have to be really drunk before I do it. That I need the alcohol so that a) I have a good chance of passing out, b) I can relax so it's not excruciatingly painful—not that he is well endowed (although a nurse he went out with kindly said that he was 'average'. She lied)—and c) I feel I need a drink.

It's verrrry painful. I try to position myself in a way which is least painful. Which is sort of what I imagine giving birth to a baby is like. Keeping back straight or slightly arched. I try to drink more port, which I hate but it makes me drunk and hopefully more relaxed so it's less painful. Try to avoid brandy coz that makes me cry. But I want to cry anyway, so what's the difference? I know Paul wouldn't stop even if I did start to cry because I've learnt he's that sort of person. So here I am. On all fours in birthing position, but as if to have the baby inserted rather than taken out. Paul's small but it still hurts. The three glasses of port I downed help. Paul thinks it's sexy to pour another glass of the sticky, sweet, eighty quid a bottle mess over my back and let it run down my spine to my neck, dripping down my front to my nipples. I now find going to the loo more of a turn-on than this is turning out to be. Somehow with John this might have been sexy, but it's not with Paul. I find myself thinking about John in an attempt to get relaxed. To get turned on. To feel something. Anything. Passion. Lust. Instead there's nothing. Just anger. Anger at myself for agreeing to do this. With him. Anger at him for being him.

I'm in tears. Silent tears. Letting the tears run down my face and onto the floor. Like so many times on the rare occasions I make love to Paul. Crying silently in anger for allowing myself to do this. But feeling this is the bed I made, so should lie in it. I deserve it. This is what I deserve. And Paul is a good catch. And fun and steady and romantic and honourable. My mum says he is very honourable, putting up with me, taking me off her hands, and will always be honourable to me. I think of Anthony in *Julius Caesar* talking about Brutus and saying what an 'honourable' man he was. And I don't think Paul is honourable.

And I get angrier, enraged, but this makes me tense and it hurts even more. And I almost sense Paul is angry at me. For the past five years. For the abortion and the fact he feels I've tricked him into believing I'm something I'm not, don't want to be and never can. And I'm angry at putting up with him for so long and he's pushing harder to hurt me. As he's

really hurting. And thank God he comes. Coz I think I'm
going to split or scream out in pain and overwhelming anger
and hatred. More self-loathing than loathing for him who,
strangely, at that moment I pity because he's pathetic as he
kisses me on the back and hugs me round the stomach as
I'm bent over on all fours, crying silently and uncontrollably
and wishing myself somewhere else. Preferably in the arms
of John, kissing me gently on the neck, running his fingers
through my hair, just loving me. Just being gentle and loving me for me. But how can he? He doesn't know who I
am. And I see in my mind's eye Guy mouthing 'Don't do it'.

Paul—'I love you, Sarah.'

He says it almost as a thank-you, turning me round and
kissing my tears away.

Paul—'With pleasure there is always pain.'

At this point I want to kick him in the balls very hard
and put into practice all my kick-boxing techniques. And
make Nicholas not the only one-balled wanker in the area
that night.

Sarah—'That's nice. Now I had better go to shower.'

Paul—'Let me know if you fart cum.'

So witty. I don't laugh. Prat.

And I think back to the trip through France and dancing on the steps of Versailles and the drive back to the pub
when he said those sweet things. And then I think of what's
just happened. And I wonder where the gentle man I loved
has gone and wonder if he was ever there. And don't know
whether to feel duped or angry or guilty. Because perhaps
I've changed him. Or it's just time that's changed him. Or
it's experience. Or it's a combination of everything. Or the
fact he's doing well at work. And it's his environment. Anyway, he's not as sweet and loving as he was. And perhaps I'm
being idealistic and perhaps all men are secretly into anal

sex and don't admit it because it's unnatural. Illegal. And all women do it and don't admit it. And nor will I.

23rd April

Morning after the night before. Paul and I compare notes on the anal sex. He enjoyed it, but not as much as he thought. Great, perhaps he won't ask me to do it again.

Paul—'It's more a case of curiosity for men. Want to see what it's like. Sort of tick the box. Some men like it; others don't. It was OK. Didn't think it was as great as I thought it would be.'

I said I hated it and it made me feel degraded, and it's not because I'm frigid or not a game girl. It's nothing to do with affection. Or caring. Er, at a push, it's 'fun'. But couldn't help think of Italian's words, describing the 'sandwich', as he called it. Thing is, people think he's such a lovely guy as well. Just like Paul.

I've done it now. Sort of tick box for that one. But it's one that wasn't on my list in the first place. I'd rather have done a bungee jump. Or naked free fall. Or run round the supermarket naked screaming 'cream me'. Less humiliating. Not a turn-on. He listened and said he apologised if it had made me upset. But, looking back now, I don't think he was sorry. Just felt it was the right thing to say. Then, half way round the M25:

Paul—'Are you OK about the wedding?'

Sarah—'What do you mean?'

Paul—'I mean, do you still want to get married? I've just felt recently you've been more distant. I know we've had our difficult moments, Sarah. Our difficult times. But it's worth waiting for. I know how you've felt about not having sex. And I wouldn't blame you if you had had an affair because I know it's been a lot to ask. But it's worth waiting for something very special and we have something very special.'

I felt like shit.

Sarah—'I know. It's just that sometimes I feel you don't love me. I've needed the physical affection and it's not there for me. And when we have an opportunity to be intimate, and show we care about each other, we do something like last night. Which was horrible. Perhaps I wouldn't have felt the same if we had had a normal sexual relationship. But, Paul, this is weird by anyone's standards. It's not normal and it's not natural and it hasn't been for a long time. And you won't see anyone about it. Not a counsellor or anyone. And you won't tell your parents and you need to talk to someone.'

Paul—'I don't need to see anyone. You know why we're not having sex. We're not having sex because I don't want to go through an abortion again. I don't want to risk that. It had an incredible impact on me and I don't want to repeat that. Plus the fact that you're bad with money means I respect you less, and I need to respect you. I trust you, Sarah, but I don't respect you as much as I should. The guys I work with have girlfriends and wives who earn good money. They have a good living to look forward to. You could earn good money, but you flit from one job to another and it's not good for starting a family.'

Sarah—'I don't want to start a family. I've told you this. Not at the moment anyway.'

Paul—'Let's not talk about it.'

Sarah—'I think we should, Paul. I do have doubts about the wedding if we can't resolve this, but you seem to think it will all be resolved by marriage. I don't.'

Paul—'But think how special sex will be on our wedding night. How we can make love and it will be special.'

Sarah—'It doesn't work like that. Think how much I have grown to resent you. Think about that. And go and see someone.'

Paul—'Let's not talk about it.'

Sarah—'Can't you discuss this with your parents? You say you're close.'

Paul—'No way could I talk to them. They're Catholic, for God's sake.'

Sarah—'They're also human beings, aren't they? Aren't they realistic as well? These things happen. You need to talk to someone, Paul. I don't think our wedding day is going to be the panacea for all evils you think.'

Paul—'I don't want to talk about it. Sorry I brought it up.'

Sarah—'I'm not. We need to. I love you, but you need to deal with this. It's not natural to sleep with a woman whom you love and not want to hold and touch and make love to her. It's not natural.'

Paul—'Shut up and drop it.'

I dropped it. I arranged to see John on the following Friday, who wanted to make love to me and hold me and touch me. And didn't think much of anal sex. And, no, he didn't want to do it. Even when drunk. He just wanted to kiss me and stroke my hair and listen to me.

28th April

Picnic with John. On Box Hill. Made excuse to Paul was looking for wedding shoes, when in fact know ones I want and ones I want to get Catherine. Break golden rule and go to Tesco and buy olives and fresh figs and cherries (which are extortionate) and kumquats and champagne and Badoit and chicken and poached salmon and samosas. And it's warm and there are few people about in the early afternoon and we find a place by a tree. Which is semi-secluded and I can't keep my hands off him.

I want him to slowly undress me. And he teases me and says he won't, while he does. And his words don't match his actions. Lying on top of me, he occasionally blocks out the light and all I can hear is the wind through the trees.

There are even bluebells, and it's my *Ryan's Daughter* moment—albeit without the voluptuous breasts. And there are ants, and a few bees buzzing about. And I don't care. And as I breathe out he breathes in, and as I breathe in, he breathes out. And he's inside my head and body and I feel lost in his arms and in time and don't want to go and wake up and remember who I am or why I'm there. Just know that I am. And it's real. Of sorts.

John—'You rarely mention your past boyfriends.'

Sarah—'It's not exactly a turn-on for the current one, is it? I know you do it with yours, but I take it in my stride as you seem to get a kick out of it.'

John—'Well, I don't mention them now. Amanda is going out with someone else now, I think. She may even be pregnant.'

Sarah—'You don't keep in contact, then?'

John—'Why should I? She's good with the cats, and occasionally comes round to see them, but I think she's over me now.'

Sarah—'How do you feel about that?'

John—'Fine.'

Sarah—'No ego, then?'

John—'No.'

Sarah—(taking risks)—'What would you say if I said I wanted marriage, kids, the lot?'

John—'I wouldn't believe you. That's not you. You're too independent.'

Sarah—'Perhaps.'

John—'Well, do you want to get married?' (Looking surprised.)

Sarah—'No—' (first honest thing said in a long time) '—but one day, perhaps.'

John—'When you've found the right man.' (Putting his right hand slowly between my legs and stroking very slowly.)

Sarah—'Yes.'

Mobile buzzes with a text. In the bag. I reach for it. John moves for another olive.

Message received:
Hope you've found something you like. Miss you. P xx

Feel like shit again.

Message sent:
Still haven't found what I'm looking for. Miss you too.
S xx

John puts his mouth to mine and blows champagne into it. Then kisses my eyes and nose, telling me it's my best feature. That and my bum. And that he is amazed I'm with him and I tell him (jokingly) so am I. And that I don't want to get him more arrogant than he is. And he says Is this possible? And I say probably not. And we go back to his house and don't eat and drink or go to the pub or watch TV. We go to bed and stay there—just sleeping and making love when we are awake. And sleeping again.

29th April

John is getting good at knowing my body. And I his. He likes me to dress in short skirts. Flirty short skirts. As summer is approaching I have an excuse to wear short skirts. As in just below the lacy pantyline. This means I must wear knickers, which John says is fine if the skirt is *that* short you can see them. He says he loves my legs. That when we go out he likes walking behind me so that he can look at them. I say he must look perverted. He says he doesn't give a fuck.

I begin to dress for him. Wear colours he likes. Wear skirts he likes. Wear perfumes he likes. He enjoys massage. His feet.

His back. Stroking his hair. I teach him to kiss me when I come so that my energy isn't wasted into the air but absorbed by him. He says he likes this and tells me it's Tantric sex. I say I know nothing about this, but that I know Sting practises it. We breathe for each other. When I breathe out, he breathes in. Sometimes we're so close I want him to enter my body. Not just sexually but all the way.

We break the bed one time he is pushing into me so hard. He has fun asking his friend to find another strut for the bed.

'How did you break it, John?'

'Having sex with Sarah. We got carried away.'

He says he was very proud when she asked.

John—'I wouldn't have told her if she hadn't asked.'

Sarah—'Of course not.'

Home life is limited and limiting. I can't face Paul's face, so I don't. I told Anya I have decided to drop John and go back with Paul. But she notices I am on a high.

Anya—'You look good.'

Sarah—'Thank you.'

Anya—'You still seeing John?'

Sarah—'Maybe.'

Anya—'Be careful. You look good. You look in love or in lust or both. Be careful. Postpone the wedding, Sarah. You must postpone the wedding or come clean with John.'

Sarah—'I will.'

I don't.

MAY

ACTION LIST

Go to gym every day.
    Have fun.
    Be nice to Paul.
    Be nice to me.
    See more of friends.
    See less of John.

IMMACULATE CONCEPTION

I'm pregnant.

Five weeks. I feel sick. How can I be pregnant? I'm on the Pill. Perhaps having too much sex means the Pill doesn't work as well. Anyway, I'm pregnant and I can't tell anyone.

Plus I've lost my job at the advertising company. The journey was awful. And I'd already worked there for over two months, which was a breakthrough for me after the two-day fiasco before. They said I was great, and had achieved a lot, but perhaps wasn't right for the position. I wasn't good with systems and procedures. Good way of saying I didn't stick politics and bureaucracy and didn't see the value of things like Year of the Pier and having meetings about meetings—or, more obscurely, who should attend the meetings to make them of more value. All bollocks. Forget the tax payer, what about the wasted talent who has to manage this crap?

But as one door closes another opens. Radio station wanted a travel correspondent. I had been interviewed several times by the Travel Editor, Alastair, and he liked the way I spoke. Good talking head. Or was it good head? Can't remember. Anyway, he called me. In short, I kept going until he wanted me to stop and I talked sense. So he asked me to produce some reports for him. Initially in the UK, then overseas. First was to a balloon meet. I took Paul. We went up with twelve dignitaries, including the Mayor. We landed in a freshly manured field on our side. The Mayor landed on top of me. His medals pushing into my cleavage. Last report made to microphone:

'We're landing in a field which has been freshly manured and the Mayor has landed on top of me…aghhhh.' Descriptive or what? Anyway the editor liked it and I was sent to France next trip. To the Dordogne. No Paul this time. Just myself and ten other journalists, all of whom smoked and drank and threw up and had opinions about everything, including what a lot of wasters journalists are and how they are all up their own arses. And they swore a lot. And some got off with each other. I just recorded the lot of them and threatened to use it when they were famous. If they ever got famous.

The trips away meant more time away from Paul. Only short trips—three or four days. But some got longer. John also didn't like these long trips, and it was perhaps because of spending so much time in different time zones that the Pill failed to work, or I didn't take it at the right time. Anyway, I was pregnant. Ten tests couldn't be wrong. The clinic confirmed it. Three hundred pounds poorer I found myself at seven a.m. on a Friday morning in the middle of May waiting to be 'seen'. I had told Paul I was in a meeting. I had told John I was in a meeting. No one knew. I told Catherine, who was horrified but said if I needed money she would help me. I said it was fine. I hadn't made provision for this. It was to come out of the wedding fund. It was sick. I felt like shit. I was shit.

In the ward before I went into the operation theatre I wondered if I was doing the right thing. Could I have the baby? After all, only thirty and a second abortion. That's bad. Very bad. But I couldn't have John's son and bring him up in a marriage with Paul. Plus, did I really want John's child? I lusted after John and perhaps, just perhaps, was falling in love with him, but did I want his child? No. I was doing the right thing. But, as ever, what timing, Sarah. What bloody awful timing. Two days before Paul's birthday. What a lovely present. Three months before the wedding. I couldn't have sex for two weeks after the termination. Would have to make an excuse to John. John would dump me. Perhaps this was the reason this had happened. Perhaps it had all been for the good. John would get sick of not having sex with me for two weeks and dump me and pick someone else up. Yes, that's what would happen.

I was the oldest in the ward. Everyone else appeared to be a teenager. Except one woman who looked about forty.

'Hello, I'm Edith. I'm forty and feel a bit of an old-age pensioner in here.'

'Hello, I'm Sarah, I'm thirty, and so do I.'

'Where are you from?'

'Chelmsford.'

'So am I. I manage the Ashby Arms. You know that restaurant?'

'Never been, but I'm told it's very good.'

'It is. If you come in, say hi.'

'If it's with my husband, I won't. He doesn't know about this and if he asks me how I met you I will have to lie.'

'Hmm, I understand. Say we met at the doctor's surgery. It's sort of true.'

'Sort of. Why are you having a termination?'

'It's my fifth pregnancy and we can't afford five. I have four lovely children and have always preferred even to odd numbers. And you?'

'Too early into the relationship.'

I didn't want to tell her how I felt. The fact that this was my lover's baby, that I was due to be married in three months' time to a man who hadn't made love to me in five years but whom I loved. And that I was very confused and that this would make matters worse. I kept thinking, Perhaps this happens to lots of women and they don't talk about it and perhaps I should tell her. But then I stopped myself. When I heard myself talk back about the past nine months I sounded like a slut. But it wasn't like that.

It wasn't like that.

Honest.

General anaesthetic should be sold at Boots. It is fabulous. I am told nitrous oxide should also be sold at Boots. My friend, who had just had a baby, said it was the closest she had ever got to euphoria and that it was like when you were first in love or in lust with someone. I said I knew how she felt. I thought, This is how John makes me feel when I am with him. With the GA I completely relaxed for the first time in a long time. It knocked me out completely. The last thing I remember seeing was the doctor's face leaning over me, saying, 'You will be fine. You will be fine. You will be

fine. Count backwards from ten.' I made it to eight. I remember nothing else.

Awoken by another face. And a cup of tea. I felt relief.
They say you feel relief and I did. They explained that you
might bleed and that if there is consistent bleeding you
should contact your GP. With a GA you have to have someone to drive you home. I had no one, so I waited a few
hours and drove myself home. I turned on my mobile to
receive seven text messages and two missed calls.

Message received:
How are you?

Message received:
How are you?

Message received:
How are you?

Paul. John. Catherine.

Message received:
Have been thinking about you.

Message received:
Have been thinking about you.

Message received:
Have been thinking about you.

Paul. John. Catherine.

Message received:
Can you go to Canada in two weeks? Alastair.

Messages sent:
Am fine. U2
Am fine. U2
Am fine. U2
Yes please.

I explained to Paul I needed some space to think about what I was doing and that although Canada looked as though it was close to the wedding date, it was a good time to get away. Plus I had the hen party to arrange for August, and then September second we would be married. Time had flown.

Paul said it was a good idea. He felt that we hadn't been close and that I was having second thoughts and doubts. He didn't like the fact I was starting to travel and that from working in a job locally, earning a good regular income, I had now become a travel journalist—earning some money—and he didn't see much of me. This wouldn't be conducive to married life. I said if he loved me it wouldn't matter. Point was, did he love me enough? He knew that I had always wanted to travel and that, in many ways, this was a dream job—not just mine, but anyone's. After all, I had started off in a bank. A clearing bank, for goodness' sake. I knew what good looked like and this was it.

He said he knew that but also knew himself and that I should think about it. He wanted children and just to be content and happy.

I said I knew this but that I wanted more. He knew I was ambitious and that eventually I would like children but not now. Not now. Images of the clinic and talking to Edith and counting back from ten kept echoing in my mind as I spoke. Anya's words, like ghosts, haunted me during the day and night. I even began to get snappy with John. It would take hours for him to calm me down and make love to me and relax me, and kiss away the self-imposed stress.

As I became more stressed, John became more relaxed about us. More open about how he felt. Then, end of May, he said:

'I know I love you.'

Sarah—'You think you do, but you don't.'

John—'I love you. I lust after you as well. But I love you, Sarah. I care about you. I have never felt like this about anyone. I even went to see my mother to talk about you. She says it sounds like love. I love you. We don't have sex, we make love, Sarah. I want you. Not just sexually, but emotionally and spiritually and completely. I don't want other women now.'

Sarah—'You do, it's just because you've seen less of me recently and you feel you're losing me, but you're not.'

John—'I'm not a child, Sarah. I'm a man who has known many women and has lusted after many women and who hasn't treated them very well. I admit this. But I want to treat you well, Sarah.'

Sarah—'So you want me to marry you?'

John flinched.

John—'Well, that's not what I said. I said I love you.'

Sarah—'What if I said I want to get married? Like next week? Would you do it?'

John—'No, of course not. That's different. Can we take one stage at a time, please?'

I got aggressive.

Sarah—'You say you love me but are unable to commit. It's a cliché, John. It's a cliché which I didn't think you would fall into. It's like one of those silly romantic novels where the girl is weak and feeble and the man is big and macho and the girl believes everything the man says when he rescues her and she is saved and fulfilled because she is loved and married with kids and a mortgage and a personal pension plan. Well, that's rubbish. It's not like that any more.

I don't want to marry you, but it's a commitment, and it's more than just saying I love you. That's easy to say. Harder to prove and harder still to show. Just because you enjoy sex with me doesn't mean you love me or want me or need me. I know you enjoy my company, which is great. But get real, John. Do you really love me? You don't know me.'

I sounded like a man. A selfish, bigoted, self-protecting man.

John responded. Calmly.

'Sit down, Sarah.'

I sat down on the leather sofa in the yellow cottage.

'Are you OK? You seem very stressed recently. Very stressed and very tense. It takes me a long time to calm you when I see you and I'm worried. You've lost weight. A lot of weight. Your legs are still great—' (he smiled) '—joking, just in case you think me flippant, but you have lost it everywhere else. There is something wrong. Do you want to tell me something? I'm worried and I do love you—not just as a lover but also as a friend. You've offered me good advice and been a comfort to me. You've made me trust and respect women again. Thank you for that. And I want to give you something. What can I do? How can I help?'

Aghh. I felt a complete bitch. I had managed to change this amoral man into a loving human being who actually liked women. Women are forever wanting to change men. I didn't want to change this man and he had changed. Or perhaps he was always this way, just pretending to be bad. Perhaps he had deceived me. Perhaps he thought I had money. Perhaps the fact that I was unattainable, that I hadn't been at his beck and call, made me more attractive. I couldn't always see him at weekends. I had to be with Paul some of the time and was genuinely working other times, and that made me more attractive. More elusive. More mysterious. I wanted him to stay bad and selfish and sexual and uncaring and dump me, but it was now nearly June and he had just told me he loved me and I was getting married in—hey—fourteen weeks' time. And two of those would be in Canada.

Sarah—'I need space, John. I'm going away to Canada in two weeks and I want to think about our relationship. This has happened very quickly. And you will have time to think about what you want to do as well. OK?'

John—'OK. Can we have sex now?'

Sarah—'Yes, please.'

That was more like the John I knew. Completely focused on one thing. His dick.

SUMMER

JUNE

ACTION LIST

Be very nice to Paul.

See less of John.

Go to gym.

Go to tarot card reader, Doreen (who tells me to not marry Paul and not see John).

Go to spiritual healer, Hazel (who tells me to not marry Paul and not see John).

Chill.

PAST LIVES

1st June

I had always wanted to go to Canada. Had never been. Had no relations there. But had always wanted to go. One of those places which was always prohibitively expensive, and full of things like Mounties and mountains and moose. I liked the images I saw and the Canadian Tourism Commission had a fabulous PR person who I liked liaising with when organising the itinerary for the trip.

I was to spend the two weeks crossing Canada. It was a sort of journo-challenge. My radio station was pitted against *Loaded* and the *Telegraph*. So a diverse spread, one might say.

I was the only girl of the three journalists going. We were each given five hundred pounds, had to take part in six outdoor sports, use five modes of transport to cross the continent, and sample five varieties of cooking. Then we had to go back and write about it or broadcast it. I'd start off in Vancouver, then to Calgary, then to Banff, then to Winnipeg, then to Quebec, then to Toronto, then to Montreal and finally to Newfoundland, the most easterly point—only five hours' flight from London Heathrow.

I was excited, as I would be using the internet to stay in touch with everyone back home, and would be getting ideas from radio listeners as to where to go and what to eat and where to stay. Hopefully not too many rude ones.

Flight to Vancouver was great. I carried only hand luggage, the heaviest item being my tape recorder and mobile laptop. I couldn't lose them that way, and with so many connections and timing imperative I didn't need luggage going missing anywhere. So it stuck with me.

Stayed at B&B in Vancouver. The place looked nothing like the place on the internet pictures. Home cooking meant bought pre-prepared from the supermarket and cooked at home. Not quite the same. It was about one mile from the centre of town, so I took a bus and went to Chinatown, third largest in North America. Live frogs croaked for me and a guide explained why the Chinese believe eating them is good. Some of the other foodstuffs for sale I had never seen in Sainsbury's or even Waitrose. I ate Chinese food. One down, four to go. I ate a frog. Not a frog's leg. A frog.

It tasted great. 'I'm not surprised the Chinese love eating frog,' I said with gay abandon to the microphone.

Ten minutes later I was vomiting into the restaurant toilet.

One down, four to go.

3rd June

Down to the harbour and a touch of jet skiing. 'It's like riding a bike,' the twenty-something beach bum guide reassured me. A motorbike.

I'd ridden one of these things in Corfu on an early holiday with Paul. It had been fine. But that was a tricycle compared to this BMW zooped up version. One touch of the accelerator and I thought I would be in orbit. Three times in the water and the guide decided perhaps I should just hold onto him for dear life. I did. Nice guy. Nice chest. Didn't want complications so didn't give him my number or my card. I got both of his.

I didn't take my mobile with me (it didn't work overseas), nor did I log on to e-mail at this stage. I wanted space completely and didn't want to think about what would happen when I got back. I hadn't made my mind up yet what to do, but this would clear the cobwebs. I hoped.

5th June

Next stop Calgary. It was approaching stampede time. I was interested in something called the Ball-Busting Festival, where men who are men ride bulls. I interviewed the guy who beat them all, who was smaller than I thought, but obviously had nerves of steel.

You don't need muscles to ride a bull. You just need nerve. Lots of nerve.

7th June

Next stop Banff, where the winter sports are at their best, but in the summer months the wildlife wanders through town. The moose especially like to window shop down the high street. The town of Banff is situated in Banff National Park. It's a wonderful place where you can go skiing and snow-shoeing in the winter and hiking and kayaking in the summer. I went hiking and kayaking. Got bitten to death by insects called no-see-ums—coz you can't—and saw four moose and a cougar and several eagles. I met a First Nations guide who told me that he was a spiritual healer and that at one stage I had been a Native American and my name was Silver Trees and that I had been very wise. And that I should listen to him because he would tell me what to do. The Native American said I had a big decision to make ahead of me. I had two paths and only I would know which one to take. He told me to listen to Silver Trees who was there as my spiritual guide.

I kept thinking both Paul and John would think me completely bonkers if I told them this story so decided to keep it to myself. But would write it up and broadcast it on radio. Neither read my stuff nor listened to my reports—so I didn't fear repercussions. The guy had been uncannily right, though, about my life to date, even saying I had lost two children. He didn't ask if I had wanted them. He said I would find happiness but not in the way I thought, and I would have many life lessons to learn. I asked him if I should get married. He told me to listen to my instinct. That would tell me. We had moose stew. It was good. Not just saying that for microphone. It was genuinely good and I asked for more. Three down, two to go.

After the unexpected spiritual encounter in Banff, I moved on to Winnipeg, in the centre of Canada. I expected it to be some backwater but it's fun and funky and ten thousand Canadian geese can't be wrong as when they flock south for the winter, they stop off there and the sound on the outskirts of town is amazing. Like a gaggle of women who've just been told the hunk of the month is in town. It's a town right in the heart of the prairies, which means it's freezing cold in the winter and very hot in the summer and there is a lot of light. The food there is normal, so I didn't have to eat frog, or moose or bulls' testicles. I was happy with fresh salmon caught from the river. It tasted of fish. It tasted good. But it wasn't odd enough to go in the article, so it didn't count.

I interviewed a famous sculptor who was originally from Surrey, England, and who had decided to travel the world and had for some reason flown into Winnipeg by accident when he'd meant to get a first stop to Toronto. Had liked it so much and had stayed and was chilling out nicely when I met him; told me Winnipeg was a wonderful place to chill out and find myself. So many people travel to lose themselves, to forget, to escape. But travelling is all about learning and clearing the mind and seeing things as they truly are, he told me. 'This journey will clear your mind, Sarah. Life is a journey, not a destination.'

Was everyone in Canada a spiritual philosopher? A band called the Crash Test Dummies were performing in town. They all came from Winnipeg so it was a coming home concert, and they sang a song which consisted predominantly of the lyrics Mmmm Mmmm Mmmm Mmmm. It was very good. They gave good interview.

10th June

After Winnipeg, I headed for Quebec, where everyone speaks a sort of French, but French people don't understand them. I understand when a former French president once visited the province he couldn't understand a word anyone was saying. So everyone spoke in English, much to the annoyance of everyone except the Canadian government. I spoke French, and just about understood their French, and found the old and new cities delightful and fun and the food wonderful. I ate French. Nothing weird. Just salmon (fresh caught that day) with olive oil and garlic and maple syrup ice-cream to finish. Just one foodstuff to go, and several modes of transport and sports to cover.

11th June

Down to Montreal. The Grand Prix was taking over the town. I couldn't interview anyone there as everyone wore earplugs and it was senseless to even try. I stayed at a B&B called Marmalade run by a lovely French Canadian called Monique who told me I should eat more and who had a dog called Fifi who wasn't a French poodle but a lovely golden Labrador. I liked Monique but thought her cruel to call such a wonderful dog such a naff name. I visited Schwartz's, which sells salt beef to the good and the great. President Clinton has eaten here, as has Celine Dion. I don't eat meat, but for the sake of the report I ate a slice of salt beef. It was my last food challenge. The Montreal underground was wonderful to travel on. The bars and especially the jazz clubs were wonderful. Montreal is famous for its Jazz Festival as well as its Grand Prix and it also has a comedy festival as well, which takes over the streets. A very pretty city with a lot to it. I liked it and was sad to go.

12th June

Last stop was Newfoundland. An island with a history and islanders who consider themselves more apart from

Canada than Quebec. They are a tough breed, but they have had to be as winters are harsh and summers are very short. If you like birds it's a good place to go, and I met local ornithologists who told me about the puffin. How, if ever there was proof that good looks don't go with good personality, it was that bird. The bird was a bitch. Used to beat up other birds. And it's about the size of my fist. In Iceland they eat puffin. I always thought the Icelanders were cruel for doing that. Now I had more sympathy with them. The island is also famous for its whales. So I decided to go whale-watching. But with a difference. Here you can swim with them. Staying close to the boat, of course, but bobbing about in a wet suit. I was sure I was wetting myself, but I couldn't tell. So very, very cold. Then this humpbacked whale lifted its head about five hundred yards from me, looked at me with its great sagacious eye and lopped back into the water. I was speechless, which is unusual for me. Unique experience.

Last meal on the last day, I sampled some cod's tongues, which are the bottom lips of the cod, rather than the tongues themselves. They taste like pork scratchings and you can have large ones the size of your palms or small ones the size of Hula Hoops. Not the greatest taste, but I loved Newfoundland. The people were finely etched and had character and colour and life and respected nature and the sea and somehow I felt more at home here than I had in any of the places I had visited *en route* during my journey.

I hadn't spoken or communicated with either man during the two weeks. I had made my mind up to stay with Paul. I would tell John on my return of my decision. I would be open with him. I would tell him that I loved Paul and that I had made my decision.

★ ★ ★

15th June

My birthday with Paul. Takes me to supper. At the Punch Bowl. I don't take the mobile. I don't want to be texted by anyone—especially John. Wear something elegant and simple and long. Paul approves. Sole and salmon for me. Lamb for him. Will I try something new? No, not even this time round. Champagne and fine wine. Montrachet in a year it was supposed to be sublime. Can't remember which one. Paul does. Simon, *maître'd,* looks suitably impressed. Says how lovely I look. And looks as though he means it. Poignant being here. I now sit and look at Paul talking at me, and remember the first time, and wonder has time made my eyes clearer or made me appreciate him less, love him less, take him for granted, resent him more? Or just a combination of everything. I don't see as many of my friends these days. Or not with him. Our friends are his friends. My friends stay resolutely my friends. Is this because I'm selfish with them? No. They don't like Paul. They think he's controlling and would rather see me by myself. He breaks my thoughts and asks about the dress.

Paul—'What is the dress like?'

Sarah—'Lovely. But I'm losing weight. I don't want to look like a blind-man's stick by September.'

Paul—'You won't. You will look stunning. Are you happy with the music I've chosen?'

Sarah—(can't remember the music he's chosen)—'Yes. "Toccata", and entrance to the "Arrival of the Queen of Sheba". Right?'

Paul—(smiling)—'Yes, something like that.'

Sarah—'I'm pleased about "Lord of the Dance". It's very cheerful. And "All Things Bright..." is always good. People usually sing to that.'

Paul—'We've got some strong singers in the congregation. Freddie and Nick are OK. Matthew is a professional, so we'll be in good hands.'

Sarah—'I know.'

Paul—'I'm pleased we made it, Sarah. To this day. There were times when I think it was almost touch and go, but I'm pleased we're doing this. I love you. I don't think there is only one love in one's life, but I know together we will make a very strong team.'

And with that he handed me a little box. A little gold bracelet. Very simple, with the date and words: 'All my love always. Your Paul'.

I cried.

Paul—'Don't cry. I love you, Sarah. We're a strong team and it will be us two against the world. You know it will.'

Paul always returned to the theme of 'strong team' and 'two against the world'. For such a long time I hadn't felt part of a team. I had felt excluded and cut off and belittled and humiliated by the captain, if you like, who'd taken me for granted and ignored me and made me look and feel small. And I didn't feel as though it was just us against the world. I felt as though I was increasingly battling Paul, for my freedom within the relationship, for wanting space—to find out more about myself but ideally not fall into the arms of someone else. Especially not someone like John.

But at least John wouldn't fall for me. And Paul would never meet him. Why would he? The passion would fade, as it does in all relationships, John would get bored with his little bit on the side, and Sarah would go down the aisle, live happily ever after with three kids, two dogs and a husband who played golf with the guys, loved to cook and didn't beat her up. Not physically anyway. Oh, yes, and probably a house in France to boot, and a big house with huge fuck off garden in leafy suburbia somewhere.

Paul—'Where are you?'

Sarah—'What?'

Paul—'Where are you? Sometimes I feel you're not with me at all. Your mind is totally somewhere else.'

My mind was not on Paul. It was on how to tell John that I couldn't see him any more. That it was impossible and that I had met someone else. How do I tell him the truth? Hi, excuse me, well, you know I said I was single, er, well I'm not. Actually, I'm getting married in September and I know I told you a pack of lies. But you will forgive me, won't you? Coz you're a bit like that anyway, aren't you? A bit emotionally immature and you use women for sex, don't you?

Think he'd understand. Not.

Sarah—'Oh, nowhere.'

Paul—'You're dangerous when you think. Don't think too much.'

Sarah—(smiling)—'I'll try not to.'

Paul—'Fancy going to the cricket pitch when we finish and seeing if they are playing a game? Just like old times?'

Sarah—'That would be lovely.'

Coffee. *Petit-fours.* Hand-made. Sweet trolley groaning with creamy chocolatey gooey fab stuff. Bill paid. Thank yous. Kisses on both cheeks. Walking to the pitch. Sun shining. Warm day. Similar to the first time. Sat in the same spot. Game nearly finished. Cuddling. He takes my hand and writes 'I heart you' on the back of it with his forefinger, just like he did when we first met. And all the happiness of when we first met floods back to me and overwhelms me and I want to cry and think what a stupid selfish bitch I've been and how the hell do I get out of the mess I've got myself into?

Do other women get into such messes? I'm sure they don't. But perhaps I should read more agony columns so I would feel that either I'm not alone or I should get my act together. Most columns I read involve stuff like my mum wants to shag my boyfriend. Nope. Don't have that problem. Or I'm pregnant and don't know who's the father. Er, no. Won't have that problem. So is my problem banal or so commonplace it doesn't make the leader letter?

How can I do this to him? How can I betray him like this with a man like John? But John isn't all bad. I'd discovered that. He isn't the total amoral bastard he's painted as. Well, perhaps he is. But perhaps he's met his match. He's caring in his own way, I thought. And passionate. And John is not fucked up by sex or guilt or religion, which Paul seems to be. One or all of the above. But, lying in Paul's arms under the trees, I started to feel happier with him. Perhaps there was hope and he might change back to the Paul I knew five years ago. Perhaps.

16th June

My birthday with John. I met him at Redhill Station. In the afternoon. He'd taken a half-day. We went to lunch at the Italian restaurant where he'd first taken me. He gave me a little box which contained an antique silver box inside.

John—'I got it in the Lanes in Brighton.'

Sarah—'It's very beautiful.'

The box was very delicate and had a little elf-like creature on the front. It ironically reminded me of how Paul called me Pixie, and rarely did these days. I smiled.

John—'You like it.'

Sarah—'I love it.'

I've got to tell him now. I've got to tell him now.

Sarah—'I've got something to tell you.'

John—'I love you, Sarah. I didn't think I could ever say that to anyone and mean it. But I love you. I just feel very close to you. Not just physically, but emotionally, mentally.'

Sarah—'Bullshit.'

John—'It's not. You're bright. You're brighter than you look and you act. There's more to Ms Giles than meets the eye. Much more. And what you see is not bad either.'

I smile. So does he.

John—'I don't know if I can commit to marriage, and that's being honest of me, but I know I want to spend a long time with you and can't imagine not having you in my life.'

Sarah—'I'm very happy and content when I'm with you.' (Being honest.)

John—'I know you are. I can tell.'

Sarah—'We will be able to see lots of each other—' (being dishonest) '—in the future. I'm not the marrying kind—' (What the flying fuck am I saying? Girl, talk about digging the hole deeper than it already is, if that's humanly possible. Fill it in a bit. Fill it in a bit.) '—but I would like to get married one day. When I meet the right man. And perhaps have children and dogs and stuff.'

John—(looking surprised)—'That's not you, Sarah. Don't kid yourself. You're not the marrying kind. You're a free spirit. You'd hate being tied down. Who was that ex-boyfriend of yours? Peter or Paul or something? He sounds completely controlled up. Weak. Wanting to make you into something you're not. Probably very nice. Think you said he had loads of friends. But probably not yours. You never talk about him much, which I understand, but I think he influenced you a lot. Your perceptions of yourself and what you were supposed to want out of life.

'And I don't think your dream was his dream or anyone's, really. I think your dream is on a different level. You're a mixture of child and woman. You've got a very childish, naïve attitude towards life in many ways, but also a very gentle, kind attitude towards people. You're much more compassionate than me. Think you're a natural giver, but you've been hurt and don't give as much of yourself away as you used to. Which is perhaps to be expected. Especially with a rogue like me.' (John frequently acknowledged his arsehole tendencies.) 'You seem to have been used as some sort of trophy by all your boyfriends. But they didn't really see you, Sarah, did they? They saw what they wanted to see and, just like men, were too lazy to dig deeper. They want someone to look after them and someone to look after and keep life simple. And that's not what you're about. You're different. You're interesting. There's more to you. That's why I'd like to get to know you more. And I think it would take more than one lifetime to get to know you, Sarah.'

How true! I can't break in with, Er, you know that Paul guy? Well, I'm marrying him in September.

Sarah—'Paul has his wonderful qualities. He loved me in his own way.'

John—'He loved you and wanted to change you. Sarah, I've realised you can't be changed and I can't be changed, but you can bring the best out in people and I don't think he brought out the best in you. He swamped you. You've got a strong fiery spirit. You need space to breathe. I think if you weren't given it you'd go off and have affairs. Wouldn't you?'

Sarah—(turning red)—'Probably. But that's not the way to deal with it. You've got to confront an issue, not go off and have affairs. Because that doesn't resolve the situation. It's just hiding from it.'

Ha! Why couldn't I ever take my own advice? It was only ever as this 'other' Sarah I became with John that I could look at Paul's Sarah and think, This is not the way to handle it. But I was in too deep. Eating the sole (two days on the trot, getting bored with it, but hey), I tried to work out scenarios to disappear from John. Or perhaps I should disappear from Paul. But, no, there was too much good history there to waste. Work on the bad stuff. Work on it. That's what relationships are about. You have to work on them.

John—'He didn't have sex with you, either, that Paul, did he?'

Sarah—'No, well—you know. I told you about the abortion.'

John—'That's serious stuff, Sarah. A man doesn't not sleep with his girlfriend for years coz of stuff like that.'

Sarah—'But there were also the financial matters.'

John—'You say he said you spent too much money, got into debt? Stuff like that?'

Sarah—'Yes.'

John—'Sorry, Sarah. That's a cop-out. Man doesn't not sleep with his girlfriend because of that.'

Sarah—'This one didn't. He was sensitive.'

John—'Fuck that. He was fucked up. Did he ever go and see a counsellor or something? Or his priest?'

Sarah—'I suggested it, but he said no, he didn't need it, and that I probably needed it more. Which I think I did.'

John—'Perhaps. But I don't think it was healthy for you to be in a relationship with that guy for so long. It would fuck anyone up. Got to remember, no matter how much you love someone, the resentment grows. Not saying sex is everything. It's not. And we have sex the amount we do because, hey, we don't see as much of each other as we would like, so it becomes more intense. But this guy used to see you most days, right?'

Sarah—'Yes, most days.'

John—'And you lived with him?'

Sarah—'Yes.'

John—'Well, then, sex plays a part. But you need that physical intimacy. I know you do. I can tell when I'm with you. You don't *need* men in the way most women need men. You love the physical affection and the intimacy but don't want any of the other crap that comes with it. Can't imagine you ever ironing anyone's shirt or doing the vacuuming.'

I had ironed Paul's shirt night before, and had done vac-uuming week before. But hated doing both. So John was sort of right.

John—'You're strong. You've learnt from your past mis-takes and the future is yours.'

I'm weak. I haven't and it's not.

John—'You're wonderful.'

I feel like shit.

John—'And do you know? You're gentle and most im-portantly you're honest. I've always felt women are lying manipulative little bitches. But you're straight. I trust you, and once trust is broken it can never return.'

JULY

ACTION LIST

To dump Paul.
  To dump John.
  To have fun.
  To be myself.
  To go to the gym.
  To eat no dairy or wheat products.

PRESENT LIVES

4th July

Independence Day. I feel trapped.

I haven't told John. I've continued to see him and sleep with him and take the yellow Lotus around the M25, through the dull countryside of Essex, the lifeless land-scapes of Kent, into the lush green of Surrey and feel alive and loved and sexy when I'm in John's arms. Usually naked or in a state of nakedness. And I have continued to feel cold and unloved by Paul, who is increasingly angst ridden and worried about work and if we are doing the right thing.

I said we should postpone the wedding but he said too much preparation had already gone into it and that this was just last-minute nerves and we had to live in the present and not in the past. And what had happened in the past. With the abortion. We must—he must—forget about. But he hadn't. Because he brought it up at every chance he could when we talked. And in the end I became numb to the mention of it. With John I was able to ignore Paul's existence and pain. John made me feel stronger and better about myself, although it was wrong. Paul made me feel weaker and wretched. And I was increasingly confronted by the guilt.

I started to have facials from a local beauty therapist and it was here I noticed a leaflet advertising a lady called Jenny who was a spiritual healer. I didn't really know what a spiritual healer was, but I decided to visit her to ask about my career. If travel would take off. If I would win the Canadian award. Unimportant things like that.

Jenny was all of five foot, with bright sparkling eyes and a warm round lovely face. She greeted me in her small room at the beauty therapist's and sat down and looked at me.

Jenny—'I'm very pleased I've met you, Sarah. You're a very special person.'

Sarah—'I feel better already.'

Jenny—'No, I mean it. You are very special. You have a very wise old spirit in you. An old Native American. A man called Silver Trees.'

I froze.

Jenny noticed.

Jenny—'Have you been told this before?'

Sarah—'Yes. Last month I was in Canada and was told this.'

Jenny—'He's very wise. You should listen to him. You should trust your instinct. You should listen to him and know that he is right. You have a young child in you as well, who is naughty and restless, and sometimes you listen to her.'

This was becoming weird. I laughed to myself quietly as I imagined the young child running rings round the wise old Native American. Sometimes I felt this was happening in my head with my decision making.

Jenny—'You have a lovely boyfriend or husband. But he is very unhappy. Very restless. He is a lost soul. Tortured. This is not good. He is trying very hard, Sarah. Very hard. Be kind to him. Let him go.'

I felt hot and cold. I didn't expect this. I wanted to hear about something unimportant—like my career or my travels—but not about my personal life.

Sarah—'What can you tell me of John?'

Jenny—'John? He's using you, Sarah. He's using you more than you're using him. You are using him for some reason. Sex? Yes. Physical gratification. But it's not love. Don't convince yourself this is love. What you have is real and genuine and true with Paul. Don't lose it. But you must let him go. Only if you let him go can he ever return. But at the moment he does not have the capacity to forgive you, Sarah. Few men do. Paul does not have this capacity. He never will.'

Sarah—'But he's cruel. If you can see, really see, you will know.' (I meant about the lack of sex, the arrogance, the boorishness.)

Jenny—'He has issues only he can resolve. You cannot. Be true to yourself and he will be true to himself. And find his own way. You can't find it for him. Nor can he help you find yours. You have the chemistry. Not the ability to communicate.'

Thirty quid paid for an hour of disquieting honesty. I might have been preened outside, but I felt ugly inside. How did I get in this mess? How can I get myself out of this mess? I had a delicate, sensitive man whom I loved, was getting married to. And a potent intelligent lover who intoxicated me and made me feel real and alive and excited.

Which one? Which one? Jenny had chosen for me. Canada had chosen for me. My conscience had chosen for me. How many more fucking signs did I need?

7th July

In the church. The priest talking to both of us. Are we aware of what we are entering into?

No, I think.

'Yes,' I say.

The church is pretty and there are a few choristers practising and I wish the wedding in reality could be this small and unfussy. Without the dress and the cake and the reception and the parents and everyone. And I ask Paul if we could just elope and have a simple registry office and he laughs and kisses me and says it sounds like a good idea, but of course we couldn't. Of course we couldn't.

AUGUST

ACTION LIST

To dump John.
  To dump Paul.
  To have fun.
  To spend more time with friends.

BEST FRIEND

1st August

Hot and sticky month. Humid. No rain. When I am with John it makes the moments more intense and surreal because of the heat and the physical as well as emotional need to be naked with him. We get more adventurous. More opportunity for al fresco sex and we are taking more risks. Being seen in pubs together. Skirts ever more short and wearing red, which have never done in life. Was eternally dressed in beige and brown and green. Now it's red and purple and bright colours and semi-transparent stuff. Paul thinks I look sexy these days and says he's lucky to be marrying such a lovely girl. Which makes me feel sad, coz it's not for him and not because of him that I look and feel good. I think if it wasn't for John I wouldn't be feeling or looking this good. I would be miserable. Which makes me think again that I'm doing the wrong thing and should call the wedding off.

With Paul I now don't undress. But we hug a lot. I must look up in a dictionary the difference between love and being in love and being in lust. Is there one? Is love when you feel more pain being away from them than the pain you can feel being with them? Is that it? I don't want to read any more women's magazines. They are all full of crappy commentary about why men do things and why women do things and why we are from different planets or universes and why we can't communicate. And how love means different things. And how men can't be faithful and women are born to be. And I know women who aren't and men who are. And I think I've found one of the rare ones who is, and know I'm playing about with one who hasn't been. And may not still be. I seem to be having these commentaries with myself a lot these days.

Mornings are best for text messaging.

Message received:
Think of Tom Brown's School Days.

Message sent:
You were in my dream last night. Vigorous.

Message received:
Am I the man of your dreams?

Message sent:
Other men there 2. They were watching.

Message received:
Sometimes you scare me.

Message sent:
Sometimes you like me to.

Message received:
I'm in the office. Have temporary secretary. Medina's on hols.

Message sent:
Wot's she like?

Message received:
Big tits. Nice.

Message sent:
Should I b jealous?

Message received:
Only have eyes for you. And I fancy a shag. Miss you. Love your mind. Dream on.

2nd August

Fitting for wedding dress today. Catherine is having green. Looks stunning with her dark long straight hair. I'm having cream, but as I'm losing weight (a pound a day on average) I may have to have it taken in a few sizes. The dressmaker is cross. She speaks her mind.

Dressmaker—'What the fuck have yer done, Sarah? Yer skin and bone now. Put weight on. I usually get the brides who're pregnant and I have to keep adding more and more, but you're the reverse. You OK, girl?'

Sarah—'I'm fine.'

Dressmaker (Tracey) works from her own studio in

Colchester. Does the meringue dresses but has made something sleek for me, says at the moment I will indeed resemble a blind-man's stick if I don't put more weight on. I asked for no frills, just simple lace on cuffs and cleavage.

Tracey—'You've got no boobs, Sarah. What's 'appened to your boobs. And no bum either. I'll 'ave to put a bustle on you. This looks ridiculous. And for goodness' sake eat some cake while you're there.'

Sarah—'I will, I will.'

Tracey—'Well, you better, or your bridesmaid will look better than you and you don't want that on yer wedding day—do yer?'

Sarah—'No. Thank you.'

I feel like shit. But she's right.

3rd August

I have to talk about the situation to someone. I've got to cancel the wedding. This is getting ridiculous. But I can't get through to Jenny and Anya's fully booked up. So call Catherine.

Sarah—'Catherine, are you about tonight?'

Catherine—'Think so. Why?'

Sarah—'Need to talk.'

Catherine—'OK. About John?'

Sarah—'Yes.'

Catherine—'Wheelers at six?'

Sarah—'Done.'

Meet at six. For once I'm on time. I'm never on time. But I am this evening. We find a quiet table in the corner. Order a bottle of Chardonnay and two salads. Niçoise and Greek. And talk.

Sarah—'I don't know how I got myself into this situation, Catherine. I loved Paul. He was all that I wanted. I knew from the moment I met him—well, almost from the moment I

met him—that he was the one. But now I think back there
has always been someone else in my life when I've known
him. Someone else there to compensate when he had something missing. Like the sex, or the caring, or the support I
needed. Somehow he didn't give everything and I felt I had
to change myself into what he wanted at different times.

'I feel as though I'm holding my breath. And it's been five
years now, and that's a long time to try to be someone you're
not. Or try to become something you're not. I thought I'd
evolve into what he wanted. The little wifey at home. But
I'm not, Catherine. That's not me. Perhaps I don't know
what is yet. But I can't help thinking I want to live a little.
Travel a lot. Meet a lot more men. Have more relationships
before this. I've met him at the wrong time, perhaps. Don't
know. Perhaps I have. Perhaps I haven't. But I have a gut feeling that I'm doing the wrong thing. For Christ's sake, I'm
fucking someone else and it's a month to my wedding day.
Surely that's not right? Not to say not ethical?'

Catherine—'I've known you for a long time. I know
Paul. I don't know John. So it's not fair of me to comment
on John. Gut instinct is you're doing the right thing by marrying Paul. Yes, there are problems but you've known from
the start he is the one for you. Don't throw that away.'

Sarah—'But aren't you throwing it away with Freddie?'

Catherine—'Perhaps. But that's my choice and this is
yours. And I think you should stick with Paul. John, although he makes you happy, sounds like a lust thing. Just a
fling. Forbidden fruit. Sarah, you want to have your wedding cake and eat it as well. And you can't. Men can, but
women can't. It's double standards in this game. You know
it is. And it is a game, whatever people say. Dump John.
Make an excuse, any excuse, but dump him. I know it's exciting, but you've got to find out if he's your emotional
crutch and take the jump. Not saying I could do it. Don't

think I could. But you're a risk-taker, Sarah. Your cliff-edge is way past most people's and you need to decide which way to go. And do it now. Before it's too late.'

I tell her about Guy at the wedding. Miss out bit about anal sex.

Catherine—'Guy is right, but he doesn't know the good side of Paul, nor all about you. Stick with Paul. He will come round. Perhaps you can get him to see a counsellor. Perhaps. I've got to go now.' (Looking at watch and realising we've been talking for over three hours. Most of the time, she's been listening.) 'Got to go. We can talk more at your hen party.'

12th August

Catherine has organised my hen party. Belfry. Ten to go. Same as birthday bash. One difference. They can all get drunk. Stag parties surrounding us. We are a group of ten girls amongst a sea of black-tied handsome hunks. Nice. I make a goodie bag for every girl. Containing condoms and chocolate Maltesers and cotton buds and tweezers and edible knickers and Alka Seltzer. Basically everything a girl needs on a hen party night. No one got me a stripper, but that was fine. There were plenty of men who were prepared to take their clothes off. I got drunk, but not honesty drunk. Rang John from my room at two a.m. and told him I loved him and why I loved him and told him I was at my friend's hen party and he told me I would never get married because I was too independent and I said I might do and that he didn't know me well enough and he said he did.

And I said nothing. Blew him a kiss. Seduced him in my drunken slur over the phone and clicked off at four a.m. Think I ordered Room Service and opened the door naked to a young waiter with two salade niçoises and no dressing or dough balls and extra tuna. I'm not sure, but think I did.

Anyway, there were no complaints in the morning. But there were two empty trays at the end of my bed, so perhaps I did.

Facial at nine a.m. Followed by salt rub and full body massage. Light lunch of lettuce leaves and seared tuna, followed by kai bo, then yoga and Pilates and then home. We had toxified and detoxified. Catherine and Colleen had pulled men. Claire had pulled a muscle dancing too aerobically, and Helen had disappeared with the best man from a stag party. Despite being married with child. Lots of flirty harmless fun.

13th August

Driving back from Belfry with Catherine. Everyone seemed to enjoy themselves.

Sarah—'Everyone seems to have enjoyed themselves.'

Catherine—'Yeah, did you?'

Sarah—'Yes.'

Catherine—'I think I told two guys about Liam and how I lusted after him and all the things I want to do with him.'

Sarah—'Oh? What did they say?'

Catherine—'They gave me their cards and said that if I ever got bored with him to call them. Both of them.'

Sarah—'Sounds as though you told them a lot.'

Catherine—'Can't remember. Wish I could. Perhaps I should just tape myself. Sure I come out with better chat-up lines when I'm pissed than when sober.'

19th August

Paul's stag party in Ireland. He invited ten and they played golf and I think there was a stripper and he snogged a girl on the dance floor but I think that was it. I wasn't really interested. I wasn't really there at all during August. I was in another place. My mind was in turmoil about making decisions and living lies. But which life was a lie?

Catherine, my best friend, was in a turmoil too. Liam had said that he didn't want to see her any more. Freddie, her boyfriend, wanted her to move to Richmond with him. She didn't want to go but she didn't want to stay. I suggested she move with Freddie and take a risk. He has been there for her for over seven years, so why not try? She said she wanted Liam, so stayed, and Freddie went to Richmond and met someone else. He didn't tell Catherine. But Catherine knew. Used packets of condoms in the bedroom. Perfume bottles in the bathroom, shepherd's pie dishes in the kitchen. Freddie told her it was the cleaner. She knew better. But didn't care then. She was in lust and in love with Liam. Who didn't want her. I didn't want to make the same mistake. I didn't want to lose Paul.

So…

20th August

Have invited Catherine and Karen round for Witches of Essex session, watching *Witches of Eastwick* on DVD. Bagsy me be Michelle Pfeiffer. Catherine—Cher. Karen—Sarandon. We got cherries, just like in the movie. Big bowl. Cost about forty quid but worth it. And sat. Paul still away with his mates.

Karen—'Are you excited about the big day?'

Sarah—'Yes. Bit dazed, actually.'

Karen—'Thought you would be excited. I suppose it's been a long lead-up.'

Sarah—'Yeah. Suppose so. But it will all be over in two weeks.'

Catherine—'Everything's organised, then?'

Sarah—'Yes.'

Catherine—'Have you dealt with *everything*?' (Looking at me knowingly.)

Sarah—(lying)—'Yes.' (Looking at her knowingly.)

Catherine—'Good. All for the best. Group hug.'

We sat and watched Jack Nicholson expound his wisdom on why divorced, deserted or widowed women are the sexiest, most powerful women on earth because they don't have men in their lives. And how men wake up with their wives and girlfriends and wonder where the spirited women they married have gone and they don't realise that they're the wankers who've killed them. We all nodded in agreement. Then giggled, because, hey, I was getting married in two weeks' time.

We then watch *Dangerous Liaisons*, with Michelle again. She's being told that men can only feel the love they receive and women can only feel the love they give, so any relationship based solely on love is doomed to failure. And we cry when Michelle dies of a broken heart and probably the myriad leeches all over her body.

Paul returns to a group of girlies who look at him as though he's stabbed their mothers.

22nd August

I ignore all John's text messages. I ignore his phone calls. I say I'm busy on a course. I can't see him before the wedding. I will just have to let it ride. He won't find out about the wedding. I will just come back from holiday and say I want to finish the relationship and everything will be fine. Come back with a tan, completely loved up with Paul, and everything will be fine and John's pheromones won't work on me any more. That's the way it will be. So I ignore the messages.

Message received, eight a.m.:
Where are you? I miss you. I love you. Where are you?
J xx

Message received, nine a.m.:
Don't you love me any more? J xx

I give in.

Message sent, nine-ten a.m.:
Am very busy this week and next. Then on holiday for
two weeks. Have got lots to do at work. Sorry S xx

Message received:
Can't we meet up just briefly. Am in your part of the
woods this week. Just for a drink. J xx

Drink? Last time I will see him and he will not look at
me with utter contempt in his eyes? OK. Will meet. Six p.m.
at Hylands Park on Sunday.

23rd August

Want to cancel meeting on Sunday. But don't do anything
about it.

Have to collect cake, make arrangements for flowers and
chef and catering and make sure still fit into wedding dress.
Dressmaker furious as am now size six. John texts.

Message received:
I miss you and love you J xx

So does Paul.

Message received:
I love you and miss you. Can't wait to be your husband.
P xx

I'm losing more weight.

24th August

Want to cancel wedding. But don't do anything about it.

Have final fitting for dress. Dressmaker says I will have to wear padding if I lose any more as she is not going to put it in *again*. See Catherine in her dress. She looks fab. Wedding present list arrived. Most things have gone. Except five people want to give us fish kettles, so we bargain for two and get some Villeroy & Boch wine glasses which break too easily but Paul likes. Organise hair colour and cut and arrange for massage day before wedding so am relaxed. Are you kidding me, Sarah!

Go to priory to make sure the hall is as we like it. The band know where they have to be and we know their set. Mostly Dire Straits and rock 'n' roll. Similar to GBH wedding. Think of Guy and wonder where he is now and if he still remembers our meeting. Probably not. Try to eat something but everything going straight through me. Go to aerobics. Two hours in a row to get rid of worry. Can't. Go to Anya to have reflexology. Even the pain doesn't take the pain away. Anya says I'm strangely quiet but that's to be expected. Last-minute nerves and that. And she still says I should postpone it. Gives me a hug and doesn't charge me.

'It's my wedding present to you. Be good.'

25th August

Want to cancel John. Paul been really sweet and sent two dozen wonderful red roses to house. With wonderful card. Saying how lucky he is and he's so sorry he's treated me the way he has and it will all be different when we are married. And how I will make him the happiest man in the world. And I don't believe he believes that. And I don't believe I can. But I still want to cancel John, because John isn't the way out either. And I haven't been sleeping well, or eating, and I will need padding for the dress.

At five p.m. my friend Katrina calls and tells me she is getting divorced. That her man of eight years has been seeing another woman, ten years her junior. And they have a three-year-old little boy. And she's devastated and doesn't know what to do, but can't—just can't—come to the wedding, and of course I understand.

Katrina—'Sarah, I don't know what to do.'

She sounded completely wired. Two octaves higher and talking without drawing breath and seemingly not needing to. I'm worried.

Katrina—'I didn't expect this. OK, we hadn't been getting on terribly well, but every marriage has its off times. You know, the passion goes and you try to make it work. But, hey, Gerry—' (three-year-old) '—takes up a lot of time, and I wanted to get my figure back and worked out in the gym and Henry—' (bastard fuck-face of a husband) '—didn't think I was spending enough time with him.

'And I love him, Sarah, and I want him back, and he's suggested that he needs space and that Gerry and I should move out of the house and he'll buy us a little house nearby so he can still see Gerry and I can get a job locally just so that I can prove I can do stuff on my own. And I don't know what to do. And he hasn't been coming home, and sometimes he calls and sometimes he doesn't, and I was at a total loss, and then last night he came home and was drunk and I asked him if everything was OK and he said no, and that he thought divorce was the only way out, and I asked him if there was someone else and he said there was, and I'm devastated because he said he would always be there for me and trust me and love me, and we have Gerry, and, Sarah,

I don't know what to do. And I love him. And I want him back. And…'

I need to calm her and focus her.

Sarah—'And you need to see a solicitor and find out what your rights are. And Henry is a banker and he's always been money-focused. Paul even told me this. So he knows exactly what he's doing and don't you dare leave the house and you stay in the house, Katrina. Don't you leave that house. If he wants space he can find it in a little flat in London and share it with this bitch from hell, but he may not have told her the whole truth, in which case she isn't. And I understand you can't come to the wedding, but you need to see someone. You need support and it's difficult for me at the moment. But I can come over. Are you going to be in for the next few days?'

Katrina—'Yes.'

Sarah—'You mustn't leave the house and you must stay with Gerry. I can come there.'

Katrina—'You've got the wedding to prepare for.'

Sarah—'You need me. You need someone. You don't have close family. You're an only child, like me, and, like mine, your mother's a complete cow. She's never supplied you with emotional support in your life. When the shit hits the fan like this she might, though—have you spoken to her?'

Katrina—'Yes. She screamed at me for half an hour and told me it wasn't her fault and she had a fabulous relationship with my father and that it was nothing to do with her and I felt like shit and didn't hear much of the rest of what she said.'

Sarah—'Have you spoken to anyone else?'

Katrina—'Some of Henry's friends at work. His boss's wife, who I know fairly well, and she's absolutely shocked. When I suspected something I contacted her and she said no way would Henry have an affair, and she asked Henry's boss and he said no way would Henry have an affair. And, Sarah, he's having a fucking affair, and when I get my hands on this bitch I'm going to kill her.'

Sarah—'Katrina. Did you see this coming? I thought you and Henry had the perfect marriage. One gorgeous little boy. A big house in the country. House in Italy, isn't it?'

Katrina—(sobbing now)—'Yes, in Umbria. Very pretty. Rustic. Not much needed doing to it. We bought it because—well, Henry thought it would be nice to retire there, and things were getting a bit stressed with work and stuff and he thought this would help. But it hasn't, obviously.'

Sarah—'Has he said he loves this girl?'

Katrina—'No, he says it's just an affair and that it's nothing to do with the divorce, and he doesn't feel guilty and doesn't want to be forgiven because there's nothing tacky about it. And that he's moved on and I must too. And out. And that these things happen.'

Sarah—(thinking on feet here)—'Katrina, what you do is you contact a good London solicitor. I don't know any, but I know there are ones that specialise in this sort of thing. Go to see one. Tell him what you've told me. Tell him everything. Warts and all. Tell him what you know about how much money he's got—which you probably don't, coz he's a mean old git—and listen to what he says. Word for word. And if I were you I would take his advice. Do you think it's worth saving? The marriage?'

Katrina—'I love him, Sarah. I love him. He's my life. He was so wonderful when I first met him, and then we eventually got engaged and married, and we've had our ups and downs and redundancy, but we've pulled through and he's doing well now. And he started to go to the gym last month and he's never done that. Sarah, he's even got a personal trainer, and he looks great and then this happens.'

Men are such a fucking cliché. I didn't want to insult Katrina by asking, Got new underwear too, then, did he? I wanted to get hold of Henry and bash his head in. But didn't think that would be constructive to say or do at the moment. Not with a friend as wired as Katrina. She needed to be calmed down and needed some TLC and so did Gerry and she didn't have anyone to turn to. I called Catherine.

Sarah—'Catherine?'

Catherine—'Hi, there. How you? Excited about the big day?'

Sarah—'No.' (Not realising how blunt I sounded, but realising how honest the answer was.) 'I'm phoning about Katrina. Henry's found someone else and wants her and Gerry to move out of the house.'

Catherine—'He *what*? No, surely not. Not Henry. He's as sweet as they come. He's like Paul.'

Sarah—'Yeah, well. Worm has turned and all that. He wants out. Wants space. Wants her out and wants his house back. Told her to see a solicitor but don't know any. Your sister got divorced. Who did she use? Coz she did OK, didn't she?'

Catherine—'Yeah, think she used Ottley, Studd and Parsons. Becoming like ad companies, these places. Anyway, she used them and did OK. Got just under half. You don't get over half, but they've been married what—for seven, eight years is it now? Went to their wedding, I think. Big fuck-off affair—six tiers to the cake. Bloody thing nearly fell down. Big band. Long honeymoon. Marriage made in heaven and all that. And now this. What's he gone off with?'

Sarah—'Dunno. Girlie ten years younger. Traded in for a new model. He told Katrina that it's not tacky and their marriage was over already.'

Catherine—'Convenient and fucking worthy of him. Bet he told her to move on. They usually do. That's what my sister was told by her ex. "I've moved on; now you should." Men don't deal with things, they just compartmentalise and say, "Hey, dealt with it." Wankers.'

Sarah—'You sound aggressive. What's happened to Liam? Surely he's different?'

Catherine—'He's gone off with some woman. I think someone else in the yoga class. More money and better flexibility than me, probably. Anyway, don't talk to me about it at the moment. Still sort of seeing him, but I don't know any more.'

I think, you *do* know. Just not admitting it. And you're not ready to deal with it yet.

Sarah—'He will come round.'

Catherine—'I can go and see Katrina. Do you have time today?'

Sarah—'Think so.'

Catherine—'Let's go, then. I'll call her and ask her what time's convenient.'

Must admit, don't think this is a particularly good omen so close to wedding day. What with John and abortion and now this, my view of marriage is getting more warped by the second. I'd been to weddings where the groom had said 'till death us do part' and it was the groom's third marriage and I'd been to the previous two. I'd started to get cynical about the institution of marriage. Not just the men who were getting married, who were making mistakes, or didn't want commitment, or had chosen the wrong girl, or had grown apart from them, or whatever excuse my male friends came up with every time they decided enough was enough and happened to find someone else at the right time and, hey, they'd moved on.

But was I any better? Come on, girl, look at yourself. What are the foundations for your marriage? Isn't a good start, really, is it? Last fling before tying the knot is not turning out the way I'd planned—not that I'd particularly planned it. I've fallen in love with John and it's inconvenient, and I don't know if it's real because it's not a real situation and I don't know if my feelings for Paul are real coz how can I do that to him? But perhaps this is just my way—so it's not him at all, it's me. And it's not that he's controlling, it's that I allow myself to be controlled. So deal with it. Preferably before the wedding day, darling.

Catherine texts:

Message received
Thnk we should go round now. K's in state. C u at her place or I can drive you there. R u ok for that?

Message sent:
Meet u there. xx

Katrina lives in Surrey. Same journey as had done with John on what it seemed like hundreds of times. Over the bridge. That beautiful bridge where now involuntarily I get butterflies at the anticipation of seeing and being with him. Like some druggie who gets high just with the anticipation of having a fix. Knowing the high is just round the corner. John's my fix. Sexual, emotional and intellectual. But he doesn't have it all. That's why I'm going to marry Paul, right? Right, Sarah, right. Just remember that. Keep it in your head. God, I was doing lots of this head-talking these days. Thinking too much, as Paul would say. But perhaps should have done this at the beginning of our relationship and wouldn't be in the crap I've put myself in now. Anyway, forget self and focus on Katrina, who needs help.

Katrina lives in Barntley Road. Middle-upper suburban class. Big houses with big fronts and big gardens and big interior-designed rooms. Most commute into the City and most wives either work in the City (how they met husband) or stay at home and look after children. Katrina works part-time and looks after Gerry. Who is adorable. And probably a bit confused at this moment.

Catherine's car not in drive so I'm first. Knock on door. Katrina opens it.

I haven't seen Katrina for months. What with preparation and John and Paul and dinner parties with mainly Paul's friends haven't seen her. Spoken but not seen. She's thin. As in seven stone and five foot ten thin. Bones. Her usually smiley round face is gaunt. She has supermodel cheekbones and her wrists are thin enough for me to get my hand around—meeting little finger to thumb, with room to spare. I want to cry but I don't. I'm shocked. Horrified. Angry. Very angry. How could Henry do this to her? I'm so very, very angry.

But I don't know the whole story. Sarah, you don't know the whole story. Cool it. Are you angry just because of Katrina or are you taking some of your own baggage, your own guilt into this? Keep it simple. Just be there to support, not to give advice. Just support. That's what she needs. That and a fucking good lawyer.

Sarah—'You look great. Thin, but great.'

Katrina—'Liar. I feel like shit. Come in, Sarah. I need a hug. Big hug.'

Give Katrina a big hug. Not too tight. I don't want to break her.

We go into her perfect interior-designed kitchen, with Aga which fits in perfectly with the setting. And sit at the table with the centrepiece of flowers from Harvey Nichols. Present to herself, she says. She wants pretty things round her at the moment that make her happy. Gerry is upstairs, asleep already. She says she doesn't know where Henry is.

He hasn't phoned, but probably won't be back. Or may be back but will be drunk and they're now sleeping in separate bedrooms. So she wouldn't know anyway.

Sarah—'Catherine should be over soon. She's got the name and contact number of a good solicitor. Not saying you need one, Katrina. But just in case. You can see them and they will tell you what is what.'

Katrina—'I've already seen one, Sarah. I know I didn't tell you, but I've got a male friend who works in town and I've told him stuff in the past. About how unhappy I was in the marriage. And I had a fling with him in the past. Henry found out about it, but said he forgave me, and that was about two years ago. I thought it was all sorted, but it obviously wasn't.

'Anyway, he threw that up in my face and said that he couldn't cope with me having an affair, thought he could but he couldn't. And I said that was two years ago and why couldn't he cope now when he felt he could then? Why the delayed reaction? And he said it had just taken time to make him realise that he was unhappy as well and that he had to move on and it was best we split now for the sake of Gerry than try and make it work and wait until Gerry was a teenager and that that would be a worse scenario.'

Sarah—'Do you know anything about the other woman?'

Katrina—'No. Well, not strictly true. He was seen with her by a mutual friend and he's been introducing her to some of his broker friends as his new girlfriend. He's been telling them that we're getting divorced because I had an affair and making it sound very one-sided. So I haven't really called anyone.'

Sarah—'Did you tell him about the affair or did he find out?'

Katrina—'He found out. He read my e-mail. I had a virus on it and he wanted to sort it out and find out who sent it to me and this guy—well, he'd sent me an e-mail saying how much he missed me and, well, you know, loved me and wanted me, and got, well, quite explicit and Henry read that and it was obviously very hurtful and he was angry and I thought he was going to chuck me out then and there but he didn't.'

Sarah—'Perhaps he didn't because he couldn't, and now he's thought about it. But I think after a certain number of months—don't know how long for—you're seen to condone the affair so you can't cite it in divorce proceedings. Read about it somewhere. Anyway, he can't cite that. But you can cite his. If you want to. Do you want to divorce him?'

Katrina—'No, Sarah. I love him. He's the only one for me. When I first met him he treated me beautifully. I thought my prince had come and all that. Know it sounds so corny. I'm not stupid. You know me, I'm a cynic, but he changed my view on men. Thought he was different. I've met my fair share of emotional fuck-wits. Never gone out with a married man myself, but met many "happily married" who were prepared for more than a one-night fling. Those insecure pricks who have lovely wives to go home to and yet still play away. Coz they're insecure, or their wives don't understand them, or don't have sex with them, or won't have the right sex with them, or they've grown apart, or whatever or whatever. The ones you don't think are like that but they are. But you never think you're married to one. But I am. I am.' (She bursts into tears.)

Message received:
Running late. Shd be there in 1/2 hour. C. xx

Message received:
How u? Miss u. Love u. J xxxx

Can't text now. Rude. I'll text J later. In the loo or something. Always good place to text.

Sarah—'Do you know anything else about the other woman?'

Katrina—'He met her in the gym. Think she was working out too, or something. She works in publishing. Financial publishing, I think. One of our friends met her. He's been introducing her as his new girlfriend and saying we're considering divorce because of my affair, but it's not like that. He's painting himself as the victim. My friend says this girl is the total opposite of me. As in completely. She's just over four foot. Sarah—that's a fucking munchkin. Not that I've got anything against short people. Only the ones that are fucking my husband. She's dark—red hair. I'm blonde. She's quiet, I'm told. But I don't think she's quiet. I just think she's quiet now coz she's in a shitty situation. Think of it. There is a young child involved. It isn't just me. It's Gerry as well.'

She sobs again. For five minutes. I go over to hug her and feel her pain, and she's shaking and I think she's going to be sick, but she says she's fine.

Sarah—'Have you eaten?'

Katrina—'Yeah. I'm eating, but it's going through me. I can literally feel the stress burning it off me. No diet has anything on the Divorce Diet. I've lost two stone in a month, Sarah. Two stone. And I've got to keep it together for Gerry coz I don't want to lose him. Not through ill health. And I can't even beat up the bitch coz she sounds as though she's only a bit taller than my three-year-old and I could lose Gerry if I attacked her. And Henry is being such a bastard. I've never seen him like this. A real dark side. And I've been to clairvoyants and tarot card readers and spiritual healers and they all say that I have to move on and that Henry has moved on and is like a racehorse and wants out and that's that, and he's surrounded by friends who will tell him to move on, coz he's not telling them the whole story so they're just validating what he's saying about the marriage and himself. And, you know, not one of the two hundred people who turned up at our wedding have contacted me to say, Hi, Katrina, just ringing to see if you are OK. Know Henry has told me his side of the story—but what's yours? Or, Do you want to talk about it? Or, Are you still OK?'

Sarah—'People get embarrassed, Katrina. You know what people are like. And then others are just nosy and like a good gossip. They lead such little lives themselves they have to live vicariously, off other people's lives—or through soap operas—to make them feel, Hey, I haven't such a shitty or boring or conventional life myself. I'm OK. You need genuine friends around you—and, Katrina, at least they've made your choice for you. They've made it for you. They're *not* your friends. You'll see them with better eyes now. And you have Gerry.'

Katrina—'Oh, yes, I have him. He's wonderful, Sarah. And Henry's so stupid. He's missing out on such a wonderful time with Gerry at the moment. He's becoming a real little person. So wonderful. And I want Henry to see as much as he can of Gerry. Not for Henry's sake, but Gerry's. He needs his daddy. Needs to feel his daddy wants to see him. To be with him. It's so unfair.'

Sarah—'So, your mother was no help?'

Katrina—'You joking? She's like yours, Sarah. She's barking. From a different age. But at least she believes in marriage and stayed married to my dad. But perhaps he was the one who believed in marriage and now it's the men who don't believe in it any more. I don't know. *I don't know.*'

Sarah—'How about Henry's parents? Do they know?'

Katrina—'Yes, they know. But they've heard Henry's side of the story. You know, like Paul's, they're a close family. Well, I say close. The children don't tell the parents anything, but they all stay close together. They only live five miles from here. Doubt if Paul will ever move far from his parents, Sarah. Take that into account. These close families are really just insular and isolated. I've never felt a part of their family and this has made it worse. You know Henry's Catholic too?'

Sarah—'Yes, I know.'

Katrina—'Well, I'd thought they would be all anti-divorce, but, no, they think it's best that he moves on and finds happiness. Perhaps even with this midget, and these things happen, and it's very sad for Gerry. And I've become this non-person and, for God's sake, Sarah, I've been married to the guy for over eight years now. How superficial is that?'

Sarah—'It's to be expected, Katrina. He is their son. Favourite, I think. I've got it with Paul and will always have it with Paul. He can do no wrong. You knew what you were getting into when you married Henry, didn't you?'

Katrina—'No, I didn't. Didn't think he was such an arsehole. Could be so cruel. You know he went on holiday with her? Went on holiday with her and missed Gerry's third birthday party two weeks ago. He went to the Caribbean. Some big island. He wanted space and wanted to go on holiday and wanted to go with her. And told me he was. But said he wasn't asking my permission, just how I felt about it. How I fucking felt about it! Well, I said I wasn't very happy about it and he said he wouldn't go and I said thank you but the wanker did anyway.'

Sarah—'Why do you want to stay married to this wanker?'

Katrina—'Coz I love him.'

Sarah—'Doesn't sound as though he loves you, though, Katrina. Men are different from women. They handle things—or rather don't handle things—in a different way.

It's the only way they can. That's why I've got to find work, a career, a lifestyle that will make me happy, totally independent of Paul, though I love him. Because I know he's human and he'll let me down—' (and has already) '—like I will probably let him down.' (Have already.)

Katrina—'I know—I know. But I'm thinking of Gerry, Sarah. This is so unfair on him. Why do we bring children into this world if marriage becomes so throwaway? So cheap? So disposable? Well, this one didn't work, let's try again—there is only one life. You know what he said? You know when the Twin Towers came down in New York? It made him re-evaluate his life and made him think about everything, what he wanted in life, and he woke up one morning and looked at me and thought, I'm not happy. I'm not happy with you and I'm not happy with this life and I want out. I want out. That's what he said to me, Sarah. And he said it's taken him this long to do something about it.'

Sarah—'No, Katrina. It's taken another woman for him to find the balls to do something about it. Men—not saying all, just most—only have the balls to go when there is another woman involved. Especially those who've been so close to their mummies. They need another carer in their lives. They can't be by themselves. They need someone. Not necessarily to do their ironing and cooking and cleaning, but to say they are wonderful and number one and the best. And with marriage you have to work on that. And when you had Gerry—well, Henry became number two, and that happens in lots of marriages and you felt it too; that's why you had the affair. And you had it for a reason, right?'

Katrina—'Yes, I was unhappy. And it was exciting. I don't know if you would understand, Sarah, because you have such a wonderful relationship with Paul, and it's so perfect, and I'm very happy for you, and don't know if I should be sharing this with you right now, but I need to speak to someone and feel that you'll understand coz you're not conventional and you're marrying—well, you're marrying quite a conventional guy, really. And, well, just be careful. Just be careful.'

Methinks, Is this a message from God, or something? Do things just fall into your lap to teach you a lesson and you ignore them at your own cost? Here was Katrina, utterly distraught, with a gorgeous house and home and little boy and a seemingly lovely marriage and it was a complete sham. And she didn't want to divorce him and wanted to stay and work at it for the sake of Gerry, but Henry wasn't having it any more coz he'd gone off with a trog-bitch-from-hell, according to Katrina—who was painting her smaller by the minute.

By the time Catherine arrived I imagined her as this incredible shrinking woman who lived in a doll's house.

Catherine—'Sorry I'm late. Had trouble with the car.' Aside to me, 'Bastard Liam. Wants to get back together, but won't. Well, want to, but won't.' To Katrina again, 'I've got you a very good solicitor. Specialises in divorce law and was great with my sister. Go and see her. I've contacted my sister already and told her the story and she says that she'll fix up an appointment for you tomorrow. It will help. She will be able to tell you what to do. It will help. She can deal with the financial side of it. Henry is money-orientated, and if he's reachable it's through his money. You're not just thinking about yourself now, Katrina. You're thinking about Gerry and his welfare. The new girlfriend—' (methinks of doll's house again) '—may want children and will put hers first. So you've got to get as much security for yourself and Gerry as possible. Think about it.'

We stayed there for another couple of hours. Katrina was nervous Henry would walk through the door any moment, but I said he wouldn't. I had the instinct he'd stay out with his Pippa doll that night. They were due to come to the wedding, and I told Katrina that she still could if she wanted to. She said that Henry had said they should go just to show face. But then he had started to introduce the girl-friend as his new partner so that might prove awkward. But that they should be grown up about things.

Sarah—'Grown up? What the fuck does he know about being grown up? If ever there was a little boy with broken-toy-and-want-a-new-one-scenario it's this one. Wanker. Do you want us to stay the night? We can. I can.'

Katrina—'You have a wedding to get ready for.'

Sarah—'This is important, and I don't think you should be by yourself tonight.'

Katrina—'No, Sarah, I'm fine. If I need anything I will call.'

Sarah—'Promise?'

Katrina—'I promise.'

Sarah—'OK. But you promise to call? You can call at any time. Middle of the night. Four in the morning. Any time. Promise?'

Katrina—'Promise.'

As Catherine and I go.

Katrina—'You're almost as thin as me.'

Sarah—'Wedding nerves.'

Katrina—'Yes, I remember when I…' (Bursts into tears.)

We hug. Our emaciated bodies clinging to each other.

Drive back. Thinking of dropping in to see John because I need to see him. But I couldn't tell him everything. I'd have to spend a month telling him about everything and then he'd hate me and then it would be destroyed anyway and I'd lose both men. But perhaps I wasn't meant to be with either. And look at Katrina.

I didn't want to go into too many details with Paul about it. But Paul wanted to know where I'd been that night and I told him.

Paul—'Oh, yes, I've heard. Katrina had an affair and Henry can't deal with it. It's understandable. I think he's found someone now, and she's dealing with it OK and being grown up about it. People have to move on. Henry's putting a brave face on it. I feel sorry for Gerry.'

God, that made me so angry. I'd just come from seeing Katrina, totally distraught, and her husband was painting such a woe-is-me-I've-been-cuckolded attitude with his friends and colleagues. It made me sick. So I spoke.

Sarah—'Just one minute, Paul. You only know part of the story. I've just been with Katrina. She's distraught. She's by herself. Henry's been behaving like a pig. He's asked her to leave the house with Gerry and move into a smaller house. Leave the marital home. He doesn't come home. When he does, he's drunk. And he went on holiday with this little bitch when it was his son's third birthday party.'

Paul—'Oh, she mustn't leave the house. She should get a good solicitor. But she's probably feeling guilty for her own affair, Sarah. You must consider that.'

Sarah—'That affair was two years ago, Paul. Two years ago. Why's it taken him such a long time to realise he can't cope with it? That's an excuse. It's bullshit. He's met someone else and is passing the buck. He's a complete wanker. And she's all alone. Her mother is no help at all and his parents are being complete prats. Treating her as a non-person and protecting their he-who-can-do-no-wrong son. Ugh, it makes me sick.'

Paul—'She shouldn't have had an affair.'

Sarah—'She shouldn't have married the prat. Why did she marry him, then?'

Paul—'For the money.'

Sarah—'He didn't have any when she married him. They've made all their money during the marriage. Something he'll have to take into account with the settlement, if it goes that far. She'll get a percentage of everything.'

Paul—'He works very hard.'

Sarah—'So does she. So has she. And she's had to give up her career to look after Gerry.'

Paul—'What career did she have? She worked as a part-time teacher, or something. Didn't earn very much money. And Gerry goes to nursery now, doesn't he?'

This is getting too close to home. This is getting too close to telling Paul that perhaps we shouldn't get married and that, hey, I've had an affair, and he won't be able to deal with it because he's from a similar background to Henry and me-thinks in a few years' time he will turn round and say, Hey I can't cope. And marriages are cheap anyway, so why bother. And if two supposedly nice people can break up a seemingly perfect relationship with all the trimmings…

I'm so angry. I'm so angry for Katrina but think I'm also angry for me. Coz I know this is where I'm going if I'm not careful.

Sarah—'Perhaps we should postpone the wedding.'

Paul looks shocked.

Paul—'Sarah—we have a week to go. We can't postpone the wedding. The wedding is in one week. One week. One week, Sarah.'

He repeats it for his own sake, methinks, as much as mine.

Paul—'Why postpone it? Just because of Katrina and Henry? But we're not Katrina and Henry. Everyone is different. They grew apart. He wanted one thing and she wanted another and this happened.'

Sarah—'Well, it could happen to us. This is bollocks, Paul. It's a complete cop-out. It's a complete cop-out to say children will be OK if it's handled right. It's selfish of the parents. I feel so sorry for Gerry and so sorry for Katrina, because you didn't see her and I know she wants to make this work. You didn't see the state she was in. She's so thin. Really thin. And she doesn't want to divorce the wanker. And I'm not married to him and I want to kill him for doing this to my friend. Bastard. Complete fucking bastard. And everyone thinks he's so nice and you tell me he's coping well. He's thinking from between his legs. Well, I hope there is such a thing as karma and he gets what is coming to him and she gets what is coming to her.'

Paul—'I've met her. She seems very nice.'

Sarah—'She is nice. What do you mean, she seems nice? Katrina's your friend as well as Henry.'

Paul—'No, Katrina married Henry. I knew Henry before I knew Katrina.'

Sarah—'Does that make a difference?'

Paul—'Yes, I think so. It's difficult not to take sides.'

Sarah—'But we were at their wedding. What was all that about bearing witness, and that nothing should pull them apart? I know I've just come back from there and given her details of a good solicitor, but I want to try and make it work for them. Perhaps he'll get over this bitch.'

Paul—'She doesn't seem like a bitch. She seems very nice. Short. Not like Katrina at all.'

Sarah—'Well, anyway—us. Don't think we should get married in one week. Don't think it's a good idea. I'm very anti-marriage at the moment, and not in the right state of mind to get married.'

Thinking on my feet. This may be my way out. I may have to use Katrina's situation and say this is why I feel cynical about marriage. I'm not being hypocritical. I do. I am. Just that it's not quite the reason why I want to stall. But I think I should. Know it's gonna be inconvenient, but think I should.

Paul—(tears in eyes)—'Sarah, I love you. I love you. We've waited such a long time to get married. To get to this stage. We've gone through so much together. Through thick and thin. And I love you. And I know it hasn't been easy, and I know I wouldn't blame you if you had an affair…'

He said that. He actually said *I wouldn't blame you if you had an affair*. It rang in my head and I knew the bell to be hollow and his words to be hollow because never for one second did he think I would ever have an affair and be unfaithful so he could say it, because he would never believe it, because he was arrogant and thought I was his little pixie and only his and I wanted to cry now.

Paul—'I know we haven't made love properly for years. But we do other things. We hug and express our love in other ways. And I know it's been hard for you. But the best things in life are worth waiting for and you're worth waiting for and *we* are worth waiting for. You know that, Sarah, don't you? And I've never met anyone like you and you're so special and I know I don't always show it but I always feel it. You're the one for me, Sarah, and I'm so happy and proud to be getting married to you, and Katrina and Henry's situation is totally different. So don't let that spoil it for us. Not our day. Not our day. Not our life. Not the rest of our lives.'

And I am in tears now. And I think, How can I get myself out of this mess?

Can't sleep for rest of the night. When I sleep I dream I'm on this huge see-saw. One way, then the next. Up and down. One way with John, then with Paul, and then thinking, Hey, I just want to get off and leave the playground and go somewhere else to play—or not. Just not be there. And thinking they both have their fine qualities, and then thinking of Katrina and thinking Paul would never be able to deal with it and he'd turn into another Henry. And I couldn't be open with John because he'd hate me and he's principled and how could principled people want anything

to do with me? I'd been lying to him after all. And there I
am again on that see-saw when I close my eyes. So I keep
them open and don't sleep. Until I hear the birds tweeting
and realise I have. And realise I haven't texted John back.

Message sent:
Sorry haven't text back. Love you. Miss u. Want u.
Thinking of u. aching for u.
Xx

Lying to you.

26th August

Want to cancel John and wedding. And sleep without dream-
ing about being chased. All guests have said yes to invites. Few
on holiday. But others say yes. Sit people next to those they
get on with, we think. Or have something in common with.
Most of Paul's side are City. They can talk gilts and equities
and house and car size and ignore their wives. Most of mine
are in every field imaginable, so can talk about life. My mother
and mother-in-law-to-be are trying to outdo each other on
dress. All ushers have been given orders to be at church at a
certain time, and distribute orders of service and know where
they are supposed to be at what time. Flowers done. Cake
done. Dress done. Hair and massage organised. Numbers
known. Reception briefed. Choir paid. Rehearsal done.
Honeymoon am told done. Photographer and video done.
Car done. Everything done and running smoothly, I'm told.
    Katrina calls. In tears.
    Katrina—'Been to that solicitor. She was brilliant. And
it was scary.'
    Sarah—'Did you tell her everything?'
    Katrina—'Yes. You know I had an abortion while we
were still going out? I told them about that too.'

Sarah—(shocked, but not for reason I thought)—'I'm shocked. But it happens.'

Katrina—'It does, and I told Henry, and Henry said it wasn't the right time to have children and we'd only been going out for nine months or so. I wanted it but he didn't so I had the abortion. But he's Catholic, or his family is, and he went to confession and came back a bit strange and I didn't want to tell anyone about it and he told me not to tell anyone about it. And so I didn't. Well, except some friends who I've known since school.'

I'm not alone. My scenario is not unique and how many women out there are going through this? Making this mistake. Making this mistake over and over again. And they should be talking to one another. There should be a helpline. The 'Don't Marry Catholic Bankers with Hangups About Sex' helpline. Unless you are a nice Catholic girl, and most of them I know have told me they don't want to marry Catholic boys because they look at their fathers and think, Hey, don't want that. I don't know, perhaps they are not all the same, but I think women should talk more. More about stuff like this. Fuck the shopping.

Sarah—'And what did the solicitor say?'

Katrina—'Well, I sat in there for an hour. Cost me three hundred pounds, it did, but think it was worth it, and think I will hire her.'

Sarah—'You're right, Katrina. That's the right thing to do. And come to the wedding, and bring Gerry if you like. You'll enjoy the party. Just come. I need some friends there, Katrina. Most of them are City colleagues of Paul's. They're not my friends. They may be his, but they're not mine. I won't see them again. I know that. But I would like to see you again, and I think you might find it amusing. But then again it might be too upsetting and remind you of your own wedding. Perhaps not. Perhaps not.'

Katrina—'Thank you, Sarah. I want to be there for you, but I think it will be too painful. And I think Henry has asked Paul if he can bring his new girlfriend with him.'

Sarah—'Has he really? Well, I'll have something to say about that. She's not coming, Katrina, and he doesn't have to either.'

Katrina—'Thanks for being such a good friend, Sarah.'

Sarah—'That's what I'm here for, Katrina. There's two sides to every story. Perhaps you shouldn't have had the affair and should have dealt with it differently, but I think marriage is a commitment and you should work harder than this if you decide to do it. If you don't think you can, don't do it at all.'

Katrina—'Good luck.'

27th August

I think I'm losing weight in my sleep. I haven't weighed myself in ages, but think I'm stressing out so much I'll be as thin as Katrina by the wedding day if I carry on at this rate.

Meet John at six p.m. in Hylands Park. He picks me up at Brentwood Station and drives me to the park. Sunny day. Much like when Paul and I went to cricket ground. John looks shocked when he sees me.

John—'Christ—you're thin. You've been working too hard. Are you well? Are you OK?'

Sarah—(lie)—'I'm fine. It's so good to see you.' (Truth.)

John—'Come here.'

He holds me close and I realise how thin I've got when he presses into me and I can feel that he feels my ribcage and that for once I have cheekbones. But not the way I intended or where I intended. I feel fragile, and he senses that he needs to be gentle with me both physically and emotionally today.

John—'Are you sure you're OK, Sarah?'

Sarah—'I'm fine. Can we sit down over there?'

I point to a large oak tree up a hill. It takes twenty minutes to reach the tree, and we don't talk. We just walk in silence. I keep holding his hand and touching his arm. When we arrive at the top I sit down on his lap and snuggle up. I don't want to leave the tree or his arms. I don't want to go back down the hill or home or to bed, because I know I've only got another few days before *the* day. The happiest day of any girl's life. But not this one. John tries to pull away after ten minutes to see my face and talk. But I don't want to talk. I just want to hold him in silence under the tree in the sunshine. But I'm so weak now he's able to undo my arms around his waist quite easily. Cupping my hands in his and looking into my eyes.

John—'Something's happened. What is it? This isn't the Sarah I know or recognise. You're not OK, Sarah. What is the matter? You can tell me.'

The fuck I can.

John—'You can tell me anything, Sarah. Anything. I would understand.'

The fuck you would. Actually, you probably would, but you'd hate me for ever and probably kick me down the hill and I would deserve it, so, no, I'm not going to tell you.

John—'I love you.'

Sarah—'I love you too. But I can't tell you why I'm in the state I am. I can't. And if you ever found out you'd know why. I do love you, John, but this is serious stuff.'

John—'You're not into drugs are you? Not pregnant? Haven't killed anyone?' (laughing) 'Not getting married tomorrow?'

Sarah—'All of the above.'

He smiles.

John—'Whatever it is, I would understand. I trust you

and hope you have grown to trust me. As I said, you've changed my perception of women.'

Christ, not only am I going to make him realise what a cow I am, but I've damned all women now in his eyes as lying bitches. There must be some honest ones out there, surely?

I think in my mind how I will explain myself. How I can possibly explain this deception. And whatever scenario I come up with it always ends in death or injury—usually mine. I was unhappy in my relationship. My boyfriend alienated me and started to bully me emotionally after I had an abortion nine months into our relationship. I gradually resented him for it. He refused to have sex with me. I felt I deserved it. When I met John he changed my notion of what makes me happy and made me see that I should expect more and that Paul and I weren't right or compatible for each other. But John also had a bad reputation, so I trod carefully. And I didn't want to rock the boat with Paul either. So I two-timed. And then Paul proposed and I said yes. And then John seduced me and I said yes. And then it was exciting and there was never the right time and I made excuses not to tell either or both and now the wedding is a few days away and I'm thin and tired and full of self-doubt and loathing and it's all my fault—or how I've reacted to circumstances is all my fault. And I've got to deal with it. And I don't want to hurt anyone. Don't care about myself. But don't want to hurt either of these men.

John—'You're in your own little world again.'

He interrupts my thoughts.

Sarah—''Fraid so. But you are in them. I love you, John. Whatever happens, I will always love you.'

John—'What do you mean by that?'

He's sensing there's something final in what I've just said.

Sarah—'Nothing. I have to go now.'

He kisses me. Long, lingering, breathing in and out kiss. And I melt into him and want there to be nothing of me and want him to take the breath and responsibility and guilt and fear and anger away from me with his breath. Coz I think he can, but I won't let him. And tears run down my cheeks on to his and he opens his eyes, still kissing me and I look into his and he's puzzled but continues to kiss me because he knows that I want to and can't let go of him and don't want to go despite saying I do.

Walking down the hill, we hold hands and I play with his fingers in mine. And I kiss his palm occasionally, raising his hands to my lips. At the bottom of the hill, by his car, I cup his large hands over my face. Spreading his fingers so that they completely cover my face and kiss them. Individually, one by one. Holding his hand tight as though the rest of his body is superfluous. He takes his hand away and strokes my cheeks and then under my chin. My face follows and responds to his touch.

John—'I'm sure you were a cat in your past life, Sarah. You're a sensual creature. You like curling up and making love in front of the fire. You prefer outdoors to indoors. You love basking in the sun but also enjoy the sensuality of the shade. You were a cat, Sarah. Not a dog. Don't think you're that loyal.' (He smiles.) 'Don't let anyone call you a dog. Jessica and Hannah give you a big lick. Wish I could now.'

He moves his other hand to my thighs and gently, through my skirt, starts to stroke and fondle. With the other hand he holds me at the base of my spine, pushing me to him. Again gently. And, still kissing me, he very slowly brings me to climax and breathes in my pleasure.

John—'Have a lovely holiday, Sarah.'

Sarah—'Thank you. Can I…?'

Sarah, you can't do this now. You can't do this now. Don't do it. Deal with the guilt. Deal with it. Your issue, not his. Deal with the guilt. Shut up, girl.

John—'Yes?'

Sarah—'Can I kiss you again?'

John—'Of course.'

We kiss again. It's long and sensual and I want to be naked and in his little cottage in his bed with his cats. Or perhaps I just want to be away from this situation and not there at all. Just not here. And not me.

SEPTEMBER

To dump John.
   To dump Paul.
   To escape with grace.

FINAL CALL

2nd September

Wedding Day. I haven't told John. He thinks I'm on holiday for the next two weeks.

Nine a.m. have to be at the hairdresser's to get my hair coloured and cut. It takes an hour longer than I think.

Eleven a.m. facial with Lisa, beautician.

Mobile phone rings.

'Sarah? It's John. I have just had the weirdest phone call. I phoned your flat. Karen answered. I asked where you were. She said you were busy. I said I needed to get in touch with you. She said she doubted if I would be able to. I asked her why. She said you were getting married today and would probably be otherwise occupied. Is this true?'

Lisa noticed my skin change colour and stopped massaging my face.

Lisa—'Sarah—are you OK? I can't work on you like this. You are completely stressed. Are you OK?'

Sarah—'I'm fine. Fine. Just fine. Rather stressful phone call. Can you stop for a minute?'

Lisa leaves the room and I sit up, half naked, and talk to John.

Sarah—'It's true. I'm getting married today to Paul. I'm marrying Paul.'

John—'How can you be marrying Paul? You've been with me since April. How can you have been seeing him as well? What...?'

Silence.

Sarah—'Are you still there?'

John—'I'm still here. I just collapsed. I couldn't stand up. My legs just gave way. Sarah. I'm devastated. How can you do this to me?'

Sarah—'I wanted to tell you. I tried to tell you. But time just fled by. I couldn't tell you. Every time I saw you I would look into your eyes and you would start to undress me and I would think, Hey, next time, I can't tell him now. Not before we make love. Not after we make love. But every time I saw you we made love. We spent most of our time horizontal.'

John—'Marry me. Marry *me*. Don't marry him. Don't marry him, Sarah. He doesn't love you. He wouldn't treat you the way he has if he loved you. At best he's fucked up; at worst he's punishing you. Building up resentment over the years. He'll make your life hell. He won't change. For God's sake, if he's not sleeping with you now he won't change just because he's married to you. It doesn't happen like that.'

Sarah—'He's tortured. He's a tortured soul. I know it and I can't help him and I don't know who can. God, perhaps. But he doesn't believe in God, and all I can do is try to love him—and I love him, John. I have always loved him, despite the problems we've had. I've always loved him truly and deeply and you don't want to hear this.'

John—'He's not a tortured soul. He's a wanker, Sarah. He's a selfish, self-serving wanker who's punishing you and will continue to do so. Can't you see that?'

I could hear John start to weep down the phone.

John—'Why have you done this? Why couldn't you have saved me the pain?'

Sarah—'Because I wasn't strong enough. I don't have the emotional strength or maturity to deal with this situation. A situation which I created but didn't have the foresight to get out of or not get into in the first place. I wanted you and didn't realise the implications. I thought you were a womaniser. Someone who would dump me. Grow tired of me. Learn to hate me. But you didn't. The fact I was unattainable made you want me more. The fact you couldn't see me at weekends made you need me more. I was different from the rest because I wasn't there at your beck and call. But it was for a reason. John, I love you, but not in the same way I love Paul. I am very sorry I have hurt you, but this is my decision.'

Change of tone on the phone. More stern and angry.

John—'Where are you getting married? I'm going to come to the church. Why didn't you ask me to the wedding?'

Sarah—'Are you nuts!'

John—'Where are you getting married?'

Sarah—'I'm not telling you, John. Don't come. If anyone must tell Paul it will be me.'

John—'Drive over to Surrey—just meet me and talk about this.'

Sarah—'No.'

John—'Please?'

Sarah—'No.'

John—(pleading)—'Please, Sarah, I love you. Don't do this. Don't marry this man. You wouldn't have slept with me if you had loved him. You wouldn't have done this. Think about it. Why did you do it? Because you knew it wasn't right. You knew it wasn't right for you and you wouldn't have done it if you had been happy. Would you? I know enough about you to know you wouldn't have done it if you had been happy.'

Sarah—'I know, John. But that is past and I have to live in the present and deal with the situation. I have made my bed and must lie in it. I've confided in people about us and about you. Anya and Catherine, neither of whom have met you, both say you sound nice and that I needed you for a reason and that was as a catalyst to identify the strength of my feelings for Paul. Whether it would work or not.

'Perhaps when the priest asks me to say I do, then and only then will I know for sure. And if I can't say those two words then I won't go through with it. And, before the eyes of God and everyone, everyone will know my feelings. But I know and believe I love Paul, and what I have done with you has been for physical gratification and no other. I believed you felt the same way.'

John—'It started that way, Sarah. But it's not like that any more.'

Sarah—'You just think that. You just think that. But you're not thinking straight.'

John—'I am. This is so unfair, Sarah. You allowed me to fall in love with you, knowing this. Do you realise the pain this is causing me? Are you aware? I've never felt so much pain.'

Sarah—'I didn't think it would be this way. I didn't think

you would care or fall in love with me. I wanted you to, but didn't think you would. Relationships always seemed a game to you.'

John—'They were, but this one wasn't, Sarah.'

Silence for thirty seconds. Quiet sobbing.

Sarah—'Are you still there?'

John—'Yes. Perhaps you've treated me the way I've treated other women in the past. And I've learnt my lesson. Learnt how much pain I've caused. You've taught me a lesson. Well done. The way I've—well, compartmentalised them in my life and literally switched them off, like a light, when I'm finished with them. Men do that. I've done that. That's the only way we know how to deal with things. We move on, pretending it didn't happen. Our arrogance pulls us through. But this time my arrogance can't pull me through, Sarah. Because you've got to me. And I love you. And it's real. I'm distraught, but I've got to go and I'm going to find out where this fucking wedding is.'

Click.

Sarah is stressed. Sarah is so stressed she can't do anything and just sits. Sarah Giles is completely wired and worried and, on supposedly the happiest day of her life, she is a wreck and wretched and miserable and losing weight through nervous tension. Lisa tells Sarah that she is too stressed to work on. Legs are waxed so Sarah drives, and manages not to crash, back to her parents' home. She is half an hour late. The video man and photographer have been pacing. As has Sarah's mother, who is agitated and tells Sarah that Paul has got her a lovely honeymoon so at least she should be at the wedding on time. Sarah knows why she can't confide in her mother. Perhaps if she told her about John she would say the same thing. *You can't leave Paul, Sarah. He's got you such a nice honeymoon.*

Sarah gets dressed and made up. She looks in the mirror.

She looks stressed. She needs John to unstress her and kiss her and make love to her. She has to settle for a vodka and orange instead. Double—on an empty stomach. She walks down the stairs. The video man says she looks lovely. The photographer tells her that her bridesmaid looks prettier. Sarah has photos taken in the back garden with her father, who is smiling but notices Sarah is not herself. And is not there. But says nothing. The bridesmaid leaves. The video man leaves. The photographer, thank goodness, leaves. The man with the black Sunbeam and Sarah's father remain. Another vodka. Sarah smiles and says nothing.

Dad—'You don't look sure about this, Sarah.'

Sarah—'I'm not.'

Dad—'Bit late now.'

Sarah—'I know.'

Dad—'Just last-minute nerves, I expect.'

Sarah—'Yes, just last-minute nerves.'

Dad—'It will be fine. Paul is lovely.'

Sarah—'Yes. Paul is lovely.'

Dad—'Mrs O'Brian…'

Sarah steps into the car in her long oyster white dress. Her father looks at her and asks her if she wants to change her mind. She says she does. He says it's not too late if she wants to. But she thinks about the problems it will cause. The humiliation it will cause Paul. A no-show. He's worth more than that. Thing is, so is she.

Why couldn't she do this earlier? Why couldn't she have explained to John that it was just a fling and that she was getting married and not to get involved with her emotionally? Why? Coz she wanted to get involved with John, that's why. She wanted the emotional, not just the physical. She wanted to get under his skin. Into his mind. She wanted the communication and control and contact she'd lost with Paul and desperately wanted back but couldn't find. She wanted the romance, the bluebells, the passion. She wanted him to fall in love with her. She wanted it all. To have the wedding cake and eat it.

And then she remembers Guy, who said it wasn't too late, and only after you say I do is it too late. So it's not. But she says nothing. She is driven slowly through the streets on the ten-minute drive to the village, where the bells are ringing and the pews are full of bankers and wedding presents and people she doesn't know and will not meet again. Sarah gets out of the car. She is fashionably ten minutes late. The car got stuck behind a cow. Don't ask how it got stuck behind a cow. It just did. Perhaps the cow ate a dog, who ate a cat, who ate a bird, who ate a spider who ate a fly.

I think I'm going nuts. I need another vodka. Perhaps I just need John.

Then Sarah hears the music and can't smile any more. And can't walk any more but does. She walks down the aisle and doesn't look at anyone and wants to turn back. But she doesn't. She walks and looks straight ahead and thinks of nothing. And everything. And doesn't want to look at the faces she doesn't know and even less at those she does. Her cousins who don't talk to each other are standing next to each other and making conversation and it all seems such a huge fake. A huge white wedding fake, and she doesn't want to be the character she's playing and she doesn't want to be in this act and she realises that loads of women don't want to be in this act but go through with it because it's called role play. It's just that it's for grown-ups. And she stands by the character called Paul. And he smiles at her. And she looks round just in case the character called John is walking up the aisle and shouting, I have so many just causes to say that these two should not be lawfully married that it would take a fucking year.

And I want him to. I want him to find the church and I

want him to speak and I want him to come and rescue me. Not to take and have and hold me. But to rescue me from myself. From my weakness. And then I realise that this character can only rescue herself. No one can rescue her other than herself. She is alone and she is standing alone and she must rescue herself.

Sarah repeats the lines and hears Paul repeat his lines. They have to face one another to do so. They have to perform in front of an audience of hundreds who are there to bear witness and ensure that they stay together. And are there to eat the food and drink the wine and the port and dance to the band and network and have fun and party. Which is what it is about. And dress up. And all the women look very pretty. And the sun has come out. And it's not raining and rain had been forecast and wasn't that good? And lucky. And a good omen.

Priest—'Do you, Sarah Giles, take Paul O'Brian to be your lawful wedded husband? Will you love him, comfort him, and, forsaking all others, keep only unto him so long as you both shall live?'

The book we rehearsed with says I should now say I will. It says the bride says *I will*. It's in italics. That is what it says. It says I will. I do. *I will*.

I turn around. No John in the congregation. At the end of the aisle. The faces look at me, perplexed, as though I've forgotten my lines in the play and I need prompting, and some of them quaintly and involuntarily mouth the words *I do*.

And I smile back and think of Guy's warning and Jenny's sparkling eyes and the bliss of dancing down the steps of Versailles with this man, and his poems and my poems, and the Plumtree at Peerton, and John blowing on my calves and Anya pummelling me and telling me to postpone and Catherine's excitement when she first kissed Liam and the doctor with the general anaesthetic. Fuck, I wish I had that now. I want to sleep for a year. Please, God, I want to sleep for a fucking year and wake up when the play is over and the waters have passed under the bridge and I can be Sarah Giles the person and not the actress I have been playing on a stage I never wanted to enter. And I think of the last time I saw John and how I spread his hand over my face.

And I say: 'I don't. I'm sorry, Paul. I don't.

'I don't because it's not right. It's not the right time and I'm not the right person. It's not right. I love you and I let you go now because I do. Because I love you, I let you go now. I let you go because I am not good for you at the moment, and you are not good for me. Because you will grow to resent me, as you have already done. Because you are too controlling and you would make me more free-spirited and I would make you more stern and set in your ways. And we are opposites and would push each other to extremes. And I have and would continue to make you unhappy, and you me.

'But I love you, and everything before the "but" doesn't matter. But it does in this case. On this day. In front of these people. At this moment it matters a lot. And I should have told you before, but I am telling you now, so you don't have to explain to any of these people here, who bear witness, friends, family, acquaintances, hangers-on, people I've never met before and will doubtless never meet again. I love you, Paul O'Brian, but I can't marry you. Not until I love myself. And I don't. Not now.'

I turn. I'm not the actress on the stage any more. I've not read from the script. I'm not reading from the script any more. This is not supposed to happen in the fairytale, but it was never my dream. This was not in the game plan. Never on my action lists. Never my story, my life.

I don't look at the faces at either side of me as I walk down the aisle. I am vaguely aware of shapes moving in the background but know, somehow, no one is chasing or following me. And I realise no one in the congregation knows the real me anyway. I don't look back. I just walk very slowly, without the music, to my own pace, at my own time, not knowing where I will go, only knowing that I must. And that the honeymoon is over.

I walk out of the church. The driver in the car is leaning against the bonnet, eyes closed, soaking up the warm Indian summer rays. I walk up to him, tap him on the shoulder. He looks startled.

'I've changed my mind.'

'Not getting married today, then?'

He sounds as though he's had this happen to him before.

'No, not today. Not to this man, not today.'

'Well, better now than later. That's what I say. Can I take you anywhere, love?'

'Could you just drive for a bit?'

'Sure.'

He opens the car door and I get in. I don't feel cheated I'm not a Mrs Somebody and don't have a wedding ring on my finger. Just relieved and nervous and excited.

'Can I borrow your mobile? I'd like to send a message to someone.'

'Sure. Easy to use.'

Same one as mine.

Message sent:
Decided not to get married. Not 2day anyway. Phps one day.
But not this day. Love u. S xx

Sent it to Paul.
Sent it to John.
Sent it to myself.

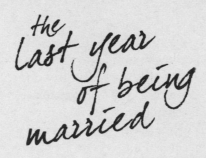

the
last year
of being
married

Sarah Tucker's intensely honest and wickedly funny
sequel to *The Last Year of Being Single*.

**A messy end to an ill-fated marriage,
and the first year of the rest of her life...**

A tipsy confession of infidelity during their engagement
hadn't been the best start to Sarah's marriage. Still,
how could her husband complain? It had taken
Paul five years to propose, and even then he'd made
only occasional guest appearances in Sarah's bed.

Now Paul had decided it was time to cut their losses.
What had happened to them? Weren't they
once the perfect couple?

Thrown into a state of denial, then self-doubt,
followed by determination not to go under without a
fight, Sarah is catapulted into an unforgettable
last year of being married.

Outrageously sexy, bitingly witty, uncompromisingly
truthful, Sarah pulls no punches as she explodes the
myth of happily ever after once and for all.

*Available in Autumn 2008
from all good booksellers.*